Alyssa Atones

SAGE MALLORY®

THE *Alyssa* SERIES

Published by Cardinal Wellingham

ISBN: 979-8-9909085-6-7

For Baby, who fuels my bewildering imagination

Author's note: This story continues the events of the Alyssa series: *Alyssa Awakens*, *Alyssa Arrives*, and *Alyssa Astray*. *Alyssa Atones* picks up immediately after the events of *Alyssa Astray*, when Alyssa confesses to Robert about her feelings for Hayden Robinson, a local realtor, and saves their marriage by promising to never see him again. They are pausing their open marriage experiment while they decide how to protect themselves from the next Hayden. You will understand the characters and plot better if you read the other books first. But if you understand that Alyssa broke their open marriage rules by falling in love with another man, you can dive into the deep end. Either way, enjoy!

1

SUNDAY, JUNE 6, HOME

ALYSSA WHISKED THE butter into the egg yolks slowly to avoid separating the hollandaise. When it thickened, she turned off the burner so it would stay warm in the double boiler but wouldn't separate while she placed the poached eggs.

I hear them moving around. It's time to bring them here. "Okay, everybody, breakfast. Come to the kitchen!" She smiled at the footsteps hurrying her way.

Clay arrived first. "Sausage Benedict. Excellent. Thanks, Mom."

"You're welcome, honey."

"Did you remember only ham on mine, Mom?"

"Of course, Susan. I've fed you for twenty years. I know your favorites."

As the kids made their way to the table, Alyssa watched the back hallway. She and Robert had made love into the wee hours of the morning, but Robert's sense of justice would require more than that to forgive her for lying about how often she'd fucked Hayden, and for how far she let him into her heart. This morning's peace offering was sausage Benedict.

He came through the archway and smiled when he saw the table. "Mm. How did you know I wanted Benedict this morning, Baby?"

She smiled back at him. "You always want Benedict, and I wanted to do something special for my family. So enjoy."

Too content to eat, she nibbled while they talked and laughed. Robert ate her second one like he always had, like she'd hoped he would. *I'll give him anything he wants if I can stay right here, enjoying this, every day.*

✍

Alyssa looked up from her computer at the sound of the door closing. A sweaty Robert came through the laundry room, toward the fridge. He had been playing basketball with Clay. She stared, unable to speak, as he chugged a glass of water. His hair was slicked back with sweat. His bent bicep bulged and the ridges along his forearm teased memories of the magic he could work with his fingers.

A tingle danced between her nipples. *Still sexy at forty-four. How did I forget that?*

Dark patches of sweat on the gray T-shirt clung to his chest and flat abs. *The gym routine shows, even if the six-pack has faded.*

Hayden has a six-pack. She remembered Hayden standing over her, every glistening muscle rippling as he jerked his huge cock to shoot hot cum on her belly. Her pussy throbbed. Her heart ached, because she wanted to be with Hayden, and for the unbearable consequences.

Stop, Alyssa. Your husband is there, sexy and loving. A better man than any you know. You have been throwing him away. Fix things.

"Clay's buddies showed up and saved me. He's better than I am."

"I watched. You did better than you think. You're a good dad, Babe." *One of the million reasons to love him.*

A long blink drove the image of Hayden from her mind, but her body refused to gear down. She let her eyes wander across the man who had thrilled her for decades as he drank. He took care of himself. So many of her friends' husbands had gotten soft, too busy with work and beer to exercise. Not Robert. He wanted to play basketball with Clay, to help Susan move from dorm to apartment, to carry Alyssa around the house after foot surgery.

He takes care of himself so he can take care of us. He works hard to provide a good life and pay for the kids' school. He is always there to help us fix what gets broken. Jesus, everything he does is for us. That's love.

Warmth filled her chest. Her belly fluttered. She walked to him and stroked a finger across his chest.

"Susan's out with her friends. Clay is outside with his. Want to continue last night's fun?"

He smirked and stroked her side. "Hm. Perhaps."

"Perhaps?"

"What did you have in mind?"

Hayden wouldn't play this game. He'd bend you over this kitchen island and fuck you like he paid you. Her mind conjured the cold granite on her chest and the wide cock splitting her deep inside. Her body felt every jarring thrust, the growing explosion building inside her. She heard his taunts: *"Your husband won't do this for you."*

She shuddered as a chill raced up her spine. *Get Hayden out of your mind. Be with Robert, Alyssa. Focus. Love him. Make it up to him.*

"Anything to prove how sorry I am. Anything to show you I can still be a good wife."

Robert stiffened in her arms. He removed his hand from her hip. His face flushed red. "I'm going to shower."

No. Save this. "Sounds fun. I'll join you."

"Not this time."

Her fluttering belly sank, leaving her empty. "Babe, please, what did I say?"

He stepped back from her. "Nothing. I remembered I have some work to do for tomorrow. That's all."

"Robert, be honest with me. I'm trying."

He sighed and closed his eyes. She let him think.

"I know you are trying, Alyssa. That's part of the problem. I wonder if every loving gesture is because of love or guilt? Worse, are you using me to suppress daydreams of him? Not trusting your motives sometimes ruins the mood. Sorry, you wanted honest."

Empty and admonished, she nodded and looked at the floor. She should have known he would see through her. He always did. "Thank you for being honest. That hurts, but I understand."

Silence filled the seconds. The ache in her gut precluded thought as she absorbed his words. The only comfort in the room came from his presence beside her. He had chastened her, but he was there to let her think and respond. Just like he always was.

She looked up at him. "You are correct. I want to atone, and I do feel guilty. That's because I love you and hate what I did to us. Doubt the circumstances, but please don't doubt my one and only motive: repairing our wonderful marriage. I'll admit you're right, sometimes you replace my thoughts of him. I don't want these feelings, but they torment me, and sometimes I'm not strong enough to drive them away on my own. I need your help to make them fade. Please help me."

"Wow. That is honest. I want to repair our marriage too. But sometimes, these feelings I have about you won't let me help with your feelings about him. Like now. I need to shower."

Alyssa nodded and moved in a haze to the back porch. For the next two hours, Hayden didn't cross her mind.

⁓

Alyssa walked to Robert's office, laptop in hand. He minimized a game in lieu of a spreadsheet as she entered. *He needs time to think. Don't get mad. Do this anyway.*

"Still working, Babe? It's getting late."

"Yeah. I had a lot to do. You can go to bed. I'll be in later."

"I can wait up a bit. Can I show you something?"

He nodded, and she put the open laptop on his desk, a mountain cottage rental filling the screen. She leaned over his shoulder so they could look at the screen and so she would not have to see his face if he rejected her idea. The knot in her stomach tightened. She rested her hand lightly on the back of his far shoulder. She took a contented breath when he didn't shake it off. *It's a good start.*

"I want to go here with you. You don't need to question my motives. I am indeed trying to make up. I am trying to ease my guilt. I'm shamelessly enlisting your help to vanquish my thoughts of Hayden. More than that, though, I want to be with you. Focus on you. Connect with you. Love you. Maybe a weekend away from home can help us get better. Would you be willing to join me?"

She held her breath while she waited for his reaction.

Any reaction.

The seconds ticked by. She let out her breath.

God, he's going to say no.

Her chest tightened. She took a deep breath and spun his

chair until he faced her. She gripped his shoulders and looked into his eyes.

"What, Robert? Why won't you say anything? Please say something."

He sighed. "I'll go. Book the cabin. We can try. Maybe a weekend of escapism will help us reset. That said, until you can deal with being here, with Hayden a mere text away, I doubt you. I doubt your motives and your willpower. I doubt your ability to stay married."

The tightness in her chest released her heart as he ripped it out. She swallowed a sob with a nod as her chin quivered and tears spilled from her eyes, blurring her vision as she left the room. She had hoped for some enthusiasm, some acknowledgment that she was trying to make amends. She should have known Robert's cold analysis would come first. And she couldn't deny his logic. She just hoped he was wrong.

Because right now, she wanted Hayden to hold her while she cried.

2

WEDNESDAY, JUNE 16, OFFICE

Noon. I feel no reason to eat. I miss the lunches with Hayden.

Alyssa turned from her computer and stared out the window.

Stop thinking of him. Let him go. Grab your husband, even if he has avoided you for ten days.

Robert had been working late in his home office, coming to bed after he thought she was asleep. She'd tried one night to roll beside him and cuddle, but he nudged her away. Their conversations at dinner had been bolstered by the kids, but he had yet to join her in the cleanup duties that had provided a chance to talk almost every night for their entire marriage. Over the weekend, they'd talked only enough to make the house function. She had stopped seeing Hayden, but they were drifting apart.

You messed it up. Fix it or this weekend at the cabin will be catastrophic.

She thought a moment. Robert had been hiding behind his

laptop, claiming to have work to do. She needed that laptop out of the way. With a flash of glee, she checked the clock on her phone, then dialed Robert's office line.

His assistant, Nancy, answered. "Robert Davis's office."

"Hey, Nancy. It's Alyssa."

"Hey, Alyssa. He's at lunch. You can catch him on his cell. You know those guys leave right at noon."

"I was counting on it. I called to speak with you. Do you have a minute, please? I need to ask a favor."

She laughed. "You two are the most romantic couple I know. You act like newlyweds sometimes. What is it this time? Surprise trip to Hawaii?"

"Nothing so dramatic. You don't need to clear his calendar for anything. Instead, can you keep his laptop at the end of the day? He's been working so late every night, and he needs a break."

Extended silence prompted Alyssa to check her phone connection.

"Keep his laptop? I don't know, Alyssa. Security takes those pretty seriously. Wait, did you say he's working late at night?"

"Yes. He hasn't been to bed before midnight any night for a week and a half. Have you noticed how tired he is?"

"I have, but our volume falls after school gets out. All the clients go on vacation. He isn't too busy here. He hasn't mentioned any special projects. Maybe he does need a break. I'll help."

Relief swept through Alyssa, relaxing her neck as she exhaled. "Great. Can you tell him there is some kind of update or something?"

"I'll tell him IT wants to run a physical scan on his unit and I made them wait until after hours. He will think I'm a hero."

"Thank you, Nancy. You *are* a hero. He needs to go to bed early tonight. I worry about him."

Nancy cackled. "I'm glad to help, but he won't get extra sleep.

Whenever I do one of these favors for you, he smiles more but barely keeps his eyes open the next day. Don't worry about the laptop, and you two have fun tonight."

Alyssa laughed, feeling some hope for the first time in four days. "I hope he will smile all day tomorrow. Thank you, Nancy."

Relief having restored her appetite, she stood to go to lunch when a delivery driver knocked on her doorframe.

"Alyssa Davis?"

"Yes?"

He held out a brown paper bag. "Here is your delivery."

"What is it?"

"It's from Junior's Roadside. It's lunch, I think."

She looked in the bag, recognizing the white wrapper on the large sandwich and a soda can wrapped in some napkins. The flutter in her stomach rose to her face as a huge grin. She opened her purse.

"What do I owe you?"

"It's already been paid for, ma'am."

He didn't leave. Alyssa handed him a five.

"Thank you, ma'am." He pulled a small envelope from his pocket. "He said if you smiled and tipped me to give you this."

Skeptical, she cocked her head. "He did, did he?"

The driver blushed. "Well, he said if you smiled. I added the tip part. I figured it wouldn't hurt to give you the chance. Thank you, ma'am."

She chuckled. "I see success in your future, young man."

The door closed. She unwrapped the BLT and moaned at the scrumptious first bite. Tomato juice escaped down her chin. She caught it with her hand before it fell to her blouse. She savored every bite while the unopened envelope beckoned to her from her desktop. She wanted to open it and feared what it would say. The sandwich finished, she eyed the envelope and sipped the coke until it, too, was gone. Unable to procrastinate longer, she opened it.

"Bet he hasn't touched you. Call me when your fingers aren't enough. H."

He knows what I need. And he gives it so well.

Her pussy pulsed and began to open. He knew the torment her memory would inflict. She could feel his cock enter her. She felt the sting in her lips as they stretched to the limit. She felt her pussy split apart deeper and deeper until his wide head tapped on her cervix, pushing her toward an orgasm. She felt him continue to fill her, over and over, faster and faster, using his fit body to make hers explode. She felt his hot cum splash deep inside her. Then she felt him hold and caress her, loving her, letting her bask in the afterglow of yet another amazing release as she snuggled next to him. She remembered feeling loved.

And she missed it.

A knock at the door stopped her just as her fingers teased her pussy through her slacks. She jerked to crumple the tantalizing note before calling for the person to enter.

"Alyssa, we need you in the test kitchen."

Her pussy ached to be filled as she stood.

It's going to be a long afternoon.

3

WEDNESDAY, JUNE 16, HOME

Alyssa grabbed Robert's arm and pulled him to the sink as the kids left the table.

"You're helping tonight, mister. Start washing."

He stepped back from her, a smile tugging the corners of his mouth as the kids laughed their way out of the room. "Is that an order?"

"You'd better believe it. You've been shirking your duties around here."

He shook his head. "I know. I have so much work to do."

"Not tonight. You don't have your laptop."

"How do you know— That's why— You set this up with Nancy."

She nodded. "I did." She wrapped her arms around him, snuggling into his chest. "I miss you. I need my husband tonight."

He hugged her back. "It's been hard to be near you, knowing

11

you are thinking about him. I'd rather stay away than think you are imagining someone else."

"It has been hard for both of us. It will only get harder if we drift apart. Please do the hard work with me. Let's do the dishes and talk. We may even laugh like we used to. We can let our work routine remind us how much in love we are. We can start in the kitchen and finish in the bedroom."

He stiffened in her arms. "I don't know…"

She squeezed him. "I do. I need to feel my husband tonight, and he needs to feel me. We need to look in each other's eyes and connect, and we need to reinforce that emotional connection with wonderful orgasms."

And I've been unbearably horny all afternoon. I need this. We need this. Come on, Robert.

"You are probably right. I do have a couple of things to do after the dishes though. Really, I do. I'll hurry."

Her heart leaped to her throat. "That's all I need, Babe. Be with me. Be in love with me. Make love with me. You can have an hour to do work if you must, but no more." *I can't wait longer than that.*

He kissed her forehead. "Okay."

She handed him a rag. "Then what are you waiting for? Wash."

Routine kicked in. They laughed and talked, and the dishes took a long time.

⧲

One hour in his office turned to two. Alyssa had checked with him almost an hour ago, and he promised fifteen minutes. She lay naked in bed and thought about the day. That lunch. That note.

Hayden thought of me when the fresh tomatoes came in at Junior's. He cared enough to send lunch, even after I spurned him. And he wants me enough to send a delivery boy with special instructions.

She looked at the open door and listened for footsteps that weren't there.

"Bet he hasn't touched you."

Robert can't put down whatever administrative bullshit he's doing when he knows I'm in here simmering for him.

She caressed her breast under the sheet and tweaked her nipple, sending a spark to her clit.

Simmering for someone.

A hard pinch this time, and her free hand followed the spark to her pussy.

Simmering and tired of waiting. Hayden doesn't make me wait.

Two fingers slid inside, a poor substitute for a thick cock, but they were available. And they went to work.

Fuck me hard. Make me come, Hayden. Fuck me senseless. The covers rustled as Alyssa's hands worked on her flowing pussy. One hand strummed across her clit while the other plunged two fingers inside to massage her G-spot. She gritted her teeth, trying to stifle any noise as she arched her back, let the small orgasm ripple through her body.

"Are you okay?" Robert asked as he came through the bedroom door only seconds later. He stopped only one step inside.

Still panting, she bit her lower lip and nodded. "Told you I'd start without you. Close the door and come taste how ready I am for you." She pulled her fingers from her pussy and extended them to Robert.

Robert crossed the room and yanked the covers down. The sudden rush of cool air tingled as goose bumps skittered across her skin, evaporating the traces of sweat. Her body heat prevented a chill, but the rapid change piqued every nerve in her skin.

Touch me before this feeling subsides.

He stood silent, the hint of a frown coloring his face as he looked her over.

Did I say Hayden's name aloud? Does he know what I was imagining? Her chest tightened. The tingle abated. She held her breath, afraid to move.

With a nod, he removed his shirt. "Put them back in. Freshen them for me."

Her body unlocked in a wave out from her chest. If he suspected or not, she knew this Robert. He was going to remind her that she was his woman. *Taking control. He knows what I like.* "Like this, Babe?" She slid the two fingers up and down her slit, then buried them inside to the third knuckle.

"Yes. Open yourself for me." He took off his pants and knelt on the bed, bringing his hardening cock to her head. He gripped her breast and tapped her lips with his cock. "Prepare me as well."

"Yes, Babe." She took the head in her mouth and swirled her tongue around it. *Salty. Maybe he couldn't wait either.* She sucked hard, not taking any more of it inside, while flicking the underside with her tongue. He swelled against her palate. *There we go. Get hard.*

Alyssa ducked her head forward to take his entire member in her mouth, then hummed. His cock twitched, and his low groan registered above her own humming, making her smile. *Ooh. Like that, do you? You're almost to full staff.*

"Give me your fingers, Baby." He held her wrist and took her two fingers into his mouth, the stubble on his cheeks scratching the insides of her pinky and first fingers as he devoured the two middle ones. "Delicious."

Robert slid two thick fingers inside her, stretching her despite her earlier vigor, finding threads of her recent orgasm and weaving them together as he moved. *I love the way he uses his hands.* "You feel ready for me. Do I feel ready for you?"

She pulled off his cock, letting him hear the slurp and a loud pop. *Know I enjoyed sucking you, Babe.* "You're ready, and I've been ready all night. Take me, Babe."

Alyssa spread her legs and lay back with her arms out to her husband. When he was in position, she used both hands to rub the tip on her open lips.

"Put this right here, Babe, and fill me." After a slight tug, she released his cock and pulled his hips forward, not stopping until his hips met hers. "Mm. Just like that."

"You like that? Here's some more." Robert backed almost all the way out of her, then slid in again. His long strokes tugged at her inner lips, stretching them in each direction as he moved. His slow pace increased the pull on her lips. The pull stretched her, making him feel even bigger inside her pussy as it clutched at the hard shaft.

"Yes, go slow. You're stretching me. Just like that. God, yes."

Alyssa began to sweat as she gyrated her hips at the same slow pace he slid into her. She locked eyes with him. He kneaded her breasts in time with his hips. The pressure of their slow grind and his firm squeeze met inside her body, building a larger release than her fingers had induced earlier. Neither of them changed a single movement. The only connection occurred at their hips and her tits, but every nerve in her body felt his touch.

You sexy devil, you, boring into me with those eyes. That look feels better than your cock. I'm your favorite meal. Devour me.

Her legs quivered and squeezed against his. Her throat opened in a groan. Her tits flushed hot beneath his fingers. Her back arched, but she maintained the eye contact driving her climax. He pinched her nipples, taking her groan to a scream and exploding the end of her orgasm through her body. She ran out of breath and collapsed back to the mattress, spent.

"Finish in me, however you want," she whispered, lacking the energy to do more than maintain their eye contact.

"I'm close." He pulled her limp legs close to her shoulders and increased the speed and power of his thrusts. Every down-stroke compressed Alyssa's body, forcing small grunts every time he bottomed out against her. His cockhead stretched the top of her channel every time. "Here it comes."

The first splash jetted against her cervix, shocking her with its force. He growled and kept his pace, depositing another big spurt every time he touched deep inside her. After four more, he stopped, pumping the rest of his seed deep inside.

That's what I like. Alyssa lay still for a while, finally breaking the eye contact with Robert when his breathing slowed. After another minute, the welcome, slick feeling of his soft cock and cum ran down over her ass, quivering her legs with an aftershock. "Mm, wonderful. Thank you, Babe. I love you."

"I love you too." He rolled off her onto his back, and she curled up against him with her head on his chest.

"I felt like you wanted to gobble me up. That's one impressive stare you gave me. What were you thinking?"

"I wanted to make sure you remembered who was making you feel so good."

She was glad her head was under his chin, though he probably felt her gasp. His insight always cut through her, and her lousy poker face always confirmed it for him. "Babe, of course I remembered that. I always remember that." *Whoever it is at the time. Tonight it's you, and I couldn't be happier. You are so much better than thinking of him.*

"Call me when your fingers aren't enough."

Robert was enough.

She raised her head to see his face. "It's good to be in your arms again. I've missed you. I love you, Robert."

"I love you, too, Alyssa."

4

THURSDAY, JUNE 17, HOME

Alyssa's phone chimed, alerting her to a text. She pulled it from her pocket.

"No phones at the dinner table, Mom," Susan admonished her mother with a smile.

"Right, Mom. You'd take our phones away if that happened to us," Clay piled on.

Alyssa raised her eyebrows at her husband. "Are you going to let your children talk to their mother that way?"

"I think so. After all, you instituted the rule years ago. They are just reminding you of it."

"Some husband you turned out to be. You won't even support a double standard."

He grinned. "I didn't say that. I support lots of double standards around here. I know what text you are waiting on. Do we have a deal?"

"Dad!" Susan laughed and pulled out her phone.

"Yeah. Me too. I need to tell Sawyer when I'll pick her up." Clay looked at his mother. "Since we are allowing phones at the table now."

Alyssa paused. The message should not have been from Hayden.

Robert had called Rosalyn, the owner of the agency, and asked that he be removed from their account, and she was handling the details until Lauren, their usual realtor, returned from maternity leave.

She previewed the message and read the highlights aloud. "Four hundred thirty thousand dollars. Contingent on appraisal, inspection, and mortgage. Close by July 30. Can't wait to celebrate…" Alyssa scrolled the message down and coughed to cover her surprise at the line revealed in the scroll. "—*by fucking you senseless.*" *Not reading that at the dinner table.* "…closing."

"Excellent. Close to asking price. Let me see." Robert reached for her phone.

Alyssa locked the screen and shoved it in her pocket, turning toward the kids to avoid the frustrated look she knew would cross her husband's face. "Nope. We don't allow phones at the dinner table. Everybody, put them away. I'm reinstating the rule right now." She grinned at her kids, hoping it camouflaged her pounding heart.

When she turned back to Robert, he was only then lowering his hand to resume eating.

"I'm glad you will be done with that house," Susan said. "I'm tired of having supper late every night."

Clay grunted. "Yeah."

"The good news is that we will buy probably four more houses. Rentals, this time. Not to improve and flip. They won't take as much supervision." Alyssa forced another grin and concentrated on slowing her breathing, but her pulse raced at the rush of almost being caught and the excitement of hearing from Hayden. Her lungs burned as the blood flowed through them faster than they could work. She took a deep breath to catch up and released what she hoped everyone saw as a relieved sigh.

"No more late suppers?" Susan asked.

Alyssa pointed at her daughter. "You could cook, young lady, if you are hungry."

Susan smiled and batted her eyes. "But, Mom, your cooking is so much better."

"Hey, what about my cooking?" Robert asked.

Clay cocked an eyebrow at his father. "Yours is good, Dad, truly. But Mom runs a training kitchen. She is exposed to more."

Robert nodded. "Okay, that's fair. But just for that, plan on helping me on the grill and Mom in the kitchen every night so you can learn." He looked at Alyssa. "And don't worry about late suppers for a while. We won't buy any new houses until we get the proceeds from this one."

Alyssa nodded and looked at her plate to hide her disappointment, understanding her husband's thoughts.

He believes I'm still attached to Hayden. If he only knew. I need Hayden to hold me, to caress me, to tell me I'm special after he fucks me to oblivion. I need to eat fun lunches with him. I need to let him pamper me. I miss him every day.

I want to stop. I need to stop for the sake of these people around this table. I love them more than anyone in the world. Why can't I stop thinking of him?

Start by talking with your family.

She snapped back to the conversation. "So I'm your captive cook for the next month?"

"It seems so, my dear. You can cook in addition to your job responsibilities, helping get Clay ready to go to college in

August, and enjoying having Susan home before she goes back to Houston."

The corner of Robert's mouth twitched up. They joked about housework all the time, but everyone did their part. If anything, her family made her life easier, especially since the kids could drive and pitch in around the house.

Alyssa pursed her lips and hardened her tone, playing along. "Oh. Is that all?"

"It will be good to have you back. You have been gone too much lately. I miss my wife."

His message landed like a punch in her gut.

She looked at his hand, unable to meet his gaze, instead pretending she couldn't grasp it without seeing it, then squeezed. "I'm sorry. Everything else has taken time away from you. I'll make it up to you, I promise."

"I know your mind has been elsewhere. Maybe this talk will help you remember that the people around this table need your attention too." That one landed hard too.

"Yeah, Mom. I go back to Houston soon, and we haven't had a girls' day." Another punch.

"And we haven't started on my dorm room stuff," Clay said.

She braced with her hand to avoid doubling over.

Alyssa looked around at her family. Susan and Clay looked hopeful. They hadn't intended to hurt her; they wanted to spend time with her.

Robert's face was harder. He knew she understood his message. He had intended her to feel the impact of putting family second, even if it hurt.

She opened her mouth to speak, felt a sob coming, and closed her mouth, nodding instead.

Robert squeezed her hand and smiled. "With the house sold

and school finished, we can get more family time and get you two ready to head out. And we all want Mom to cook more."

She squeezed his hand and recovered her voice. "I'm in for more family time, and for cooking more, especially if you guys help. There is nothing more important to me than this family."

❧

While Robert and the kids cleaned up the kitchen, Alyssa went to the bathroom and opened the text strand with Hayden. "Why are you texting? Rosalyn is handling us now."

"She's out of the office, and I know you miss me."

"Keep the texts professional. Robert almost saw that."

"All right, but I know you want me."

"Keep the conversation about houses."

"Just think about it."

I do. Every day. She rewarded her throbbing pussy by sliding a finger inside her shorts. As she touched her lips, leaden guilt filled her belly, jolting her eyes to the mirror.

Jesus, Alyssa. Touching yourself to a text with your family outside. Do better.

"I can't. Don't text again. Please."

She deleted the texts.

5

SATURDAY, JUNE 19, MOUNTAINS

Alyssa wrapped herself in a blanket as she opened the door to the back deck. Even in June, the mountain air would be cool before dawn. In the gray light, she saw Robert look toward her from his seat in the swing.

"It's unlike you to be up this early, Baby. Everything all right?"

She kissed his head, then snuggled against him and tucked her bare feet into the seat under the blanket. "I set an alarm so we can watch the sunrise."

He patted her thigh and left his hand there, warming her through the blanket as his fingertips feathered small circles. "You're just in time."

She basked in the gentle rise and fall of his shoulder under her head as he breathed. They sat silent as the sky lightened above them. His body heat seeped into her skin through the blanket where they touched. Soft sparks meandered up her arm as her fingers traced the firm chest under his fuzzy flannel shirt. She inhaled when he exhaled, happy to smell the coffee he'd sipped earlier.

We still fit together perfectly. I'll always belong right here, my head on his shoulder, his hand on my thigh. I want this more than anything in the world.

The first pinprick of sun squeezed between two peaks to the east. She stared, taking in the tiny bit of light working through the shadows. Her face warmed as the sun climbed over the mountains. Before half the sun showed, she had to look down into the dark valley where the trees remained starved for nourishment and warmth.

I'm in the sun, but only a few feet away, the darkness lingers. Such a fine line.

In just a few minutes, the sun covered the valley. Alyssa could feel the energy rising from below as birds flitted among the treetops, the leaves opened to their daytime fullness, and warmth seeped into the chilly morning.

"Just like us."

"What's that, Baby?"

She rose off Robert's side to look at his face. "This valley is just like us. We've been in a dark place. Just like the valley needed sun this morning, we need time together. I know that's my fault, but hear me out. This morning, the tiny sliver of sunlight only took a few minutes to rekindle this entire valley once it began. Could you feel it?"

"Maybe? Keep explaining."

"Anyway, once the light overcame the mountains keeping it out, nothing could stop it from revitalizing everything. That's like us. We have stayed apart, in the dark, for almost two weeks. Our sky shifted from black to gray on Wednesday, and today can be the day when the sun peeking over the mountains reawakens our entire relationship. If we can act like husband and wife, we can feel like it again too."

"You think it's that simple?"

"Yes."

"Really?"

"I know it's more complicated than that, but it is simple to start. That's why I set an alarm. We start today without wasting a minute."

She stood and faced him. "Get up, Robert. We have to hurry to have breakfast at eight."

He cocked an eyebrow. "The sun just rose. It probably isn't six thirty yet."

"I know. We barely have enough time."

She dropped the blanket. Chilly air prickled her bare skin, covering her with goose bumps from head to toe. Knowing they might be seen by the three or four neighboring cabins hardened her nipples.

The sound of a door opening next door broke the morning calm.

Alyssa remained still. The next move was Robert's. If he wanted to claim her as his wife, he needed to take her. If he didn't, he needed to reject her. Robert's hungry look smashed the chills with a heat wave from her chest. But she stood, presenting herself to him.

"Sweetheart, we can cook breakfast out he— Oh my." The cabins were perhaps a hundred feet apart, but the sound carried on the crisp air.

Alyssa resisted the impulse to hide from the voice next door. She didn't care who saw. She was offering herself to Robert; he would decide how to proceed.

"They can see, Baby."

"I want you to see, Babe. The irrelevant neighbors can look if they want. What would you have me do?"

He pursed his lips, like he was considering his options. He made a show of inspecting her body from head to toe before making eye contact.

Even without Alyssa looking, the silence confirmed the man next door was staring as hungrily as Robert was. Robert twirled his finger.

"Turn for me. Slowly."

She turned at a snail's pace. Robert had never tired of looking at her in all their years together. She knew he was envisioning how every inch of skin would feel in his hands, taste on his lips, slide under his body when she welcomed him inside.

She resisted the urge to look for the neighbor, unwilling to break the connection she and Robert were forging. But knowing she revealed all of herself to him as she spun made her turn a second time.

Robert knows I like a little public exposure. He's revving me up.

She would let Robert fuck her where she stood if he wanted. The neighbor could watch. Hell, all the neighbors could watch if Robert would start the day making love. Her pussy thrummed as she waited for Robert to speak.

Start the day inside me. Connect with me. Please.

"Jeffrey, what is taking— Goodness! Miss, you cover up right now! Jeffrey, stop staring and come in."

The hysterical lady's chatter faded into a low churr outside Alyssa's strengthening connection with Robert. He stood and looked in her eyes as the older couple next door blathered on but didn't stop watching. He kissed her gently, lingering while he caressed her hip up and down.

Alyssa moaned into the kiss, savoring it. She knew he wanted her, but he showed patience to make her feel loved and protected. He wanted her to feel like his wife again. She was ready.

Robert broke the kiss and turned toward the neighbors' deck, clearly intending to respond. She caught his chin with her fingers before he could speak and turned his face back to hers until they locked eyes.

"They're nothing. I'm here. What now, Robert?"

He kissed her again, long and slow, but hungrier this time. "We're going back to bed."

Alyssa barely refrained from skipping for joy as she followed him through the door.

"I'm glad we packed some nice clothes. When we ate here before, the dress code was more relaxed. Everybody here looks dressed up." She had brought a red cocktail dress with a low back and a hem at midthigh, with matching red stilettos. She dressed to impress for the first time in a while. For Robert, she had packed a fitted blue suit that framed his body perfectly, accentuating his broad shoulders and slim waist. With a white silk shirt, no tie, and some leather-soled shoes, Robert looked like the sexy businessman he was. Heads turned as they were led to their table. *You look all you want. He's going home with me.*

Alyssa nodded toward the band setting up beside a large dance floor. "Look, they have dancing."

Robert cocked his head at her. "Hiking all day and dancing with dinner? You are pulling out all the stops this weekend."

They had taken dancing lessons after they got married. Alyssa had enjoyed it, but Robert had taken to it like a fish to water. Perhaps it came from playing sports as he'd grown up. His light feet kept him balanced and fluid, and his hands led Alyssa with a firm control that made her swoon. He was good, even after all these years, despite their busy life affording few opportunities. That this resort had dancing tonight had been a welcome surprise when she made the reservation. She had convinced him to bring a suit by promising a nice dinner out rather than their usual low-key mountain routine.

She had planned everything this weekend to please him. His favorite hiking spots. Dancing with dinner. The cabin with a sunrise view. He needed to be happy and at ease for them to repair their marriage. And she needed to repair their marriage to stop thinking about Hayden.

The maître d' sat them at a table one row back from the dance floor.

Alyssa smiled at Robert and nodded. "How better to reconnect than some quiet conversation on the trail and some close dancing in your arms? I love you and love making you happy. Of course I planned this. I hope you like it."

"I love it. Let's eat first. All that hiking made me hungry."

"Only the hiking, Babe?"

"The lovemaking, too, of course."

She kissed his cheek. "I was worried you forgot."

"Never."

They took their time. The band started playing by the time they were on their second drink and had ordered dinner. Robert took Alyssa to the center of the floor for a fast dance. After one song of missteps while they refreshed their muscle memory, Robert led her toward the edge, and they began to dance in earnest. Traveling around the floor, Robert twirled her away, spun her close, and cuddled her from behind. His feet fit perfectly beside hers as he guided her around obstacles with firm hands nudging her waist and arm while she trusted him to move her backward. As the song ended, he pulled her in for a dip and a brief kiss that Alyssa wished could go on forever.

The band followed proper etiquette of a slow song after two fast ones. With a quick glance at their empty table, Robert pulled her against his body. His arm circled her waist until he gripped her side. He held her hand between their chests. His leg split hers as hers split his, the wool of his pants soft on her bare legs.

Looking up even in three-inch heels, Alyssa smiled at her husband. "We still fit together perfectly, Babe. We are made for each other."

"We are. Glad you remember."

She flinched like he had slapped her. She stopped dancing and pushed back from him. "That hurt, Babe. We've had a great day and a great night. Why did you say that now?"

Bewilderment furrowed his brow, then recognition widened his eyes. He pulled her hard against him. "No, no. That's not what I meant. I meant I'm glad you remember how we fit together. It's been a long time since we danced. That's all I meant, I promise."

She puffed her breath, fighting off tears, afraid to speak.

He kissed her head. "We *have* had a great day. It's been perfect, and that's your doing. I would never ruin that. I'm sorry it came out the wrong way. I should have said, 'We'll never forget how we fit,' or 'Even after all these years,' or…wow, those were bad too. I'm not digging my way out of the hole, am I?"

The chuckle blew through the dissipating sob in an odd combination of the two that sounded like an underwater sneeze. She squeezed his waist and returned her head to his shoulder. "No. But yes. Thanks for explaining, even if all you had to say was, 'We always will.'"

He chuckled and squeezed her tighter. "We always will. That's why you are better at this stuff than I am, Baby. Look, our dinner is served in time to save me from more foot-in-mouth disease."

Dinner and wine brought a return to the happy laughter and conversation that had marked the day. They finished their wine after the plates were cleared and asked to defer dessert until they had danced again. Robert guided her around the floor beautifully, but Alyssa noted that about half the other couples were quite good as well. When a couple beside them asked to switch partners, she understood.

"Are you some kind of a dance group? We've never seen a band here, and there are some good dancers."

The fiftyish woman answered. "Sort of. Once a month the resort has dancing, and we have gravitated here over the years. It's a good group. We haven't seen you before, but you dance well. That's why we asked to switch partners."

Robert smiled. "I see. It did surprise me a bit."

The woman's partner chuckled. "I bet. We like to dance with different partners to learn new things. No pressure, if you don't want to swap, we won't be offended, but if you say yes, the other members of the group will want their turn. Being new, attractive, if you don't mind me saying, and good dancers, you have created quite a buzz among the regulars."

Alyssa looked Robert in the eye. "You love to dance, but we never have time. Dance. Learn from these other dancers. Wear yourself out on the floor. We won't leave until they shut this place down. I ask one thing. Dance the last dance with me. I have to make sure you come home with me and not some lady who tangoes like Guillermina Quiroga. Deal?"

He smiled and kissed her. "Almost. We get to dance together whenever we want to, not just the last dance. Deal?"

She hugged him. "Deal. Now have fun."

Over the next two hours, they danced. True to their word, the dance group traded them off among themselves, good dancers and bad, with only brief water breaks. As the band switched to a slow song, they were near enough for Robert to pull her close. She folded into him as they swayed.

"These people are wearing me out, Babe. Maybe three-inch heels weren't such a good idea for dancing all night."

"Come with me."

With a quick release, he turned her and edged her to their table, never removing his hand from the small of her back. He held her chair as she sat, and he waved the waiter over.

"We will have a chocolate soufflé and two glasses of Banyuls. And please refill our water."

"Sir, the chocolate soufflé will take twenty minutes."

Robert nodded. "That will be perfect. Thank you."

"Thank you, Babe. I needed a break."

He laughed. "Me too. Some of these ladies are wearing me out. They're good, and I have learned some steps, but they are resting between turns with me."

Alyssa took a long drink of water. "The men are the same. I think they are competing to see who can get me to do the most acrobatic twirl. Are you having fun?"

"A blast. You planned a great day, Baby. And this has been an unexpected surprise."

"Well, enjoy it, and don't feel like you need to babysit me while we wait on the soufflé. There are some ladies ready to twirl for you."

"I'm fine right here with you. We came here to connect. The dance crowd can wait."

Alyssa slid one foot and then the other into an empty chair for some relief while they chatted. They watched the dancers and politely deferred the few who came to their table to ask. As their soufflé and wine arrived, a young blonde woman strode to the center of the floor on the arm of a distinguished-looking older man. They must have been regulars, because a space cleared around them.

The song began, and she became a red blur around him. He

moved with grace, but he was simply the pivot point for her grandeur. She added flourishes to everyday steps. She added high kicks to flourishes. She was no ordinary dancer. At the end of the song, the crowd applauded.

Robert returned to the soufflé. "She was impressive."

"She looks familiar. I wonder who she is." The answer hit her as soon as she asked the question. "I remember. She was on one of those dancing competition shows Susan used to watch. Daniela something. She's Russian, I think."

"What is she doing here? I mean, the man with her looks wealthy, but surely she isn't a trophy wife."

Another lady came to ask Robert to dance. They had finished their dessert, and Alyssa was slowly sipping the strong wine. She encouraged Robert to hit the floor for the last thirty minutes before the resort closed.

"I'll be back for our last dance," he said before walking away.

Alyssa watched him dance. He really was good. What she liked best was the way the women would gather and talk after dancing with him. They were having as much fun as he was. A warmth crept into her chest at knowing she could give him this gift, and her pride fanned that warmth into a flame as she watched him perform so well.

The band leader announced the last song. Alyssa slipped her feet back into her shoes as Robert approached her, smiling. As he reached for her hand, Daniela the Russian tapped his shoulder.

Her English only hinted at an accent when she spoke. "You are a good dancer. I will dance this one with you."

Robert smiled and shook his head. "I am flattered. You are an amazing talent, but this dance is for my wife."

"Surely your wife would not begrudge you one dance. After all, you can dance with her every day. You can dance with me tonight. You would not mind, would you, ma'am?"

Alyssa looked at Robert. He would never renege on his promise to her. And he would never mention his disappointment if he missed the chance to dance with a true professional. And she would not let him miss his chance.

"Robert, go with her. You may never get this chance again. We can dance another night."

He raised his eyebrows in a silent question.

"Go. I mean it." She shooed him away with her hands for emphasis.

Robert led the blonde beauty to the center of the floor. Everyone seemed in awe, and they hung at the edges so everyone could see. Daniela nodded at the band leader, and a tango began.

The professional tried to inject a flourish at the first step, but Robert held her firm against him. Her eyes flashed annoyance until Robert again pulled her against his torso and she raised her thigh to his hip.

Alyssa chuckled to herself. *I know that impatience. Let him lead you, then he'll drop the leash.*

He established their rhythm and pace as they learned each other. Then, with a raised arm, he twirled Daniela away from him and pulled her back, leaving his hand light on her back and signaling her to cut loose.

She draped herself over him in the clutches and never broke eye contact with him as they moved, slipping her leg between his, raising her thigh to his waist, and caressing her hand over his chest. Her smoldering look compounded the tango's natural, sensual body contact as they moved across the floor.

Their coordination was like watching two lovers who knew every pleasure point, every action, every touch to exhaust their partner with pleasure. They danced a fire that she fanned with every move. As a crescendo announced the finale, she threw her ankle over his shoulder, putting her long legs in a full split up his body.

She wants him. Hell, every woman in here wants him, but he should fuck her. Robert may be tempted to reopen our marriage tonight. Alyssa looked at Daniela's companion. *If he wants to have her, her man wouldn't be a bad diversion. No attachments to worry about tonight.*

A smirk flashed over both faces. Daniela nodded at him before Robert cupped her calf and her back, pinning her leg against him as he dragged her trailing foot in a slow circle. The hall fell silent with awe as the music stopped. Daniela embraced Robert, and they whispered beside her elevated leg. The crowd applauded when he lowered her leg and pecked her cheek.

The Russian dancer stalked off the floor, but Robert tipped the band leader before returning to their table.

"You must have loved that dance, Babe, if you tipped the band leader afterward."

"It was some dance." He offered his hand, and Alyssa let him help her stand.

When she was holding Robert's arm, Edwin McCain's "I'll Be" began to play. She stopped walking and looked at Robert.

"I promised you the last dance. Come on, Baby, they're playing our song."

He led her toward the dance floor, just as he had at their wedding. They had practiced the choreographed moves until they were second nature, and they danced it whenever the song played to this day. With a grin, she nodded, and they trotted to the center of the empty floor.

He snuggled behind her, crossing his arms over her stomach as they swayed, grinding her ass on his crotch. With a flick of his wrist, Alyssa twirled away, stopping with a high kick as she faced him. He beckoned her with a crooked finger, and she strutted in a wide circle around him before closing to press her body against his. As her hand trailed down his back to his ass, his feathered up her thigh, pulling the hem of her skirt, dropping it just as it revealed the hint of her cheek.

Alyssa looked over the crowd for a split second. Warm pride filled her chest at their power over the room. Nobody had left, and nobody had joined them on the floor. They stared, as enraptured at this performance as they had been minutes ago.

All of you want him, but he's leaving with me. And those of you who want me can't take me from him.

They circled each other as they danced, only breaking eye contact to glance at the silent onlookers and reconnect with a smile.

He spun her and pulled her back against his chest, then lifted when she stiffened her arms, spinning in a slow twirl during the long high note at the song's peak while she spread her legs in a wide split to either side. She dropped her legs together, and Robert flicked her in the air, spinning her and catching her waist when she faced him. Pulling her against him, he inched her to the ground, sharing a lingering kiss as their faces passed.

She pressed against him, swaying as the song neared its end. He raised her hand, guiding her in a slow pirouette while they held each other's fiery gaze. With a flick of his wrist, he pulled her to him, gripped her back, and dipped her low for a kiss during the final phrases of the saxophone.

As they rose, applause filled the room, and many of their partners crowded around to congratulate them. A hush fell as Daniela strode toward them.

She nodded to Alyssa and looked at Robert. "You make an impressive point. You can still change your mind."

He smiled. "Not tonight. Thank you."

She handed him a card. "If you ever want to dance."

Robert tucked it in his jacket.

As Daniela turned to leave, she leaned close to Alyssa. "He made an uncommon choice."

Alyssa didn't know how to respond, and her second of silence allowed the Russian to join her escort and leave. By the time the group around them thinned, Robert's arm fell into its familiar place across her back and his hand gripped her side. She felt her cheeks strain as she grinned.

His hot breath tickled her neck as he whispered, "Let's go, Baby. I'm taking you home."

⁓

The walk to the cabin took longer because Alyssa snuggled against Robert the entire way up the hill from the clubhouse. His thigh flexed against her hip with every small step. She imagined how it would feel flexing between hers when they reached the cabin.

Like it always does. I can't wait.

The day had gone perfectly to plan, and she knew the evening on the dance floor was foreplay for the night to come. She would run to the cabin if it weren't for the heels.

He stopped her under the streetlight and pulled her to face him. "You made today an adventure in being together, every second since dawn. You showed your desire to earn my trust. I was skeptical that this weekend could be impactful, but you have made it so. You are proving you want to stay together."

She pulled him along the side to the deck. "I'm not done yet."

Thin clouds obscured the moon, making the white cushions of the double chaise glow in the darkness. Once beside it, she turned to kiss Robert with her arms draped over his shoulders. He inched the hem of her dress above her cheeks, then gripped her ass to pull her against his body.

Alyssa nudged him backward when she broke their kiss. "You

looked so good tonight. Every woman there fantasized about what was under your suit. I won't fantasize. Show me."

Robert smirked while he dropped his jacket behind him. He turned to find the edge of the picnic table and leaned against it while he removed his shoes and socks. He stood and took three steps toward the end of the chaise. Alyssa's pussy surged with juice as his eyes narrowed with desire, and she reached under her dress to tease it with a finger.

He unbuttoned his cuffs before starting on the placket. *He's a sophisticated predator tonight.*

"That's it." She whirled her finger around her silk-covered clit as she fought to enjoy the show instead of jumping on her husband the way her body begged her to. "You're mesmerizing in the moonlight."

Now shirtless, Robert unbuckled his belt, stopped moving, and chuckled. "Your mouth is open just enough to breathe. Your eyes are wide. You're playing with yourself under your dress. If you are ready to skip the foreplay, lie back, pull your panties to the side, and I'll give you what you want." He froze, clearly waiting for her to answer. All the while, her body simmered.

He knows I'm on fire, but he's teasing me. If I lie back, he'll go even slower. He wants to shatter me. I want that too. Let's increase the tension, Babe. She shook her head slowly without breaking eye contact. "Not yet. I'm just getting warmed up."

With a smirk and a nod, he eased his pants open. He had never taken so long to lower a zipper in their life together. But she would ask him to do it again. She circled her clit faster but never touched it, multiplying the ropes of titillating heat massing in her belly without igniting them.

She and Robert locked eyes as they dueled. She tempted him with the accelerating gasps and undulating hips of a woman in heat, a woman unable to deny him any desire. He tempted her with the interminable revelation of the man she needed to take her. She knew neither would yield, and neither could wait.

As he lowered his pants, slowly freeing his thick cock, she allowed her clit one flick of her finger. Her hips bucked forward, and a quick grunt escaped her lips at the sparkling electricity that lingered over it.

She beckoned to him with her finger. "Come to me now."

With two quick steps, he reached her. In the span of one steamy kiss, her dress was bunched at her waist. How he pulled the top down and the hem up so fast, she didn't know and didn't care. She knew he loved her, and now she knew he hungered for her.

"I love your tits. You don't need a bra, so I can do this." He kissed around one breast, spiraling in to latch her nipple in his teeth, then stretching it out until it popped free.

The pain reached through her to the mounting pleasure above her pussy. Her abs tightened. She gasped. "They're yours, Babe. Don't stop."

He squeezed her ass cheeks, tugging and running his fingers below to rake her lips over the thong. Her skin crackled as he slid one hand up her back until he lifted her by her ass and laid her on the chaise. Without allowing her to move, he nibbled and kissed around her other breast, giving it the same slow tease, and gripped her waist as he bit her nipple.

The sexy night on the dance floor, the heat of his slow strip, and the lightning from her nipples fluttered Alyssa's belly above a simmering orgasm. Foreplay was over. She wanted him now. "That's so good. No more waiting. I need you inside me."

He yanked the waistband of her thong, shredding it and burning her ass as it jerked between her cheeks. He threw the remnants aside and glared at her. He was done waiting as well.

Hayden did that. Then he took me so hard.

Stop, Alyssa. Focus.

Take me like you own me, Robert.

His cock, comfortable and familiar in her hand, still excited her as much as it did the first time she'd guided it to her wet lips. "Open me."

Her lips stung, stretched by his girth as he inched inside. The curve she loved so well forced his head against her G-spot, her juices letting their skin slide frictionless until he tapped the sensitive spot beside her cervix. He plunged deeper, opening the entire length of her pussy by the time his hips rested against her inner thighs. She held him inside her as she panted, gripping his sides tighter when he tried to withdraw. Her muscles flexed against his cock as the hard intruder stretched them. Pressure and pain mingled with fullness and accumulated atop her pussy, fanning her building orgasm. With a flutter, her pussy relaxed, ready for the next step.

"Now fuck me."

His slow withdrawal rippled every vein and ridge on his cock against her lips. He stopped when his cockhead compressed her G-spot, the constant pressure swamping her body. She grunted as he slammed forward, the sound echoing off the house in the crisp air.

So good. Give me more of that. I'm coming soon.

He slammed into her three more times, and each time he stretched her channel until she screamed. Her juices flowed with each movement, and she felt it flowing down her ass to the cushion below. He sped up until he was filling her slightly faster and harder than his typical, even pace. Her breasts bounced, tugging against her chest as they resonated with his pummeling.

Alyssa braced against the back of the chaise with both hands, desperate to maintain full contact with her husband's wonderful cock. When he lifted her legs to his chest, he held her body in place with both arms. She pulled her nipples, adding their lightning to the storm about to escape her pussy. She gritted her teeth, but she couldn't contain the brief grunts that each thrust drove through her chest.

I'm coming. God, I'm coming.

"Come in me. Come with me." Her wail filled the crisp air as her orgasm flowed into her body.

"Here I come." He pounded into her a few final times, stretching her as he swelled the last bit before burying himself inside and jetting hot cum on her cervix. The sensation exploded her orgasm. She clamped her legs around him, keeping him inside. Her pussy clenched against his steely cock in waves.

He lowered his body onto hers. The security of Robert enveloping her flowed through her body in a wave that relaxed her muscles. He nibbled her neck, spasming her pussy in a delicious aftershock.

Alyssa stroked the back of Robert's head, briefly tightening her grip when he tried to rise.

He raised his eyebrows. "You don't want to go to bed?"

"Not yet, Babe. Stay on me. I love this feeling."

He smiled and relaxed onto his elbows. The hint of weight fit perfectly, holding her in place on the cushions and allowing her to catch her breath.

Perfect like always. He feels it too. It's time to test the waters.

"She wanted you, Babe."

"Who?"

"Who. Give me a break. Daniela."

"I know."

A surge of jealousy and pride mixed in her gut. "How?"

"She told me her husband gave her permission to have me tonight."

"Just like that?"

Robert squeezed her waist. "No. She displayed what she wanted to give me."

The flash of understanding washed away her moment of confusion. "Ah, with the vertical split."

He nodded and grinned. "It was a vertical split, for sure. Who knew dancers didn't wear panties?"

Alyssa cackled. *That's my husband.* "And you turned her down? Why?"

The smile left his face. "We haven't decided to reopen our marriage yet."

She nodded and caressed his cheek. "Robert, you have borne the cost of our open agreement. I would have agreed if you had wanted to have the benefits tonight." *Hayden still haunts me. Letting Robert go with her wouldn't begin to repay him.*

"When she said you could come, too, I considered it."

"Babe, you should have said something." *I would have helped.* "She gave you a card. Call her. If the offer still stands, I'll join or stay here—your call."

"I made my call. You orchestrated a perfect day, and we deserved to finish it together. Daniela is a temptation, but I refuse to dishonor your effort by leaving you alone."

A warm, confused flush flowed up her chest to her mouth, escaping in a strangled sob. Guilt and admiration wrangled to control her love for him. Neither won before she spoke.

"Oh, Robert, I love you too. But we opened our marriage to experience new things. Tonight, when I told you to enjoy dancing with all the different partners, even the last dance with Daniela, it was because I love you enough to support your opportunities to get the most out of life. That's true when you have the once-in-a-lifetime opportunity to bed a professional Russian dancer. I feel bad you passed on her because you felt guilty about our day."

Robert shook his head and kissed her before she could

continue. "Baby, I passed on the dancer because I wanted to be with you, not because I felt guilty. Frankly, after your dishonesty about Hayden, I would have been completely justified going with Daniela."

Alyssa's stomach flipped from guilt and knowing he told the truth. *And he's right. Leaving me alone at the table while walking out on her arm wouldn't have been as disrespectful as I was.*

"But reconnecting with you is more important than twenty Russian dancers could be. You have worked hard, doting on me and respecting my space at the same time. Yes, I noticed. You created a captive audience this weekend, and it is working. We are rebuilding our trust. Time together, resisting the tempting dalliance in favor of a stronger relationship, cements that process. Repairing our relationship was my choice tonight."

"Do you mean that? This weekend is working? I thought you wouldn't believe it until we were home."

"We still face that test, but yes, this weekend together is working."

Take the shot. "Babe, is it working well enough to try opening our marriage again? We both liked the variety. We'll have an empty nest when Clay leaves in August, and we may need some excitement."

"You think we will get bored?"

She felt him tense as he said it. *Clarify. He'll get it.* "I said we may need some excitement. Didn't you like that uneasy excitement of learning a new lover, or the excitement of playing together with someone?"

His silence answered her better than his nod.

"But be honest, the anticipation of coming home to reclaim each other really gets your blood boiling, doesn't it?" *You know it does. You always fuck me harder when you know I've been with someone else. You reclaim me like you mean it, and we both love it.*

He smiled. "When we get home, if you want to try being open again, I'll go along. But you have to obey the rules."

I didn't expect him to agree yet. Maybe he wasn't as upset as he acted. No. He was, but he trusts me. Some days I don't know why, but I'll earn it this time.

"Babe, I will. And I'll be selective. But this only works if you get to enjoy it. Why don't you meet Daniela in the morning? This is your big chance."

He shook his head. "No. My big chance this weekend is with you. This captive audience thing works both ways. I intend to have my fun with you."

His cock twitched against her thigh. *You're getting hard. Time for round two, Babe.* With a squeeze, she kissed him. *All right. Let's have a little fun.*

"Very well, then. Carry me to bed. See if my splits get you hard like hers did."

With a laugh, Robert stood, slung Alyssa over his shoulder, and headed inside.

6

WEDNESDAY, JUNE 23, EPICUREAN RESTAURANT

SHIT. NOT HERE. Not today.

Alyssa couldn't believe her luck. A student had delayed the morning training session by complaining that the instructor was treating him unfairly. She had observed for an hour before removing the immature student for acting recklessly with knives and heat.

Then Frank had asked her to substitute for Doug with the potential franchisee whose knowledge of their industry was the only thing worse than his manners. He ate like a pig, had derided the waitstaff, and clearly had ascertained her bra size but not her eye color.

She had looked to the other side of the dining room, seeking relief from the view of her companion's chewed food. Hayden sat

44

with a young woman by the windows. A smirk had crossed his face when he and Alyssa made eye contact.

The day would be fine if I could hide in his arms and let him push all this away.

Her gut tightened.

Then my marriage would collapse. That's a bad day.

Her companion's phone squawked with an alarm lifted from a submarine avoiding a torpedo. She decided not to try to hide her frown when he announced he needed to catch his flight and left without even a thank-you. *He probably thinks I miss his company.*

Half her food had outlasted her appetite, but she needed a few minutes. She nibbled a bit before the waiter delivered a gin and tonic.

"I didn't order this. You must have the wrong table."

"It is compliments of the gentleman across the room." He pointed toward Hayden.

Alyssa looked over long enough to nod in acknowledgment.

"I'm working. I can't drink this. You can take it back."

The waiter raised his hand. "He said I was to leave it on the table. It was your decision to drink it or not."

She sighed. *I can't even get a waiter to do what I want.* "Very well. Leave it." She stood. "I am stepping to the restroom, but I am not finished eating. Please do not clear the table."

"Yes, ma'am. I will watch it in your absence."

Alyssa let the cold water run over her hands and wrists until the cold had restored some energy. *If he's gone, the afternoon will be better. So why do I want him to hold me?*

Because you still have those feelings. Fight them, or lose your marriage. Finish eating while you settle your thoughts.

She opened the restroom door and stepped out into Hayden's chest. His hands gripped her shoulders, strong but gentle. His scent filled her nose, clean and arousing.

He kissed her, hard and hungry, his tongue tickling her lips, requesting entry.

She gave it, opening her mouth as she pressed her body to his. Red wine and chocolate teased her mouth. *He even tastes like dessert.* Her pussy throbbed, almost begging Alyssa to pull Hayden into a stall and fuck him before she could think.

Electricity crackled across her skin as his hand traced down her back to squeeze her ass and press her against his hardness. *Like I remember. I want this.*

I can't fight it. I need him. Just once.

She reached back to open the ladies' room door. As she touched the handle, someone up the hall cleared her throat. Alyssa broke the kiss to see an older lady walking their way.

She smirked and leaned close to Alyssa's ear. "I don't blame you, honey, but don't bring him in here. My church group will all need to pee over the next twenty minutes, and some of them wouldn't understand. Go to the hotel up the street to let this fine man wear you out."

She patted Alyssa's shoulder before slipping through the door.

Hayden pulled her close to him again. "That is a smart old lady. Come with me."

Do it. Alyssa tightened her arm around his waist before releasing and stepping back.

"I can't, Hayden. I crave how you shatter me, but I'll destroy my family if I go with you. We have to be done."

"You want this. Come with me and let me shatter you all afternoon. You can be home on time with a big smile on your face. And nobody will ever know."

His gaze held her, confident and comforting. Her heart wanted to cling to him, but her brain forced her to nudge her hands against his chest.

You want this. Do you want a divorce? Choose.

"No, Hayden. I can't see you."

"But you want to. You miss me, and I miss you. I care for you and need to be with you. You are clearly having a bad day. Let me help you feel better."

She pushed again, stepping back until he released her.

"All that is true, but everything I love will collapse."

"Not everything. I'm right here. And I'll never collapse with you."

She closed her eyes, afraid her will would fail if he smiled. The day had been too hard; he was too tempting. She pushed him harder and opened the restroom door. Still unable to look at him, she spoke over her shoulder, praying her voice didn't reveal the anguish consuming her from inside.

"Please, if you ever cared for me, leave me alone."

Alyssa bent over the sink, this time splashing the cold water on her face to clear her thoughts. It would do no worse to her makeup than the tears welling in her eyes. She released them, softly sobbing into her hands as she bent over the sink.

She let the small hand caress her back a while before looking up at the old lady in the mirror.

"He's the one you can't resist, isn't he?"

Still unable to speak, Alyssa nodded.

"Your husband knows? Maybe you are on your last chance?"

Another nod.

"You can't believe it, but you're considering leaving your husband for the man outside?"

Her guts wrenched. Even an old lady in a bathroom could see through her. How could she hide her feelings from Robert until they subsided? Another sob rose from deep in her belly. Both hands muffled it, limiting the sound even in the tiled room. She mentally clung to the continuing soft caresses as the only protection against the emotional tornado inside her.

"It happened to me, honey. It's not easy."

After some deep breaths, Alyssa could respond. "What did you do?"

"Lost them both. I fought my lover's temptation for a while, then gave in, then tried to be a good wife and resisted my lover again until the cycle repeated. My husband ran out of forgiveness and threw me out. By then, my lover had grown tired of me stringing him along and found someone else. I have a good husband now, but he's a distant third behind the two men I threw away."

She had never considered losing both. She wanted to finagle having both. Cold fear buckled her knees. She caught herself on the countertop.

"What should I do?"

"Do you have children?"

"Yes."

The old lady wrapped her arm across Alyssa's shoulders. "Either rid yourself of your lover or embrace a lonely life."

"How do I get free of him?"

"The same way you beat any addiction: either quit cold turkey or have one last time to get it out of your system."

After hugging the old lady and repairing her makeup, Alyssa returned to her table. A bite of the cold food turned to sawdust in her mouth, and she handed the waiter her credit card.

She looked around. Hayden was gone.

Thank god. I couldn't resist him again. Cold turkey isn't working, but one last time might not be the last time.

She picked up the gin and tonic, closed her eyes, and held the cool glass to her forehead. It pushed against the headache that was building behind her eyes. When the waiter mumbled for her to have a good afternoon, she opened her eyes, knowing there was no possibility of that happening.

She made eye contact with the old lady, who gave a wan smile and raised her drink in a silent toast.

Alyssa raised hers in return, then chugged it dry.

7

WEDNESDAY, JUNE 23, HOME

Alyssa lay her head on Robert's shoulder. She panted as fast as he did as they came down from their lovemaking. Since returning from the mountains, they had resumed interacting around the house. They'd cleaned up supper together, talked, laughed, and made love every night.

The routine had become her safe haven, especially tonight. The afternoon had been a blur after she saw Hayden. She had not told Robert of the encounter because she'd resisted him, and she couldn't risk the progress she and Robert had made. But she had needed Robert to love her tonight. And he had. During what was easily the highlight of her day, he had taken his time building her to a powerful climax, and now they lay panting together.

"Thank you, Babe. I needed that tonight."

"Glad to provide. Anything you want to talk about?"

"Nothing more than I told you already. Just a rough day."

Which was almost much worse. And much better. God, Alyssa. Get control. She raised her head, needing eye contact to connect even though their skin touched from head to foot and he was caressing her back. "What about you? Anything you want to discuss?"

"Only whatever has you in knots. You don't normally get flustered from the kind of issues you described. Are you sure that's all it was?"

Shit. What is he hinting at? Or is he showing his attention to my mood? Can he see through me like everyone else? I can't tell him now; he'll be upset that I waited. Nothing happened. Except that kiss, and almost pulling him into the restroom at a busy restaurant to get my pussy filled. But that counts as nothing for today. Keep it that way.

I need a distraction. Maybe if we play with someone, it will help.

"Yeah. That's all. Maybe it just hit me hard after such a great weekend."

"Okay."

He would ponder everything she said tonight until he deduced what was bothering her. Even though there was nothing to worry about, she clung to the progress they had made. She needed his help, and doing that meant refocusing him on the good times.

Let's see if he's ready. "You tasted salty. I thought you made love so well to get another woman out of your mind. Have you been busy today?"

"I have been busy but only working and playing basketball with Clay. Sorry to disappoint, but that was just sweat you tasted, not pussy."

"Just making sure."

"What about you? Your enthusiasm tonight could say the same thing. Any visitors you need to tell me about?"

He knows better, but he's asking for a reason. "No visitors. I've only been with you. We opened our marriage again, and I'm playing by the rules. No disclosure, no playing outside. I won't violate your trust."

He stopped caressing her back with his fingertips. "It has been good to refocus."

Remember the excitement and ease back in. "It has, though we should play sometime soon."

"You must be past being deliberate with your partners. Are you back to 'just for fun'?"

"No, I'm still choosy. But fun is an honorable intention, too, isn't it?"

Robert laughed. "Yes, fun for its own sake is worth pursuing. Did you have someone in mind?"

"I did. Why don't we invite Summer for dinner one night when the kids are out? We could see how she's handling her divorce. We would be deliberately checking on a friend and having fun at the same time."

"We can. We've seen her at the club several times, and you have texted with her, right?"

"Yes, but texts and talking in passing don't match a deliberate visit. It has been too long."

"You have thought this through, Baby. You are more deliberate than I thought."

"So?" She waited as he took a deep breath. He was considering it. *Come on, Robert. Help me and have some fun at the same time.*

"Sounds good. We helped her end her marriage. We should make sure she is getting along all right."

8

SATURDAY, JUNE 26, COUNTRY CLUB

ALYSSA FINISHED ARRANGING her towel on the pool chair beside Summer and turned to sit.

"Before you sit down, let's take a dip. I'm hot." Summer stood and patted Alyssa's hip.

"Okay." Alyssa tossed her cover-up on the chair and dove in beside Summer.

Summer surfaced beside Alyssa, away from the few others in the pool. "Robert gave you some load this morning. Or maybe someone else?"

Alyssa's chest tightened. Summer knew she had been masturbating to memories of Hayden within thirty seconds. "How did you know?"

"Light green darkens when wet."

Should have thought of that. "Thank you for not letting me flash everyone. The matrons would not approve."

"We hot mamas need to stick together. So which is it?"

"Which what?"

"Which option gave you that wet spot?"

Alyssa looked around for eavesdroppers and decided to lie. "Robert. I haven't had anyone else in a few weeks. I got too attached to my realtor."

"Your realtor? You got attached? Tell me, you bad girl."

"I saw him a lot for a few weeks." She froze her smile to cover her thought. *More than I should have. Less than I wanted to.*

"A lot? When you had Robert at home? He must be something."

"Mm-hmm. He's tall, handsome, intelligent, he is amazing in bed, like huge and inventive. On top of that, he's a great guy. He has done kind, helpful things for me that nobody else would. I really liked him in and out of bed."

"He sounds too good to be true. What's wrong with him?"

Alyssa shrugged. "His only negative was that I got too attached. I had to stop seeing him." *She doesn't need to know I still want him every day. Or that I feel like a schoolgirl when he texts before I delete them without responding.*

"Nothing? Why hasn't somebody snatched him up? Everybody has some negatives."

"I never saw his. Of course, it was hard to see with my face jammed in a pillow." They both cackled, easing Alyssa's nerves.

"You lucky girl."

Time to change the subject. "Come on, Summer. Surely men have been chasing you since you and Bryce separated."

Summer smiled and waved her hand in the air dismissively. "A few; none worth slowing down for. I stay home a lot."

"Oh my. How long since you had sex?"

"A week."

"That's not staying home too much. Who?"

Summer's smile dimmed, and she looked down at the water. "Bryce."

"What?"

Alyssa took both of Summer's hands and watched her face while she took a few breaths, clearly trying to calm herself before continuing. Alyssa scanned the pool for anyone paying attention, but nobody was looking their way. When she looked back at Summer, the pretty blonde nodded and started to talk.

"We met at his attorney's office to work through some details. After the meeting, he asked if I wanted to get together for old times' sake. He looks so good in a suit. It had been so long. I was super horny. I fucked him in that damn sports car in the parking deck."

"Are you getting back together?"

"No, no, no, no. It was good to get some dick, and god, I came like a volcano, but I felt cheap afterward. Bryce laughed and said he'd fuck me again whenever I got desperate." Her chin flexed and quivered.

"Summer." Alyssa hugged her friend.

Summer patted Alyssa's back and broke the hug with a sad chuckle. "It's all right. I learned that I can go three months before getting desperate enough to sleep with that asshole."

Alyssa cocked her head. "You guys broke up in the middle of March, when you slept with Robert and me. You've been alone since then?"

"Yep."

"Summer, had I known, we would have met earlier. I'm sorry we didn't talk. We wanted to have you to dinner."

"You didn't know, and I didn't want to invite myself into your hectic schedules or your open marriage. Is it still open?"

Alyssa nodded. "We are being careful. You are always welcome. We care about you and are here for you, whatever you need, especially emotional support when you are lonely." *And you are so damn hot we'll never kick you out of bed.* "Our open marriage can satisfy your physical needs too.

"Thank you, Alyssa. I should have known to call."

Alyssa put her hand on Summer's shoulder. "Now you know for certain. Call Robert or me anytime." She ran her hand down Summer's arm to hold her hand. "What about dinner? You want to come?"

"I'd love to. When is good for y'all?"

"Tonight?"

"Are you sure? I don't want to mess up any plans."

"I wouldn't have invited you if I weren't sure. We can hang out and have dinner." She squeezed Summer's hand. "Honestly, we helped you end your marriage. Let us help you recover. Please come tonight."

Summer squeezed Alyssa's hand. "I'll be there. What can I bring?"

"Your appetite and a smile. Dress casual."

Summer hugged Alyssa again, squeezing tight and holding a bit longer than usual. "Thank you."

Alyssa smiled at Summer's soft snore. *She's relieved she's not alone. I should have called her earlier.* Alyssa opened her phone and texted Robert.

"Summer is coming over tonight. She needs companionship and loving. Can you grab steaks on the way home?"

She looked at her friend's bare back, the bikini top unhooked for tanning. *Her perfect muscles look gorgeous and feel wonderful. I could rub her back all night.* Alyssa set a timer for twenty minutes. *Turn, don't burn.*

Her phone vibrated in her hand with Robert's reply. "Sounds fun, my naughty wife. I'll pick up steaks and wine. You bring dessert."

"Dessert is driving herself. She needs some companionship, but she needs to get laid too. Don't tell her you know. Seduce her instead. Let her enjoy the pursuit."

"Whatever you want."

"Good. Love you, Babe."

Alyssa stared across the pool, her eyes unfocused behind her sunglasses. *Admit it, Alyssa. You care about Hayden, and you can't let him go. You masturbated to his memories on the drive over.*

Don't pretend it was just sex; you know it's true. It has been for weeks. Now what? That emotional attachment won't go away. Jessica warned you. Sonia warned you. Beth warned you. Even Robert warned you, but you let this guy worm his way from your cunt to your heart.

Even weeks after she'd last had sex with him, she couldn't stop thinking about him. Even now, thinking about how dangerous he was, her nipples were getting hard and her pussy was tingling. The sex had been so good. He'd been so inventive, like when he used the ice cubes, and he'd maneuvered her into all different positions. He was willing to do things Robert wasn't, like share. Like spank. Yes, Robert had shared once, but he'd struggled. Hayden has no problem giving me what I really want. But Robert would never hurt me, even if I begged.

But why fall in love? Don't deny it. You are in love. You are the only one who didn't see it coming. What will you do? You have chosen Robert for now, and you try to fight it. But he haunts your thoughts, your feelings.

Deep down, what do you want? Robert won't abide your loving someone else. You can't have both. Choose one to love. Cut the other one out of your life forever.

How can you even consider Hayden? Robert has been your soul-mate for twenty-four years. Throwing that away for a sex partner of two months is foolish.

But Hayden is a better lover. I don't feel Robert as well after Hayden, and it isn't because of size. I still felt Robert after Cole, who is bigger, and the three business travelers, both times.

She stifled a sob, her body knowing the truth before her mind formulated the thought into words.

I don't feel Robert as well because I don't want to. I don't want to release Hayden. I don't understand why, try as I might, I don't see his negatives. Maybe he really is the perfect man.

Hayden may not have negatives, but choosing him did. She wrung her hands as she forced herself to consider them: Divorce, but she would see Robert when she saw the kids. The realization her kids would never speak with her again, nor would most of her extended family, knotted her stomach. She wondered why she wasted her time considering him.

Because being with him forever might be worth it. Could I come home every night, knowing he had some new adventure waiting for me? We could go far away, watch the sun set, and make love. He could fuck you into oblivion and wake you by stroking your hair.

And you would never see your kids again.

Intellectually, she hated these feelings. But they were such exquisite torture. *I love Robert more than anyone in the world, but I love Hayden too. I wish I could hate him, but I can't.*

She closed her eyes and counted to one hundred while slowing her breathing. She couldn't think about this here. Her own heart tore at her, and she didn't want questions about crying at the pool.

Staying away a while longer will help me adjust. Maybe playing with Robert and Summer tonight will help too.
Hayden would love to play with Summer.
Don't fuck this up, Alyssa.

9

SATURDAY, JUNE 26, HOME

"To a great dinner companion." Alyssa tipped her glass to the petite blonde.

"That was delicious. You two outdid yourselves." Summer took a sip. "To great dinner companions." Summer tipped her glass at Alyssa and Robert. "Thanks for getting me out of the house." Her face sagged as she looked at the table.

"It's been too long, but none of that moping. We invited you here for a good evening." Robert drained his glass. "Come on. Let's play pool."

Alyssa refilled everyone's glasses, knowing alcohol would help Robert seduce Summer. "Sounds fun as long as we keep drinking." *What does he have planned?*

Robert nodded as he stood. "Pool was made for drinking. You in, Summer?"

"Sounds fun. I haven't played in years."

In the basement, Robert racked the balls. "The best three-person game is cutthroat."

"Ah. A friendly game." Alyssa drew her finger across her throat while making a gurgling noise.

"Thay don't actually play for blood...in this century." Summer giggled while choosing a cue stick. "But pool is for betting. What are the stakes?"

"Why don't we play a friendly game first?" Robert chalked his cue. "Guest's break?"

"Sure." Summer sank the seven on the break. The ten fell on her next shot, then the thirteen, before she missed on the nine. She smirked at Alyssa and Robert. "I'll take one through five."

"It's been years, huh?" Alyssa knocked in the eight.

"It has. Just beginner's luck. Or rebeginner's."

Alyssa sank the six before missing the four. "I'll take the high balls. You get the middle balls, Babe. Or should I just say the nine?"

"I'm in it yet." He pocketed the two and three, then the twelve and fifteen. He missed on the five. "That looks more even. You're up, Summer."

"This shot is all the way across the table. Do you have a bridge?"

"No bridge. House rules." Robert grinned at her.

Summer leaned far across the table and missed her awkward try at the nine. "I'm too short to play on this nine-foot table. It's too wide. And whoever heard of a no-bridge rule?"

"Not our fault you are only five feet tall." Alyssa laughed, leaned across the table, then missed the one.

"Five two, thank you very much."

Robert finished the one, then missed the four. All of them missed their next three shots.

"This is more like I expected us to play." Robert filled their glasses. "We need to drink more."

Summer took a long swig, then sank the nine. "You are out, Robert. Plenty of time for you to drink some more." She missed on the fourteen, and she and Alyssa shot several rounds at the two remaining balls before Alyssa finished Summer off.

"Woo-hoo! I'm your winner!" Alyssa danced a moment. "I never play. Did you two let me win?"

"No, Baby. You just had the right shots. And I was out early. Summer, you are our guest, why don't you set the stakes for this game?"

"Right, Robert, oh master of the table." Summer smirked at him. "Twenty bucks?"

"Seems weak from a woman who arrived in a Lexus and owns a hot tub." Robert grinned at her.

"Oh, so that's how it is? Do you want to cruise in the Lexus or use the hot tub?"

"Both, but we should settle our bet immediately. Maybe we play cards at your house for hot tub use. What's meaningful and immediate?"

Alyssa fought a smile. Robert loved to play strip pool. The stakes and the distractions rose as each article of clothing disappeared. She loved when he "won" her and she "submitted" to making love on the table. He was using the game to seduce Summer, but he was letting it feel like her idea.

Summer furrowed her brow. "I don't know. Shots?"

Robert nodded. "Which way? One shot for the losers, or a shot for each ball you lose?"

Alyssa jumped in to help. "No good. The first way isn't enough; the second is too much." Alyssa fought her smile.

Robert shrugged. "Loser does the dishes?"

Alyssa lifted the hem of her shirt like she was absent-mindedly playing with it while she thought but exposing her belly to the other two to help Robert guide Summer's thoughts. "Sounds like a punishment, not a reward. We need to play *for* something, not to *avoid* something. What's a good reward?"

Summer's eyes locked onto Alyssa's belly. Her mouth hung open. Alyssa gave Robert a quick wink, and they waited for her reverie to break. A hint of pink flushed up Summer's neck to color her cheeks. Her nipples hardened, poking the thin satin shirt. She looked up and bit her lower lip like she was embarrassed to say what they knew she was thinking.

"I have an idea." She swallowed and looked from Alyssa to Robert and back. "Clothes."

Robert downed his glass of wine. "That's my kind of reward."

"Jumping to high stakes on the first game." Alyssa smiled at Summer and turned to her husband. "And really, Robert? What are you, thirteen?"

"What can I say, Baby? A vision of you two stripping haunts me."

"You and your imagination." Alyssa winked at Robert. "You might see more playing for shots. We can win, you know."

"Maybe, but you said 'reward.' Besides, isn't it more fun to get naked when you choose the stakes of the bet than to get drunk and let your inhibitions fall? Summer knows. That's why she suggested it. Are you in for the stakes, Baby?"

Summer looked at Alyssa. "Before you answer, hear me out. I suggested this, and you two have an open marriage, but I won't play for clothes unless you agree. We all know what happens after the clothes come off."

Alyssa nodded. "Thank you for saying that. You won't hurt our marriage, but I won't play for clothes unless you want to. You have had an emotional few months. Are you sure?"

Summer nodded and turned to Robert. "Strip pool it is. But in case I change my mind, I set the stakes for the game after that."

"Deal." Robert shook her hand.

Alyssa hardened her tone and scowled at the other two. "You didn't get my answer yet."

Robert and Summer looked at Alyssa.

"Just kidding. I'm in. I set the stakes after Summer does." Alyssa took the cue ball from Robert. "And since I won, I break."

"One second, ladies. Since we are playing one article of clothing per ball, should we assign numbers before the break, or does the last one to pick have to catch up?"

Summer grinned. "I don't know. The break is random."

Alyssa bent to Summer's ear while looking at Robert without trying to whisper. "What do you think? Do we get him naked all at once, or a little at a time before he even shoots?"

"A little at a time. Plus, if I get you naked along the way, you might distract him if he does get a shot. You break and take one through five, I'm six through ten, and Robert, since you shoot last, you are eleven through fifteen." She patted Alyssa's ass. "Shoot well. I really want to see your husband naked again. No offense."

Alyssa patted Summer's ass in return. "None taken. I want to see him naked too." She broke well, sinking the seven. "You first."

Summer hiked her skirt until she could reach the waistband of her yellow thong, slid it down her legs, and stepped out of it, all while staring into Robert's eyes. She walked to him with the panties extended before her. "Is this what you wanted? Me out of my panties?"

Robert took the panties from her. "It's a start." He displayed the darker yellow in the crotch before placing them on the bar. "Moist. I think you wanted these off as much as I did."

"Ha!" She caressed the top of Alyssa's chest through the

cutout in her shirt. "I'm wet because your wife's cleavage has teased me all night."

Alyssa pulled Summer's hand out of her shirt. "Wet because of me? I'm flattered, but it's only half true, isn't it?"

"Keep shooting and find out."

Alyssa missed on the eleven.

Summer didn't. "One article of clothing, mister."

"I'm only wearing four. I shouldn't take anything off for the first ball to keep it even."

"You should have thought of that before wagering your clothes. Strip." Alyssa twirled her finger at him to spur him along.

Robert put a shoe under the bar. "If that's the way it's going to be, I'll just have to win."

"Good luck with that," Summer said as she sank the thirteen. Robert removed the other shoe as she missed on the one.

"I hope you have enjoyed wearing your clothes, ladies, because now they come off." He finished off the one. Alyssa put a sandal beside his shoe. "Hardly fair. Your beautiful feet were already on display in those sandals." He put the four in the corner pocket, and Alyssa removed the other sandal. "I like that red toenail polish, Baby."

Alyssa moved across the table from his shot on the eight and stretched her leg along the rail. "This red toenail polish, Babe?" She leaned over to trace her finger along the tips of her toes, staring at him.

Robert smirked and sank the eight. "Mm-hmm. And that gorgeous leg too." He turned to Summer. "Dropping a heel, Summer?"

"Not if I want to reach across the table." She smirked at him as she lifted the tank top over her head and tossed it on the bar. "These boobs aren't as good as your wife's, but I bet they make you miss on the five." She moved behind the shot he was lining up and tweaked her hard nipples.

Robert missed. "They didn't make me miss, but they are beautiful, right, Baby?"

Alyssa smiled. "Beautiful and every bit as good as mine. Don't sell those firm and perkies short, Summer." She cupped one as she walked by the petite aerobics instructor and smirked at her husband. "And they absolutely made you miss." Alyssa sank the fifteen. "Show us some skin, Mister I-Want-to-Play-for-Clothes."

Robert pulled the hem of his blue polo shirt out of his shorts.

"Slowly. We want a show," Summer said.

Robert smiled and worked the hem up one side a bit before moving the other side above it, all while swaying his hips. He added it to the pile on the bar.

Alyssa watched, always enthralled by her husband's hard body, even in his forties. She rubbed her hand along his firm, flat abs when she walked by him.

"This was a good idea after all." She missed the twelve, but it knocked the three in on the rebound. "That's mine. What do I do?"

"Take off some clothes, slowly, like Robert did," Summer said. "We want a show from you too."

Alyssa moved so the table wasn't between her and Summer. She danced, swaying her hips and unbuttoning her shorts before working them down her legs and off, sticking her ass out at Summer. She dropped the shorts on the growing pile.

"That would be sexier if you weren't wearing those big boy-short panties. I'm a little surprised." Summer patted one of the cheeks still thrust toward her. "Still very sexy though. And still your shot."

"You'll understand shortly."

Alyssa missed on the six. Summer sank the twelve. "Drop 'em, big boy."

Robert unfastened his shorts, held the waistband away from his body, and let them fall to the floor. His erection, purple and full, pointed at the two women standing side by side. "Alyssa's chest may have made you wet, but my cock is making your mouth hang open, Summer."

"Yes, it is," Summer whispered without averting her eyes.

Robert chuckled. "Still your shot, if you can find your wits." He moved in line with her shot on the two and laid his cock on the rail.

Summer recovered enough to smirk at him and hit the two hard, stopping the cue ball dead and slamming the two into the pocket.

Robert jerked back at the loud clack. "Careful, you may yet want this tonight."

"Oh, I do. But first, I want to see your wife's gorgeous tits. Alyssa, if you please?"

Alyssa shook her head. "Not yet, you don't. I choose what's coming off." She hooked her thumbs in the waistband of the panties and pulled them out from her hips. She turned her back to Summer and Robert, who had joined her for the show. Alyssa worked the panties down her straight legs, bending at the waist until her head was near her knees and her panties were on the floor. The cool air kissed the insides of her lips, confirming that they were flowering open.

Without straightening, Alyssa stepped out of her boy shorts, then stood and walked them to Summer. "The big panties were to catch Robert's big load from before dinner. You can have it if you want it." She displayed the wet crotch.

Summer leaned her stick against the wall and took the panties in both hands. She put the crotch in front of her mouth before shaking her head with a laugh and tossing them on the clothing pile. "I'm not that drunk yet, but keep trying." She grabbed a wine glass from the bar and drained it.

Summer frowned at the table, then smiled. She raised her right knee, put it down, and hiked up her skirt, then placed her knee on the rail to lean in for a shot. She looked over her shoulder at Robert and Alyssa watching her bare ass from behind.

"She's as wet as you, without a load of cum." Robert nudged his wife and pointed at Summer's pussy.

"Don't shoot yet, Summer. We have to make sure you still have one foot on the floor." Alyssa stepped behind Summer and placed both hands on her exposed butt cheek. She knelt and ran her hands down, dragging her fingers along Summer's slit before caressing the inside and outside of her leg all the way to her ankle. She ran her hands back up, this time sliding a finger inside the trembling blonde. She stepped back and patted Summer's ass. "You're official. You can shoot now."

Summer missed on the fourteen. Her knee stayed on the table while she panted. "Thanks for checking me."

Robert lined up and sank the six. "Let's have that skirt, Summer."

Summer walked to him, turned around and lowered her skirt just as Alyssa had done with her panties. She put her head on her knees and grabbed the back of her ankles. Her pussy lips spread, crisscrossed by a gray web of lubrication. "Like this?"

"Yes." Robert grabbed her hips and slid his cock inside her pussy, burying most of his length on the first try. They both moaned. He stroked her five times, then pulled out, his cock shiny in the bright light above the table.

"No. Come back. Please."

Alyssa laughed. "Stand up and watch. I think he's about to win."

Robert sank the nine, then the ten, and Summer moved to the bar to remove her heels. "No, leave those. You look even sexier with them on. But you are out of the game."

As Robert lined up to sink the five, Alyssa and Summer moved behind it. Alyssa nodded at Summer, and they kissed. Their hands roamed each other's bodies. Summer moaned when Alyssa pulled her nipples. Summer dipped a finger into Alyssa's pussy, then pulled it out, making Alyssa's lips throb. She broke the kiss, looked Robert in the eye, and said, "Take the shot," before sucking the wet finger into her mouth and moaning again.

Robert laughed and resumed what he had been doing before getting distracted by the two hot MILFs in front of him. He shot before they could resume, and the five dropped into the side pocket. "My dear, please show us your tits."

Alyssa stretched the shirt down so her nipples peeked through the cutout above her breasts.

"Not good enough. Take it off," said Summer with a wag of her finger.

Alyssa pulled the shirt over her head, then wiggled her chest as she dropped the final piece of clothing onto the bar.

"Amazing. That big and no sag. They get more perfect every time I see them." Summer cupped one in her hand and sucked the other nipple into her mouth. Alyssa gasped, and Summer switched sides.

She cupped Alyssa's mound and squeezed. The pressure across her lips would have made them open on their own if Summer hadn't been holding them in place. Instead, they tingled and pressed against each other as they swelled.

Summer stood. She kissed Robert and fondled his cock. Alyssa knelt beside Summer and sucked the tip of her husband's cock into her mouth. He tasted like sweat and pussy. She flicked her tongue around and over him, savoring the flavor of fucking.

As she took more, her lips nudged Summer's hand. Summer released Robert's cock and wove her fingers into Alyssa's hair, gripping it and cupping the back of her head. The strong hand in her hair pushed a little when Alyssa bobbed down, forcing her to take more than she intended on each pass.

Alyssa bobbed her head until she swallowed her husband's entire cock. *She's guiding my head with her hand. So hot.* Ceding to the tactile instructions tingled her clit. She rewarded it with light brushes from her fingertip. She held his cock in her throat until she needed to breathe, then pulled all the way off. She looked up at Summer. "I expect to taste that pussy from the source very soon."

Summer broke her kiss with Robert. "You will. I set the stakes this time." She pulled Alyssa's hair to guide her to stand, then traced her fingers down her spine to cup Alyssa's ass. "This time, when a player goes out, he will obey the player who sank the last ball for five minutes. The final winner controls both losers for twenty minutes. You in?"

Robert gripped Alyssa's other cheek as the three of them huddled close. He held more of the cheek than Summer, and his fingers dug into her, where Summer's pressure came through the palm, lifting the cheek where Robert squeezed it. Alyssa imagined those hands all over her body and moaned into her kiss with Robert.

Robert broke their kiss. "And when she goes out?"

"Feeling confident, Babe? We are ganging up on you."

"I just won. I'm hard from thinking about the possibilities."

"I thought you were hard from just being down my throat."

"And in my pussy."

"True enough, but the thought of you obeying me keeps me saluting."

Summer gripped his cock. "So you in?"

"Not yet, but I will be."

"Maybe. What about you, Alyssa? Are you in?"

"Mm-hmm. Sounds like fun. You won, Babe. Break."

Robert broke, sinking nothing. "You're next, Alyssa."

As Alyssa walked toward her shot, Summer stopped the taller woman by placing a hand on her abs as she tried to pass.

She caressed them from ribs to mound, sending sparks to gather low in Alyssa's belly, where they churned and grew. "Don't miss."

Alyssa shot at the fifteen. It rattled between the pocket facings and stayed on the table. "That's your fault, Summer."

"I know. It's a trick I learned in college." Summer cracked her knuckles and chalked her cue stick. She proceeded to sink the one, two, and three in order, moving quickly from shot to shot before banking in the four.

Robert chuckled. "Baby, we've been had. Summer really knows how to play."

"I learned in college. A couple of alcohol-induced blackouts taught me that I was too little to drink with big guys playing pool at the bars. If I wanted to remember going home, I had to win. I practiced as much as I studied. I haven't played in years. This is where you go out, Robert." She banked the five off the rail and the eight right into the pocket.

Summer walked to the couch along the wall and reclined on her elbows. She crooked her finger at Robert and said, "For the next five minutes, kiss me, lick me, suck me, make me come with your mouth. Alyssa, time us."

Alyssa winked at her husband as she moved so she could see. "She suckered us, Babe. I hope you aren't scarred by having to nibble such an incredible body."

Robert nodded back at her. "This is the best way I've ever been conned. Remind me never to play her for money."

Robert climbed onto Summer and kissed her while he slid his hands down her sides to cup her ass cheeks and pull them apart before kissing down her neck to her breasts. Their small size meant they stood straight up from her chest with little sag, and he nibbled around them before sucking the hard nipple into his mouth.

Summer moaned and hugged his head tight to her chest.

"Getting mashed flat against his rough palate shatters your nipple, doesn't it?" Alyssa whispered in Summer's ear.

"Yes."

Alyssa pinched Summer's other nipple and looked at the clock. "Three minutes left, Babe."

Robert pulled Summer's nipple up with his mouth until it popped out. He kissed his way down her abs, leaving Alyssa to tease Summer's tits. As Robert reached Summer's cleft, he pushed her thighs up and back, opening her.

He licked from the bottom of her opening to the top, flicking the clit when he reached it. Summer gasped, and he licked down the outside until he reached the bottom, where he repeated the trip up to flick her clit. He licked down the other outside lip this time, then stuck his tongue inside before sucking the right inner lip into his mouth and pulling it.

Summer's abs pulsed as she breathed in ragged gasps punctuated by staccato, low yips when Robert's tongue crossed her clit.

"One minute," Alyssa said.

Robert licked up Summer's pussy and sucked her clit into his mouth. Summer's eyes flew wide open, and her mouth opened in an *O*. Alyssa knew how powerful Robert's move felt, and her pussy throbbed in sympathy with what Summer experienced. His teeth kept the hood back, and the bare nub was sucked and flicked against his teeth. Summer yelped and gripped Robert's hair, clearly wanting more explosive contact.

Alyssa pulled both Summer's nipples up as the small woman pressed her head back against the sofa and closed her eyes. Summer's neck flushed pink as her breathing accelerated. Robert made eye contact and nodded.

"That's time," Alyssa said just as Summer began humping her hips upward. Robert released her clit and rose.

"No. Don't stop. Make me come. I'm so close."

Alyssa cupped Summer's cheek. "Five minutes is the stakes. You got every second. Was it good?"

"God yes, but I need thirty more seconds. I'm so close. Please."

Alyssa rose from beside Summer's head. "You will have to win the whole thing. Good luck with your pussy on fire. It is on fire, isn't it?"

"Yes. That was so good. Please let me finish."

Alyssa chuckled. "Nope. And it is your shot. You can take a minute to get your breathing back to normal if you'd like. Or you can finish yourself off, if you prefer."

"No. I'll shoot. Then I'll leave *you* wanting more."

Summer sat up, closing her eyes and shuddering before returning to the table for her next shot. She shook her head and sank the six, seven, and eight. After sinking the nine, she put one leg on the table, showing her open pussy to Alyssa. "Do you see how wet I am? How it runs down my legs? Your husband did that to me, and you are going to clean me up…right after this shot." She ran two fingers up her pussy, spreading it further.

"This is where I win." Summer shot the ten, knocking it into the side pocket. The cue ball rolled toward the corner. "Stop!" she yelled at the white ball to no avail. It fell neatly into the pocket. "Dammit."

Robert laughed. "Never gloat before you win. We each get a ball on the table." He put the three and the nine on the spot.

"Ball in hand to me." Robert finished off the fifteen, then the twelve and eleven. As he walked by Summer to shoot the fourteen, he patted her ass. "Twenty minutes for the winner. Should be fun."

He pocketed the fourteen and lined up on the thirteen. The shot left the thirteen on the lip of the side pocket. The cue ball caromed to his three, knocking it close to the corner pocket.

Alyssa cackled. "How perfect!" She clicked the cue ball off the thirteen, pocketing it. "Come here, Summer. I'm in control for five minutes." She patted the couch. "Lie on your back. Spread your legs."

Summer did. Alyssa sucked her clit into her mouth as Robert had moments earlier, exposing it with her teeth and flicking it with her tongue.

Summer grabbed Alyssa's hair. "Wait. Don't you want me to do you? I'm the one out."

"What I want is to taste your cum and then make you come again before the time runs out. We invited you here so you could feel good tonight, and I'm going to make that happen. Robert, play with her tits while you watch the clock."

Alyssa returned to her high-intensity cunnilingus, sucking and flicking the overstimulated nub. She pushed two fingers inside Summer's slick opening, pressing down toward her back and moving in and out. Summer clamped her thighs on Alyssa's ears. She quivered as her orgasm crashed.

Alyssa sustained the assault on Summer's pussy. She looked up over Summer's flushed torso.

Robert pulled and rolled Summer's nipple with one hand and caressed the whole breast with the other. Summer took her first deep breath since the orgasm had begun. After two more, Robert kissed her. When he pulled back to check the clock, Alyssa saw the veins in her neck straining against the skin.

"One minute, Baby. Work fast."

Alyssa nodded, then twirled her fingers inside Summer to press all sides of her tunnel before pushing deep inside to rub the sensitive spot beside her cervix. She sucked Summer's clit one last time and smiled as the strong, sexy legs clamped onto her ears yet again. She lapped at the juices that flowed from the spasming pussy while moving her fingers just enough to prolong the orgasm. When Summer's legs relaxed, Alyssa kissed above Summer's slit and smiled at her.

"Thank you."

"You give orders well." Alyssa stood and walked to the table. "Let's see if you will follow orders as well, Babe, when I put you out." She lined up on the three.

Robert moved into her view and waggled his cock at her. "Don't miss."

Alyssa bounced the cue ball perfectly between the cushions to tap the three into the pocket while avoiding the scratch. "Yay! I win again!" She placed her stick on the table and repeated her jig from earlier, then stopped.

Standing still, she hefted her breasts in her hands. She strode around the pool table to Robert. "Summer, come here." She pulled Robert in for a kiss. "You two, suck my tits."

Robert and Summer each took the closest nipple into their mouth, sucking and licking. Her nipples crackled with electricity that bounced between them before massing low in her belly. Robert dragged his fingers up Alyssa's leg from her knee to her pussy and guided two fingers inside, stretching her lips and firing sparks up her walls to join with the mass sitting atop it. Summer caressed Alyssa's abs with one hand, simmering her orgasm through the skin.

"That's it. Please me." When Alyssa's knees weakened, she pulled the two heads off her chest and sat on the pool table.

"Summer, sixty-nine with me. Babe, fuck me hard, but don't come. I have plans for that."

She lay back on the table with her ass on the edge.

Summer climbed on the table and picked up the nine ball, brandishing it above Alyssa's face. "You're going to love this." Summer straddled Alyssa's head and ground her pussy onto Alyssa's face before bending forward. Alyssa tongued between the lips, spreading them and letting the juices flow into her mouth. Summer's body folded down onto hers, lighter and smaller than a man's, yet still enveloping her the way she loved.

Ah! Cold!

The cold, smooth surface spread her, sliding and rolling, too big to slip inside but making her want it to. She begged for more pressure, but Summer pressed down, her pussy burying Alyssa's mouth. As the ball rolled up and down the lips, Alyssa yelped each time it crossed over her clit, mashing it and sending cold electricity into her belly.

Different and good. Keep going. Rub my clit with it.

When the ball warmed, Summer jammed it into Alyssa's clit, grinding it until she wailed into Summer's pussy before removing it. The thunk of the ball hitting the table met Alyssa's ears just as Summer dove into Alyssa's overwrought pussy, licking and nipping the lips and clit with her teeth.

When Summer dropped the pool ball, Robert put his wife's ankles on his shoulders and entered her in one stroke. He ground slowly inside her, finding her G-spot and cervix the way he always did, even as she moved under Summer's tongue. As she had requested, he pounded into her, leaving her empty in brief moments too short to miss the exquisitely stretched feeling she got every time he slammed her channel apart. After a few, he pulled out.

Get back in there! She slapped Summer's ass cheek and made some noise into her pussy. She thrust two fingers inside Summer, making the small hips grind on her face. Then Summer's mouth left her pussy as well. Muffled slurping sounds reached Alyssa's ears, and pride bloomed in her chest at knowing Robert wanted to pay some attention to Summer.

As soon as her two lovers abandoned her pussy, they returned. She no more than felt Robert's tip nocking between her lips before it filled her to the brim, with Summer's lips latching onto her clit. The sudden assault fired her coming orgasm to a higher level in an instant and boiled it within her.

The pattern repeated three times before Robert pushed Alyssa's legs closer to her shoulders while Summer sucked him. Alyssa moaned when they returned to her, being more vulnerable to Summer's nipping mouth and positioned to let Robert in deeper, stretching her pussy into her guts.

Yes. Stretch me.

Summer stopped lapping at Alyssa's pussy, tensed her legs, and grunted as she came. Alyssa lapped the nectar that trickled from her opening.

There you go. Now to keep you going.

Alyssa worked Summer's clit and pussy, prolonging and strengthening the orgasm. Summer jerked twice against Alyssa's face, knocking her head against the hard table. The pain rattled inside her skull, but she continued drawing juice from her friend. Summer's body relaxed in one fell swoop, and her head fell onto Alyssa's pussy.

Ouch.

Robert continued fucking her. After what could have been two minutes, Summer resumed licking. Robert pulled out, and Summer licked from Alyssa's asshole across her slit before settling in on her clit again while Robert slid inside to resume his hard fucking. The cauldron of pleasure inside her boiled over.

God, I'm going to come. Alyssa tensed, unable to move under Summer's weight and Robert's strong grip on her legs. She pressed against them as the climax strengthened, spasms firing from her belly out through her limbs. Her fingers straightened and spread inside Summer's pussy as her head pressed forward into her clit.

Summer sucked on Alyssa's clit, flicking it with her tongue. She slid a finger around Alyssa's leg to rub across her anus as Robert pounded into her, never breaking rhythm.

Robert shifted so the curve of his cock toyed with Alyssa's G-spot as he moved.

Fuck. So good. Alyssa flexed, pushing against her lovers, the climax having its way with her. Alyssa relaxed after a few more thrusts, glad that Robert held her legs so they didn't collapse onto the hard table.

Through the fog of her afterglow, Alyssa heard Robert address Summer. "Don't stop. Keep doing exactly what you are doing, and she'll come again." Summer nodded without releasing Alyssa's clit, the tiny jiggles making her jerk.

More. Yes. More.

Alyssa's legs regained their strength. She pushed against Robert's hands as she bucked her hips against Summer's mouth. Robert stayed inside her, drawing the next climax closer. Additional pressure against her legs bent her a little more, pressing her pussy into Summer's face and grinding his cock harder on her cervix.

Alyssa could no longer lick or finger Summer as her body braced for the next eruption. *Close. Keep going. Now.*

The climax took her.

Not as powerful as the previous one, it still jerked her hips against the big cock inside and the frenetic mouth on top. When she breathed again, her pussy emptied, though Summer's mouth teased out the last of her pleasure. Summer finally released her throbbing clit and rolled off. Alyssa lay still to catch her breath.

Robert pulled his wife's legs toward him and laid them on the rail instead of letting them dangle and hurt her back. "Summer, come here. Bend over all the way like you did before."

Summer hopped to the floor and grabbed her ankles. Robert stepped behind her and slid his cock inside, her position letting Alyssa see his cock stretch her lips. "God, I'm so full. So deep. Fuck me like this. Fuck me hard."

Robert gripped her hips and pounded into her, swaying her body as much as he did his. Her feet stayed on the floor as her head reddened as the blood flowed into it.

Alyssa sat on the rail, leaning back on her hands, loving the view. "That's it, Babe. Give it to her. Fuck her good. Make her come." The pride in her chest grew at knowing her husband was building Summer's explosion.

Summer put her hands on the floor as if bracing against Robert as he continued. Even as flexible as she was, being folded in half with her head down made Summer's face redden. She would come soon, and big. Alyssa watched, waiting for her friend's release to wreck her.

Robert held Summer in place by the hips. He maintained his pace and looked at Alyssa. "You said you had plans for my cum. Where do you want it? I'm close."

"Deep inside her, Babe. Point-blank on her womb itself. Let her feel everything. Let her feel how deep you can love a woman."

Robert shoved deep inside, the muscles in his sides and butt flexing while he came.

Summer jerked as a shock racked her body. Two followed less than a second apart. A throaty groan came from her as the redness in her face spread up her neck, which was stretched taut over bulging veins.

Alyssa hopped off the pool table when the room went quiet. She gave Robert a soft peck on the cheek, then knelt beside her friend.

"It feels good doesn't it, Summer? To be filled so deep?"

Summer nodded.

Alyssa helped her friend stand. They shared a kiss, Alyssa caressing Summer's hard and rippling back muscles. "Sit on the pool table. I'll finish you off."

"I'm finished already."

"Not quite. Up you go."

Summer hopped on the pool table.

Alyssa dipped her head to lick Summer's breasts, sucking on the swollen nipples, enjoying the salty sweat. She looked into Summer's eyes before moving in for another kiss. She pushed Summer's shoulder, encouraging her to lie on the table.

Summer raised her spread legs into the air, holding her knees in her hands.

Alyssa sucked Summer's clit and pressed two fingers inside her, pumping and pressing down hard.

Summer gasped and moaned in hitches while Alyssa pleased her. Alyssa let Summer watch her suck Robert's cum off her fingers before licking and slurping the cum from Summer's gaping pussy. Her legs quivered against Alyssa's shoulders as Alyssa reinserted her fingers and licked Summer's clit side to side and up and down, hammering her with sensation in search of a climax.

Summer groaned and slammed her thighs against Alyssa's ears. *There you go. That's how you wanted to finish.* Alyssa smiled into Summer's pussy as she drew the orgasm out over several seconds. When Summer pushed Alyssa's head back, she lowered Summer's legs to the table rail. Robert pulled Summer's hand to bring her upright again.

Alyssa hugged Summer, stroking her hair with one hand.

"How do you feel? You wanted to finish that last orgasm, didn't you?"

"Yes. I feel so good."

"You don't feel dirty? You did some dirty things tonight."

"No. I feel like you always make me feel. Loved. Thank you for bringing me here and sharing with me."

Robert kissed Summer on the head. "You are one of our dearest friends. We shouldn't have left you alone for so long. Never feel like you are intruding by requesting our time."

"I know, but I still don't want to overstep."

"I just slurped my husband's cum out of you. How exactly can you overstep? Come on. This has been superhot, but it would be more comfortable on a bed. We can fuck ourselves to sleep."

"That would be overstepping. You told me you don't have overnight guests."

Alyssa looked at Robert, who nodded. "We do sometimes, and we'd love for you to stay."

"She's right. Please feel welcome to stay."

Summer's chin quivered as she nodded. Leaving the clothes on the bar, they went upstairs to the bedroom. As they turned down the hallway, they heard the laundry room door open, and they scampered to the bedroom.

10
SUNDAY, JUNE 27, HOME

"Susan, do you want to make breakfast?" Clay asked his big sister.

"Sure. Plan for five though."

"You brought your date home?"

"Not me. Mom and Dad. I saw Mom and Mrs. Cullen running to their bedroom when I got home. Based on the clothes in the basement, she's still here."

"They were naked?"

"Yeah. Not what I wanted to see."

"Oh, I don't know."

"Clay! Gross!"

"Eww, not Mom. But Mrs. Cullen is hot."

"Your amazon girlfriend will kick your ass."

"Hey, she doesn't like it when people only see her height.

Her height is beautiful, but she's been seen as 'the tall girl' her whole life."

"Being short, I consider it a compliment, but I understand."

"And Sawyer wouldn't kick my ass. Looking is fine. Going beyond is not. That's our deal. And Mrs. Cullen is worth looking at."

"She is quite pretty, if you like petite, fine-featured blonde aerobics instructors. I didn't appreciate Mom walking her to their bedroom last night. I thought they weren't bringing people over. It feels weird to have their hookups here."

Summer's quick move from the back hallway to the basement stairs caught Clay's eye. "Huh-oh. I think she heard us."

"Was that her?"

"Think so."

Summer emerged from the basement, dressed but disheveled. "Hi, kids. I'm going to leave. Please tell your parents I said goodbye."

Susan turned to her. "Mrs. Cullen, wait. Can we talk with you a minute, please?"

Summer stepped toward the kitchen island. "Sure. What's on your mind, Susan?"

"How much of our conversation did you hear?"

"Enough to know you both think I'm pretty and unwelcome."

"Mrs. Cullen—"

"It's okay, Susan. I overheard a private conversation. I got what I deserved."

"No, Mrs. Cullen." Susan palmed Summer's shoulder. "If what I said made you feel unwelcome, I'm sorry. I'm trying to understand my parents' marriage, but their guest list isn't up to me. I'm not upset that you are here; I'm confused about why *anyone* would be here. Please don't leave on my account."

"That's sweet, Susan, but I can go."

"No. Please stay. I don't want to throw you out."

Summer cracked a smile. "You could try, young lady." She looked at Clay. "What about you, young man? Would you rather I go?"

"No. Susan's right. We know better than to make friends feel uncomfortable. Please stay."

"Is that because I'm a friend, or so you can ogle me?"

Clay swallowed, embarrassed that she'd heard his assessment of her. "No, ma'am. You're a friend."

"Now that we have that sorted out, two things. First, call me Summer. We are all adults. Second, what's for breakfast?"

"We were deciding." Susan pulled the bread from the pantry. "French toast for five?"

Summer shook her head. "Your parents were sleeping hard. French toast for three."

Summer prepared the toast while the other two prepared the rest. As the griddle heated, she spoke. "Guys, your parents have included you in adult conversations as long as I've known them, and they never let us treat you like children. So, Susan, would you like to talk about what you are holding in?"

"This is awkward."

"More awkward than you seeing me run naked to your parents' bedroom last night?" She shrugged. "It's awkward. Say it anyway."

"Why do they need you to be happy?"

"That is both awkward and insulting."

"I don't mean it to be. You are beautiful and a good friend so a perfect bedroom partner. I don't know if they still love each other, or are they together for appearances?"

"Good recovery. Thank you for the compliment. They don't need me or anyone else to be happy. Nobody could fake their adoration for each other—no 'appearances.' Even when they entertain guests, your dad can't take his eyes off your mom, and she couldn't be prouder to share him."

Susan blushed. "I'm, um, glad…to hear that?"

"That's probably too much information, but rest assured, your parents love each other very much. They are just spicing up their lives a bit. "

"Um, yeah. Too much information."

"Clay, you are listening. Did you have any questions for me?"

He blew on his hot coffee while he watched her over the rim of his cup. She waited, watching him. Her calm face and her answers so far had told him she would be honest with them, and she wasn't trying to end the conversation by making him uncomfortable. He decided to ask the question he couldn't ask his parents.

"Does Mom talk with you about any of her other partners?"

"Why do you only ask about your mom?"

"She talked about the real estate agent a lot. Dad seemed annoyed when she did."

Summer dipped some bread and put it on the griddle. "You noticed."

"I observe and assess."

"What is your assessment?"

"She still lights up when his name is mentioned, but she tries to hide it. He's more than spicing up her life. But only you and Ms. Hedgecock come here."

Summer raised an eyebrow. "Jessica too? I shouldn't be surprised."

Susan put down her cup. "I notice you didn't answer Clay's question. Does she talk?"

"She told me he is in the past. She needed to move on."

"But…," Susan pushed.

Summer flipped the toast. "But keep your eyes out. You two

may not understand this, but even though sex can be just sex, it can become more when repeated with the same person. I think your mom is telling the truth. This guy is behind her. But if he's not…"

Susan scowled. "We'll need to help Dad."

Summer nodded. "That goes without saying. Your mom will need help, too, perhaps more than your dad. Your parents helped me when my marriage was dying. I'll be here to help them if they need it."

Clay's frustration hardened his tone before he could control it. "Why does it seem like the kids are the adults here?"

"Because you *are* adults. Your parents are venturing into the unknown, and you are their safe place to return to."

Susan placed some strawberries on each plate. "Why are we the safe place? Aren't they supposed to be our safe place?"

"You are theirs. They are yours. What does that sound like?"

"Codependency?" Clay asked with a smirk before turning serious. "Family. I get it. What if the family breaks up?" He put coffee and orange juice by each of their spots at the island.

Summer shook her head. "Your parents? Unlikely, but if that happens, the two of you are there for each of them, just like each of them will be there for the two of you when you struggle. Your parents are nowhere near breaking up, but nothing on earth would make them abandon either of you." She filled the plates and sat on her stool.

"Mom gets distracted sometimes," Susan said.

"We all do. It's part of life. Distractions provide a break between our priorities. Your mom may get distracted, but she will always refocus on your family."

"Yes, but her distraction could damage the family." Susan moaned as she took a bite. "That's really good. I'll never be upset that you stay here again, as long as you make breakfast."

"Even if you see my disgusting bare ass walking down the hall?"

Susan blushed. "It's not disgusting. It's actually amazing. I only said I didn't want to see it walking to my parents' bedroom."

"I see. And you, Clay? If I cook breakfast, can I stay over when invited?"

"I said nothing to merit inclusion in this portion of the conversation."

"No, no. I distinctly heard you say, 'Mrs. Cullen is hot' and 'Mrs. Cullen is worth looking at.' You started better than you finished, but that brings your opinion into play. Can I stay sometimes if I cook? Or maybe just stand here being 'worth looking at'?" She hopped off her stool and stepped back with her arms outstretched.

"I'm really sorry you heard that."

"I'm not sorry. My ego loves when a handsome young man calls me hot." She got back on her stool. "Seriously, do you mind if I'm here occasionally?"

"I'm with my sister. You can stay as long as you cook breakfast. This is the best French toast I've ever had."

"Wow. Hot and great French toast. Sounds like I'm a keeper." She leaned forward to hold their hands. "Guys, I'm not here to mess up your family. I'm a friend of your parents, and of yours, if you'll have me. We can work together if someone ever needs our help."

"That sounds good," Clay responded.

Susan nodded.

"What sounds good?" Alyssa asked as she walked into the room and kissed all three on the cheek.

"Summer is going to cook breakfast any time she stays over."

"Clay! First, it is Mrs. Cullen, and second, we don't make our guests do housework. Apologize."

"It's okay, Alyssa. I told them they can call me Summer, and I'll happily cook for this appreciative audience."

Alyssa looked at her kids. "Only if Summer wants it that way, understand?"

"Yes, Mom." Susan held out a bite. "But you need to try this."

Alyssa took the bite and groaned. "That is amazing. What do you do?"

Summer chuckled as she shook her head, flinging her hair around. "No way. My secret recipe, my ticket to getting invited over. Do you want some? There is batter left."

"No, thank you. We're headed to the club for brunch. We thought you had left, but do you want to join us?"

"I need to get home. Thank you for last night. I really enjoyed it. And needed it." She pulled Alyssa down for a peck on the cheek.

Susan rolled her eyes. "Last night all over again."

Clay shook his head. "The discussions we have in this kitchen."

11

SUNDAY, JUNE 27, COUNTRY CLUB

"Please keep me away from that woman." Alyssa squeezed Robert's hand as they waited to be seated.

"Who?"

"Cassandra. I can't stand her. She's headed this way."

Robert turned toward a tall, thin blonde walking toward the maître d' stand, accompanying a shorter man with brown hair.

"The tall lady with Brock Pennington?"

"Probably. Pennington's her last name. I've never met her husband."

"He's a brilliant neurosurgeon. He spoke at a chamber of commerce event last year. Nice guy."

"Yes, she is proud of marrying a world-renowned neurosurgeon. Almost as proud as she is of owning ten percent of Frank's company. She loves to show up for board meetings and brag."

"About her husband, or about owning part of the company?"

"Yes. And everything else she thinks of."

The Penningtons reached the maître d' stand. Cassandra rolled her eyes. "I have asked them to be ready to seat us when we arrive." She looked at Alyssa. "You work for me, don't you? Andrea, is it?"

"Alyssa. Alyssa Davis. We have met several times. I do enjoy working for your uncle Frank."

"I'm sure. You and, I guess this is your husband, having a special day at the club?"

"No, just brunch. This is indeed my husband, Robert."

"How nice. And what do you do, Robert?" She offered her hand palm down.

Robert shook her hand. "I'm a banker."

"Banker. I see. Useful sometimes." Cassandra looked past him, scanning the room.

"We met last year at the chamber event." Brock Pennington shook hands with Robert and Alyssa.

Robert smiled. "We met for maybe ten seconds. I remember you because you were the speaker. How can you remember me among all those people that long ago?"

"I have a photographic memory. It's great for remembering nice people like you. It's not great for forgetting the rubber chicken they served."

Cassandra pulled her husband's arm, spinning him away from Alyssa and Robert. "Brock, I don't know why they haven't seated us. Let's go to our usual table."

"Cassie, they'll be here in a minute. Besides, the Davises were here first. We can enjoy talking with them until Anton returns."

Cassandra sighed. "Very well. I like your dress, Alyssa."

"Thank you. It is one of my favorites."

"I had the designer version a few years ago, but it bored me."

You bitch! Alyssa's mouth dropped open, and her arms stiffened. She relaxed as Brock spoke.

"That's a good thing, honey. You wouldn't want to wear the same one when Alyssa looks so nice in hers." He nodded to Robert. "If you guys don't mind me saying so."

"Indeed. There is Anton. Let's go." Cassandra strode past them to the approaching maître d'.

Brock caught Alyssa's eye and gave a small shrug of contrition. "Sorry about that. I don't think she realizes how she sounds sometimes."

"It's okay," Alyssa replied, her anger dulled by his comments. "Thank you for softening the blow."

"I wasn't softening the blow; I meant it. You make that dress look better than Cassie ever has, though after seeing you in it, she will never wear it again. My apologies if I was too forward, and for what Cassie said."

"No offense taken," Robert said as Brock joined his wife.

"See what I mean?" Alyssa squeezed Robert's hand. "She's the most condescending woman on the planet, and she does nothing herself. She just rides what her uncle and husband do."

"Both of whom are the antithesis of her. Remember what you like about them and don't let her bug you."

"You mean infuriate me?"

"Your emotion, your word. I hope you feel better soon. Your smile is my favorite thing in the world."

She smiled and nestled her head on his shoulder. "You always make me better, Babe."

12

WEDNESDAY, JUNE 30, RARE BOOK STORE

ALYSSA LOOKED ACROSS the street at Poppy's before she entered the rare bookstore. *Even lunches with Hayden were wonderful. I can't shake him.*

You have to. Think of the cost.

Alyssa wandered toward the back of the shop. Clay had asked her to buy an early edition of *Pride and Prejudice* for Sawyer's birthday on the eleventh. Literature was in the back, and she browsed her way toward Jane Austen. She liked the small shop. It had the right mix of classical music, dim lighting, and claustrophobic stacks with the merest tinge of must in the air to add authenticity to the rare volumes.

She stretched up to reshelve a copy of *Macbeth*. Five thousand dollars was a bit much. When firm hands gripped her waist, a voice whispered in her ear.

"You are a greater treasure than all these books combined."

Hayden.

He spun her and kissed her before she could react. In the tight nook between shelves, nobody could see, but her brain flashed worry in the instant before her body returned the kiss and closed the small distance between them. She rubbed his muscled back as he pulled her body against him.

He was hard.

Her nipples tingled against his chest.

Her heart skipped a beat, and that light, empty feeling flowed into her body. Then it raced, and energy followed the euphoria.

She wouldn't resist today.

One last time. Bent over right here if he wants it.

She reached between them to stroke his cock through his pants.

He squeezed her tits before dropping one hand back to her ass. His fingers crawled along her cheek as he gathered the dress little by little. Cool air tickled the backs of her thighs as the hem rose.

Alyssa broke their kiss to nod, afraid to say anything in the quiet shop. She panted a couple of breaths before kissing him again.

He reached inside her wraparound dress. His warm skin ignited sparks along hers as he kneaded her breast. *Thank god for the built-in bra. I needed to feel him.*

She unzipped his pants, reached in, and gripped the big cock she had only dreamed about for weeks.

Her pussy pulsed. She felt it opening. *This will be so good.*

They froze at the ringing of the bell over the shop door. Alyssa stroked her hand the entire length of his wonderful cock before withdrawing her hand and stepping back. She caught her breath while straightening her top.

Hayden zipped up and leaned close. "Come with me. We can finish what we started. You can't deny you want to."

One last time. She listened to the shopkeeper talk. He knew his customer by name, like he knew Alyssa. And Robert. *I have to be careful. And then I'm done. Whatever hell I feel afterward, I have to be done.*

"Not today."

He smirked and cocked an eyebrow, silently asking the obvious question.

"I can't see you anymore, but I can't resist you. I want one last time to get you out of my system, but I want it to be amazing. Will you give me one last grand finale, then let me go before I ruin my life? Can you show you care for me one last time, please?"

He narrowed his eyes while he considered it. A half smile lifted the corner of his mouth. "An amazing time it is. But I can't promise a finale. You will want more of what I have in mind. When?"

"Soon. I can't live like this much longer. And it will be the last time. I'm sorry. Now go so we aren't seen together."

Hayden moved toward the front of the shop, and Alyssa meandered deeper. Her skin cooled as her sweat evaporated, eliminating that evidence of her behavior. She took measured breaths as she browsed, trying in vain to quiet the pulse pounding in her ears.

After examining a few editions to settle herself, she chose a boxed version and made her way toward the counter.

My two wants drift farther apart, like two ships in the ocean. I cling to a rail on each one, tearing myself in half. In the end, I've chosen my family, but I want more of Hayden before I let go. One last time, then I'm done.

13

SATURDAY, JULY 3, NEIGHBORHOOD PARK

ALYSSA'S PHONE DINGED with a text. *Hayden. I can answer just this once.* She smiled and stepped away from the grill.

"Come see me."

"Can't. Neighborhood party."

"Our fireworks are better."

Yes, they are. Alyssa twirled a bit of her hair and closed her eyes. Her pussy throbbed as she remembered being with him. "No. With family today."

"Tonight, then."

Can I? No. Stay away and get your feelings under control. Even though you want to. "I can't see you tonight."

"Can't? Or won't?"

Maybe I have an emergency. This last time to get him out of my system. Maybe I'll see those negatives I haven't seen yet.

On July Fourth? Don't be a fool.

"Whichever you prefer."

"When you are ready, I will remind you why you can't stay away."

"Got to go."

"I will break you in the best way."

Yes, you will. Alyssa smiled and put her phone away.

❧

Alyssa saw a man with salt-and-pepper hair at her grill when she returned. "Thanks for watching those. I'll take back over."

"No, I've got it. That way you can text and the neighborhood can eat good burgers." The stranger's comment silenced the five nearby grill masters, who all turned to watch the exchange.

"I kind of know what I'm doing. The burgers were fine for the two minutes I was away."

The stranger shook his head. "You can't leave burgers with this mix of fat. Flare-ups can happen without warning. I'll cover these."

His condescension lit a fire in Alyssa's chest. She stiffened her spine and cocked her head. "You say that like you believe I was randomly assigned to cook."

The stranger shrugged. "I don't mean to insult you. My grilling experience can help the neighbors. I certainly am more cautious of flare-ups."

The other grill masters stared, some with stifled smiles teasing their mouths, others looking stunned at the exchange.

"You can do better? Hmmm. Let's test that." She turned to the grill beside them. "Peggy, do you mind if I take over? That way our mystery chef can supervise me."

Peggy grinned as she offered the spatula and took two steps back. "Be my guest, Alyssa."

"Thank you, Peggy." Alyssa turned to the man beside her. "My burgers against yours? Our neighbors can decide what they like better."

He chuckled. "I didn't mean to start something."

"And yet you did. You up for finishing it?"

He shook his head. "Might as well. May the best chef win." He saluted with his spatula.

"Against your advice, I need to step away for a minute to text again. Please, if my grill flares up, ignore it. Let them burn so you win quickly." Alyssa walked away from her grill, the fire in her chest feeding on low snickers from her neighbors.

She returned to a normal grill, but it was clear that in the minute she had been away, word of the grilling competition had spread. People had wandered over, with more following.

A crowd of about twenty had gathered by the time Robert set a bag beside Alyssa's grill. "Here you go."

She kissed his cheek. "Thank you, Babe. Right on time." Alyssa placed a frying pan from the bag in the empty spot on the grill. She turned to the crowd. "Can somebody bring me a beer from the keg, please?"

A man gave her the one in his hand. "I haven't sipped it yet."

"Thank you." Alyssa took two big swallows, enjoying the cold flowing through her on the hot day. "Mm. Good."

She took another. "Good, but not strong enough." She scattered the beer onto the grass, then pulled a bottle of rum from her bag. She took a swig from the bottle after pouring some in the beer cup. "That's what I needed."

The stranger, quietly cooking, turned to her. "You need to get drunk to cook? You worry me.

"I'm not close to drunk. I needed something strong." She

moved several burgers onto the hot pan, searing them on both sides. She poured the rum into the pan and lit it. The crowd gave a collective aah as flames shot three feet into the air, then died off.

She turned to the crowd. "This batch is ready. Who wants a flare-up burger?"

She served the six from the pan. Her competitor announced his were ready to no response. People waited in line as Alyssa prepared hers. Burgers from other grills piled up on plates, eaten only by some impatient kids.

After an hour, Alyssa was out of burgers and rum. "That's all, folks. Hope you enjoyed it."

She put the last flambé burger on a bun and turned to her competitor. "I saved the last one for you. It's only fair that you taste the competition."

"Thanks." He took a bite. "Wow, that hint of rum is good. I didn't know you could flambé a burger."

"Glad I could teach you two things today."

"How to flambé a burger and?"

"How to underestimate someone to your own embarrassment."

He put his hands together in front of his chest and bowed his head to her. "You teach like a master."

"I teach cooking for a living."

He shrugged and gave a thin smile. "In my own defense, I'm new to the neighborhood and wanted to make a few friends by helping out. Now I'll just be the grill usurper."

Alyssa cackled. *Good sense of humor. He isn't the jerk I thought he was. And he has pretty brown eyes.* "That's good. Usurper for short. What's your real name?"

"Drew Baker."

"I'm Alyssa Davis. I coordinate the food for these neighborhood gatherings. The others have cooked with me for years and could have warned you, but it seems they wanted a little entertainment. We eat together after everyone is served. Join us."

"I've intruded enough today. You go ahead."

"Come on. You intruded, but you were a good sport about it. Join us. I'll introduce you, Usurper." She took his arm and dragged him to a picnic table where the grill masters applauded.

&

Alyssa held Robert's hand as they headed toward the lake for the fireworks. He returned her light squeeze, his strength apparent beneath the gentle pressure.

"I was surprised by your text to bring the large skillet and rum."

"I can always count on you."

Alyssa stopped and looked toward a copse of trees. "Babe, I'll meet you at the chairs in a minute. I think I saw something."

"Saw something? Anything dangerous?"

She smirked. "Not really, but I'm going to take a look. Go ahead to the seats. I won't be long."

He patted her rump. "All right. Don't be long. The fireworks should start soon."

"Oh, that they will. I'll be there."

She stepped just inside the shady edge of the trees. Her eyes adjusted to the dark, and she leaned against the tree beside her. She looked past the next layer of trees. In a small clearing, Jessica knelt in front of a man. A sliver of moonlight revealed the lust on her face; the shadows and her position slightly behind him concealed his. The man pulled her hands from his belt. "Let's see your tits."

Jessica slid her arms out of her tank top to bunch it at her waist. The natural spotlight accentuated her muscles and made her white breasts even paler.

"Yes. Lean back."

She leaned back, letting the light reach her abs below her large breasts, where the exertion of the position and the angle of the light gave her a shadowy six-pack.

Every time I see her, she's more beautiful. Alyssa cupped her own tits when Jessica presented hers to the obscured figure.

The man dropped his shorts to his ankles. Jessica engulfed his erect cock in one move. The light and shadow showed her cheeks hollow and puff as she sucked. She pulled off, gasping, leaving a string of saliva between her lip and the shiny tip.

Cocks always look good wet. Alyssa slid a finger inside the leg of her shorts. She rubbed over her lips to acknowledge their tingling. *Watching them is hot.*

Jessica resumed blowing the indistinguishable man. His hand wove into her hair and guided her for a couple of deep strokes before holding her against his belly when she had his full length in her throat. She patted his thigh twice, and he released her hair. She pulled back, panting and smiling, and his hand went to her cheek, urging her up.

As Jessica stood, she raised the hem of her skirt, revealing her shaved pussy, the lips dark and puffy with arousal. She was as tall as the man, and she leaned forward to kiss him. He cupped her ass. Jessica raised her leg to his waist and shoved a hand between their crotches, looking down and tightening her mouth as she nocked him into her opening. Her head leaned back as their hips thrust together.

The man's hands held her leg and back as he thrust into Jessica. Jessica gripped the back of his neck, clearly fighting to maintain her balance on one foot, then settled her head beside his. Alyssa reached inside to thumb her clit and insert a finger, seeking her G-spot.

Alyssa moaned as her fingers found their targets.

Jessica's eyes opened at the sound. Her coupling didn't stop as she peered into the shadow.

Alyssa chased her orgasm as she watched her friend fuck.

Jessica smiled and crooked her finger at Alyssa.

Alyssa stopped moving. *She can see me?* She looked up at a clear view of the moon between an opening in the branches. *Same spotlight on me. How long has she known? I just wanted to watch. This isn't Hayden. Maybe Robert will like hearing about this. And reclaiming me.*

Alyssa walked the few steps to the couple. He continued thrusting, apparently unaware of her presence.

Jessica caressed Alyssa's cheek. "Hey, neighbor."

The man stopped thrusting. "Huh?"

"We have company. You are in for a treat."

Alyssa looked up, seeing the salt-and-pepper hair of the man in shadow for the first time. His face came into the light, and the pretty brown eyes looked at her face. His eyes narrowed, then spread wide as they returned to her face. "Alyssa."

"Drew. Let me help Jessica welcome you to the neighborhood."

"You're married."

"Yes. It's okay."

"No." He pulled out of Jessica, setting her leg down. He turned to face Alyssa.

Alyssa looked down at the glistening cock pointing at her. *Straight. Smooth. Not too big. Not too small. I'm going to like this.* She reached for it and looked up.

He grabbed her wrist before she could grip his cock. His grip didn't hurt, but she sensed a strength in his fingers he contained. She imagined him squeezing her breast, and it tingled.

"I said no. You're married."

"And I said it's okay. Robert and I have an arrangement."

"I don't care. You should leave."

Jessica cupped his cheek to refocus his attention on her. "Drew, she's telling the truth. This could be a lot of fun. I'm glad she caught us sneaking off."

"No. Alyssa, please leave." His dick had softened. "Maybe I should go. Catch you later, Jessica. This has been fun."

Jessica grabbed his wrist. "Wait."

Alyssa raised her hand in a stop motion. "I'm going, Drew. I hope we can talk about this when I haven't surprised you. Please keep having fun with Jessica. She's magnificent." Alyssa looked over her shoulder at the pair watching her exit the trees.

❧

Alyssa plopped into Robert's lap just as the fireworks began, wriggling around to settle her needy pussy over the exact spot on his thigh to press on her opening. She leaned close to his ear so he could hear above the explosions. "You are going to get it when we get home."

"You found what you were looking for?"

"Yes. Jessica was welcoming the new guy to the neighborhood. It was so hot. She is truly the most beautiful woman in the neighborhood."

"Second most beautiful." He caressed her thigh. "And you didn't join her?"

"I planned to just watch until she saw me and invited me in."

"Do I need to reclaim you?"

"No. He wouldn't touch me because I'm married, even after we told him you and I have an arrangement."

"Scruples. I like him."

Alyssa ground her hips, letting the hard thigh muscles press her lips in and apart, but it didn't provide the relief she sought. "But watching left me so horny."

"Leaves you horny for me. I like him even better."

Alyssa laughed. "I thought you would." She nuzzled in, kissing his neck off and on as he watched the fireworks and stroked her thigh.

As the finale began, his fingers snuck inside the leg of her shorts and between her lips, still wet with arousal.

Oh god. That's good.

His fingers worked quickly in the dark, moving until she gasped or groaned, teasing that spot, then moving to another. She panted against his neck. Her thighs quivered. When the fireworks stopped, he pinched her clit hard until she ground against him, then he withdrew his hand.

"Don't stop. I'm close."

He chuckled. "I know. Everyone is heading this way with their kids. You have to wait."

"Ugh, you tease." She kissed his cheek and caressed his crotch. "Let's get home and put this where it belongs." She stood.

He stood beside her. "And where does it belong?"

"Inside me." She picked up her chair and scampered toward their house.

14
SUNDAY, JULY 4, HOME

ALYSSA GROANED AS she pulled on the toe of her shoe. *This is only supposed to stretch my hamstring, not my sore pussy. So good last night though.* She put her other foot on the step, repeating the stretch and the groan as the muscles relaxed. *I'm out of practice.* She turned to start her run, then stopped when her phone dinged with a text.

She smiled when she saw the contact.

"What about today?"

"No. I can't get away." *Still trying to cool off, Alyssa? Just say no. No last time, just cold turkey. Until you block him, you are tempted, and he knows it.*

"You can do better. You miss how I make you feel."

I do. I'm trying not to. "I'm with my family. I have to go."

"You want to squeeze me in. Come by the house."

God, I want you squeezed inside me. Her pussy, aching seconds ago, throbbed.

She looked up at her front door. *I need to be discreet.* "In broad daylight, on a downtown street? No."

"Where? When?"

"Nowhere. Not today. I can't." *I don't want to, and I do.*

She zipped her phone into the waistband pocket and took off down the driveway. As her breathing increased, she focused on the moment, relaxing control and letting her mind wander.

He's becoming more insistent. This perfect specimen of a man wants me. He still has no apparent flaws.

Are you looking, Alyssa? You never told him that you and Robert have an arrangement, but he is comfortable texting you for a hookup. Is he as honorable as you think?

He believes my marriage is my issue. He is a good man, and he wants me. He misses seeing me, and he's making his case. That's all.

So you won't text him today?

Alyssa stopped to let a car go through the intersection before she crossed the street. Several more cars whizzed by, too fast for the neighborhood, but this was the main street, and people drove faster here. She watched the traffic until she ran past the pool toward the back side of the neighborhood. As she passed the third house, her thoughts again drifted to Hayden.

I probably will text. I can't say no to him. That cock. The way he looks at me, like he never wants to be apart. He wants more than just sex, I know he does. Damn it, so do I.

And your husband? Where does he stand?

I love him. He was beyond perfect last night. He stretched me the way I love. I felt every delicious inch the way I used to. All three times. I can't live without him.

Your feelings for Hayden would crush him. How can you justify any contact with Hayden?

I'll get him out of my system.

Really?

Still working on it.

Alyssa reached her favorite part of the neighborhood. The hill in the back was the highest point, providing a view of most of the rest of the neighborhood. She could see their house and the winding wooded path to finish her run. She loved this view and this part of the run.

The downhill slope tempted her to run fast and let gravity have its way with her. The path challenged her to keep an even pace. If she rushed headlong through the woods, she risked tripping on the rocks and roots marring the forest floor, creating the possibility of a long limp home with a turned ankle or worse. Arriving comfortably at home made the trail more exciting and rewarding. *Like being with Hayden.* With a deep breath, she plunged into the woods faster than she had in months.

And why is Hayden versus Robert even a choice?

Because I want it all.

Drew was nearing the end of his morning run when he saw Alyssa trot out of a driveway and jog away from him. He was only a couple of houses down, but she didn't look his way as she ran. As he passed her house, he looked up to see a man coming out the front door. Drew ran back, meeting Robert where the newspaper lay in the driveway. "Are you Alyssa Davis's husband?"

"Yes. Are you the grill guy?"

Drew shook his head. "You heard. Drew Baker. The grill cooks call me Usurper. I am indeed the one who made a fool of himself yesterday."

"The crew set you up by not warning you. Alyssa isn't here right now if you wanted to discuss cooking."

"Actually, I wanted to talk with you." He looked at some neighbors walking their direction. "In private."

"Sure. I have water in the garage if you would like some."

In the garage, Robert handed Drew a bottle from the fridge. "What is on your mind?"

"I don't like meddling in people's business, but I learned in the military when people's business meddles with you, talk with them about it." He sighed. "I had an encounter with your wife last night."

"An encounter?"

"I was having an encounter with Jessica Hedgecock, our neighbor, and your wife tried to join us. Jessica said they would welcome me to the neighborhood. Alyssa is beautiful, if you don't mind me saying, but I wouldn't have it."

He paused to watch Robert for any reaction.

His eyes narrowed a bit, but he showed no other signs of any emotion. "Keep going."

"My ex cheated on me. I won't be a party to that. Your wife said the two of you had an arrangement. I discounted that because my ex told the same lie to some of her partners."

"I see. You are to be commended for your honor, and I thank you for having an embarrassing conversation with someone you just met."

"Thanks. I just thought you should know." Sensing no reaction, he tossed the empty water bottle in the garbage and turned to go.

"Did you get to have sex with Jessica?"

Drew stopped and turned back toward Robert. "What?"

"Did you actually have sex with Jessica, or did Alyssa's intrusion ruin your encounter?"

"We were having sex, but my reaction killed the mood."

"I bet. She owes Jessica an apology. Alyssa said she didn't

know if you would finish. You missed a great time. Alyssa and Jessica at once is a treat."

Drew couldn't believe what he was hearing. "What are you talking about?"

Robert smiled. "Thank you for acting honorably around my wife. She told you the truth. We have an open marriage, given certain rules. We are discreet about it, but since she told you, and you are being honest, I will confirm."

"No shit."

"No shit."

"So you would be okay if I slept with your wife? Or if someone else did?"

"As long as she did it by our rules, yes." Robert shook his head. "Don't worry, it still surprises me. We've only been at it for a few months."

"How does that work, if you don't mind me asking?"

"We view sex as a form of entertainment, if you will. We have an agreement that either of us can have sex with someone else, at our own option, within certain bounds that protect our family.

"Like I said, your wife is beautiful, and she came on to me, so I'm not trying to poach here, but if it happens again, what are the rules I should hold her to?"

Robert laughed and slapped Drew on the shoulder. "I would ask, too, and thank you." He counted them off on his fingers. "Be discreet. No emotional attachments. Family comes first. We tell each other every time."

"I don't know if I could get comfortable with that."

"Not everyone can. It took me some time and a night with Jessica before I would consider it."

"Oh, I couldn't have that kind of arrangement. I mean, I may not be comfortable with your arrangement if your wife comes on to me again."

"Thank you for that. Now that you know the rules, and you know she is neither lying nor cheating on me, any offer is between you and her."

15

MONDAY, JULY 5, HOME

ALYSSA SNATCHED HER phone off the kitchen counter when she saw who the text was from. Susan stood only a few feet away, slicing zucchini, and she didn't need to see. Plus, it was the first communication from him since she'd rejected him yesterday.

"Miss me?"

She typed three different responses before sending, "No. I was too busy to notice how long since you texted." *I'm lying to him too. I'm lying to protect myself this time.*

"I was busy too. Do you want a surprise?"

"Could be. What is it?"

"That would spoil the surprise. At lunch on Wednesday I'll tell you. You in?"

Her heart leaped to her throat. He still wanted to be with her. And he had a surprise. She needed to play this right. "This week is busy at work."

"You still need to eat, and no lunch, no surprise."

She smiled. He knew how to tease her. *Now you wait for me.* She fabricated a meeting. "Lunch meeting already. You lost your spot. Can I still get the surprise?"

The three dots flashed for an eternity. Just as she started to pocket her phone, it buzzed in her hand.

"Surprise: I'll send an address Friday morning. Leave work at lunch."

Sawyer's birthday party. "Must be home by five. Party that night."

The purple leering devil emoji popped up, followed by, "Better than perfect. Got to go."

Alyssa slid her phone into her pocket and returned to preparing the salad.

Susan bumped Alyssa with her hip as she sprinkled dill on the zucchini. "Who was that, Mom? You look like a kid at Christmas."

I need to improve my poker face. "Just somebody from work. Her sarcastic wit keeps me laughing all the time."

"Maybe, but you looked more like you had won a prize."

"Her jokes are a prize." Alyssa smiled at her daughter. "Can you please go tell the boys that when they finish their basketball game, we will be ready to grill?"

"Sure."

Alyssa took deep breaths to calm her fluttering stomach while Susan headed toward the garage. *One last time. I can't wait.*

16

FRIDAY, JULY 9, SEX DUNGEON HOUSE

SITTING IN THE line of traffic, Alyssa counted the minutes she was losing with Hayden. She could see the large backhoe ahead. It appeared to be in front of the address plugged into her directions, and the workers only allowed one lane of traffic to process by it at a time. On this busy street, cars would be lined up until the workers left for the day.

Ten minutes after she'd entered the line of traffic, her belly fluttered as she pulled around the backhoe into the driveway, behind Hayden's car. *Where everything started. The sex dungeon.*

Imagining her power over a man who wanted her enough to restrain her had made her horny for that entire day. She had rec-ognized the house when she checked the street view of the map. She wasn't surprised he had negotiated to use the dungeon. It had spawned a hundred romantic, heartwarming moments between them. And a thousand clit-tingling orgasmic ones.

The real thing may shatter me. What a way to go.

She shifted her weight from one foot to the other while she waited for Hayden to answer the doorbell. The workers and drivers behind her had nothing more to do than watch her wait on the porch. *Do they know why I'm here? Do they think I look desperate waiting this long?*

Never mind what they think. Remember why you are here. She thought of being blindfolded and tied to the bed while Hayden teased her with feathers and ice cubes before devouring her with his mouth until she exploded in orgasms.

Her nipples tingled, wanting to be touched. She tried the doorknob. Locked. She rang again. *Come on. Let me in.*

Only when she was ready, when her sodden pussy quivered, when she begged him to fuck her, would he fill her with his magnificent cock and make love to her until the sensations destroyed any conscious thought.

Her pussy throbbed, wanting to be filled. She tried the knob again. Still locked.

She imagined him doing these things because he wanted to please her. She imagined being released, snuggling her sweaty, exhausted body against his, and him asking, "Did I do well?" She envisioned his smile when she said, "Yes."

As she reached to try the door again, it opened. Hayden stood smiling like the host at a dinner party, not the man starving for her after an absence.

"Alyssa, good to see you again. I have lunch in the kitchen. Come in."

Still confused, she rushed to him when he closed the door. Hugging him and stretching up for a kiss.

After a shorter kiss than she wanted, he nudged her back. "Lunch is in the kitchen. This way."

Hayden kept the conversation light and mundane while they sat opposite each other, eating spinach salads with salmon and watermelon. Alyssa's body stewed, as she knew they weren't here to discuss a new industrial project on the edge of town like two developers.

Her body wanted to get downstairs to the illicit pleasures she imagined. Her pussy ached. She crossed and recrossed her legs, seeking relief. Her mind played along with the polite conversation as best she could as her body fought to control her daydreams.

After a final insufficient shift in her seat, Alyssa leaned forward. "Hayden, I'm out of energy to discuss land sales. Please tell me how you arranged for us to be here."

His gentle host's smile shifted subtly into a sneer. His eyes narrowed, and he looked at the last few remnants of her salad. "I hope you have eaten enough." He stood and took their salad bowls to the kitchen.

"It's time for dessert." He retrieved two small plates, each containing three chocolate-covered strawberries, and sat. "For dessert, you get to ask three questions. For each one you ask, you eat a strawberry, and I will eat one for each answer. When the strawberries are gone, you get your surprise. Please begin."

Her heart fluttered in her chest. He wasn't conversing; he commanded. *Mm. He's in command, but I'm in control. He's this way because he wants me. I can't wait.* She chomped a berry off its cap, chewing quickly and swallowing almost without tasting it.

"Deal. How did you arrange this place?"

"I knew that would be first."

He lifted a berry by its cap and took a bite. He returned half the berry to the plate while he chewed. He sipped his iced tea, then wiped his lips with his napkin before taking the second bite and repeating the process.

Alyssa clasped her hands together to prevent them from roaming to the parts of her body bursting into flames as she waited. *The anticipation is killing me. And he knows it.*

"I cut a deal with the owner. She let me have it for the weekend."

"What deal did you cut?"

He held up his hand. "Eat your berry first."

Mm. Commanding. I'll submit. Alyssa again bit her berry off the cap in one bite, this time savoring the slivers of chocolate that broke off and melted against her palate and the tangy, sweet juice that slid over her tongue as she chewed.

"What deal did you cut?"

He took three bites to finish his berry, his tiny grin no doubt in response to her impatient fidgeting.

"She is enjoying a beach house I control as we speak."

"Is that all? Seems easy."

He pointed to her final berry.

He got me there. Still in command. I need to remind him who is in control. Using her knife and fork, she lingered through four bites of strawberry and scraped the stray chocolate shavings off the plate before daubing her lips with her napkin. Her needy pussy clenched against the void inside her with every bite.

"Is a weekend at the beach all you traded? That seems easy for you."

His berry was gone in one bite. His eyes narrowed while he chewed. "No. She required me to learn the proper use of the equipment. It took three nights. She was most thorough."

Jealousy flashed in Alyssa's chest, rising in a hot flush up her neck to her cheeks, but she held her tongue, not wanting to spoil the mood. *He'll forget her in one afternoon with me.* Her stomach flexed, and she sat straighter, determined to enhance whatever he planned downstairs.

He raised his hand, stopping her as she began to speak.

"You have no doubt guessed the surprise. I know you crave exploring what is downstairs. For your safety and enjoyment, while we are in this house, you will follow three rules. If you do not agree to them, we will leave with no hard feelings, but we will never return. Understood?"

"Agreed."

"Excellent. First, while we are in this house, you will address me as sir. Can you do that?"

Alyssa nodded.

He stared at her as the silence swelled in the room.

"Yes, sir."

"You understand. Second, you will obey my every command. You cede control of your body to me. You are mine to use however I desire. You must trust that as I use you, my goal is your immense pleasure. Can you do that?"

Her belly knotted. *What if it hurts? He wouldn't really hurt me, would he?* She remembered his three nights learning the equipment. *I'll show him I can take whatever he dishes out, even more than her.* She locked eyes with him. "Yes, sir."

"Good girl. This is the most important rule. You will feel pain. Only you know how much you can bear. You may scream, or yell 'stop' or 'no' while we play. I will not stop for those words because they are often instantaneous reactions that you do not mean. One word will convey your wish to stop. If you say 'waffles,' you are signaling me to stop. I will stop immediately, our play will end, and you will be released from any restraints, allowed to dress and leave. This is your safe word. Do you understand?"

I knew he wouldn't hurt me. "Yes, sir. 'Waffles' stops everything."

He placed a leather collar on the table. "When you are ready to begin, stand and buckle this collar around your neck."

"Yes, sir." Her pussy throbbed as she stood. The collar lay soft against her skin as she buckled it.

"Now strip. Lay your clothes on the table. You will not need them again until you leave."

Alyssa looked through the large bay window beside them at the traffic. And the construction workers. She shook her head as embarrassment tainted her excitement with nausea. "They will see."

He stood unmoving.

"They will see, sir."

"It is light outside and somewhat darker in here. The glass may reflect. Nonetheless, I want to show them your beauty. You are not obeying my commands. This is the only time I will allow you to correct that mistake, but if you do not comply immediately, your punishment will be to strip on the front lawn."

Her nipples crystallized into aching diamonds with one breath. *He's making me expose myself, just the way I like.*

She wished she had not had a kitchen training session this morning. A sexy dress could be unzipped and dropped to the floor. Instead, her window show would take a minute. She pulled the golf shirt over her head, folded it, and laid it on the table. Putting one foot, then the other on her chair, she removed her shoes, then wriggled out of her jeans. Placing them on the table, she looked at Hayden, not wanting to strip naked by the window and yet needing to. Her belly roiled as she waited for him to speak.

"All of it."

"Yes, sir." As her heart leaped, she removed her bra and stepped out of her panties. Now naked, trembling from the nerves swirling inside her gut, she looked at him.

He reached across the table to attach a thin chain leash to her collar, then took a step toward the window. "You have been in profile to the window up to now. You will now step toward me and face the window. Because everyone has cell phones, you may choose where to place your hands. You may either cover your face or your body, but do not attempt to do both. Decide and obey now."

Unsure which she would choose as she took the first step, she raised her hands only as she turned to face the window. She was close enough to it that the sun warmed her skin, and she realized that the reflective combination of light outside and dark inside would fail because of the light reaching her.

From behind her fingers, she knew she could not be identified, and a small storm brewed low in her belly. Her legs trembled as she imagined dozens of people only thirty yards away staring at her uplifted breasts, her exposed tummy, her pussy. A drop of moisture rolled down her thigh. *Fantasize about my dripping pussy. Look all you want, but only he gets to touch.*

"Very good. You have earned a reward. Follow me downstairs."

Alyssa followed the tug of the leash, not lowering her hands from her face until she was several steps away from the window. She had not noted the dungeon's concrete floor before, but her chilled feet confirmed its status as a harsh room meant for easy cleanup. A trapezoidal wooden gymnast's vaulting bench she remembered being in a corner sat in the center of the dark room, illuminated by four bright spotlights in the ceiling. The rack of whips, paddles, chains, and sex toys straddled the edge of the ring of light.

Hayden tugged her to the end of the bench. It was about table height. He bent her at the waist until her chest rested on its padded top so her arms hung down the slanted sides. The cool leather chilled her skin, shooting a tingle from her abs around to her lower back. This wasn't the softness she expected in the bed. This might be better.

He wants to assert his dominance. He wants my power over him to diminish. He wants to take me. Deep in her chest, warm pride welled up and spread through her body all the way to her fingertips. Every inch of skin tingled as he cuffed her wrists low on the bench's trapezoidal base, then cuffed her ankles and adjusted hinged arms to spread and pull her legs back until her feet rested flat on the floor without her bending her knees. Her feet were bent up just enough to be uncomfortable.

"This hurts my ankles, can you let me bend my knees and let them straighten a little?"

The sting reached her brain faster than the crack of the slap on her ass cheek reached her ears.

"What are you doing? That hurt!"

"You will be punished when you break the rules." She heard some metallic clicking behind her. When he returned, he knelt in front of her face. He connected a clip to the ring on her collar so that her head could barely move.

"This punishment will hurt, but remember, today you will receive immense pleasure because of the exquisite pain. At any time, you may stop. Do you remember your safe word?"

"Yes, sir."

"Is there something you want?"

"Sir, may we adjust the feet? They are bent in a painful position for my ankles and calves."

"Yes, I noted your feet. We are not finished adjusting."

He stepped to her side and turned a crank. The bench moved as he cranked, which jostled her body, pulling her limbs against the cuffs low on the bench. Soon her toes barely touched the floor and her ass felt higher than her head.

He knelt in front of her face. "Alyssa, you believe that the woman in this position holds the power because she allows the man to bind her so he will eventually fuck her, complying with her wishes. Is that correct?"

A cool breeze confirmed the sensation of her pussy lips blooming open. Her body wanted sex. She squeezed her walls, then relaxed them to prepare for his thick cock.

"Yes, sir. I believe that your next actions will transform you into a ravaging marauder who fucks me senseless. It's why I allowed you to restrain me."

With a chuckle, he stood. Unable to raise her head, she could only see from his belly down. He slapped a large leather paddle hard against his hand. With a squeal, she jumped, surprised at the loud crack. Her knees and elbows hyperextended when the cuffs caught her wrists and ankles. *If it feels like it sounds, this is going to hurt.*

"If the sound of this paddle makes you jump, I wonder what you will think about power when it lands. You see its size? Barely over a foot long, it is a powerful tool for correcting your thinking."

He slapped it again against his palm. Anticipating the sound, she fought to remain still but failed, jerking the cuffs and hurting her elbows and knees.

"The only power you have now is the power to make it stop. Your safe word stops your pain. It also stops that devastating fuck you want, so understand the price of freedom. Are you ready to begin?"

"Yes, sir."

He stepped from her sight. Stiff leather caressed the bottom of her foot, then trailed up her calf to the back of her knee. A chill shot up her leg and traveled her spine to the base of her neck, making her shiver and teasing her pussy.

The gentle caress continued up her thigh to circle her cheek twice, sending soft chills into her body to mix with the lingering pain from the first blow low in her belly. When the leather left her cheek, she smiled, ready for the same treatment to begin on the other foot.

An explosion of pain burst through her body as the paddle landed hard across her ass. Pain radiated down through the back of her knee and over through her asshole, moving from there to tighten her shoulders and jerking her arms against the cuffs with a metallic clank. Alyssa shrieked, then whimpered as the sting dulled to a lingering ache.

Hayden's hand caressed her ass where the blow landed. Its gentle warmth dissipated the ache in her cheek in a few seconds. Alyssa hummed, enjoying the contrast, and Hayden turned his hand to brush along her pussy lips. The building fire in her belly drew the tingles from his fingertips.

"Count the strokes, Alyssa. I want you to know when you shift from pain to pleasure. How many is that?"

"One, sir."

When he removed his hand, the paddle landed across the other cheek. Pain flowed just as it had on the first cheek, then ebbed under his soft caress, the pleasure and pain again seeking the nascent storm in her belly.

"Two, sir."

The leather again tickled her sole before circling its way to her cheek. It lifted, and she braced for the strike. It landed harder, but instead of a caress, two more impacts followed, lighting both cheeks on fire as each smack enhanced the prior one. She wailed and jerked against the restraints in a vain attempt to avoid the next blow. Hot ropes of pain flew from her ass, tying a knot that pulsed as sensations fired into it with every move she made.

The spanks stopped, and she tried to slow her gasping breath.

Another loud crack filled the room as the next hit brought another scream.

"Count them, Alyssa."

She took a deep breath, her body still quivering from the onslaught. "Three...four...five, six, sir."

Goddamn, that hurts. "Waffles" will make it stop. She moaned as his warm hand caressed her cheeks, perfectly balanced between rubbing away the sting and not inflaming the ache. He continued as her arms and legs relaxed before turning his hand to stroke her lips.

This time, his fingers parted her outer lips, and his thumb rolled inside her. He rubbed her clit, pinning it between two fingers and making her abs flutter as the pleasure soothed the knot of pain inside her. He pinched his fingers and thumb together, holding her by the G-spot and converting more pain to pleasure in her belly. She writhed in his hand, seeking release in his grip.

"You're soaked. You like this. Do you want more?"

Her vagina clutched at the emptiness beyond his thumb even as her G-spot fired hot ropes of pleasure deep into her belly. *The pain is bearable. Not having him in me isn't.*

"Yes, sir. Give me something bigger than your thumb. Please."

He released his grip, and she heard the rustling of clothes. *Yes, hurry up and fuck me.*

An eternity later, he leaned close to her ear but remained out of sight. "Are you ready?"

In the silence, even his bare feet on concrete made noise. Her body crackled with anticipation, like every sense was heightened as she waited for him to enter her. She recognized the wide head tickling between her lips as he rubbed it up and down her slit, wetting it, preparing it to fill her.

"Yes, sir. Please give me what I want."

She lost contact with his head. *Oh yes, he's going to slam it inside.* A drop of her juice trickled down the inside of her thigh. *I'm wet enough.*

Two hard smacks from the paddle peppered her cheeks, making her jerk and scream.

"Seven." She gasped a breath. "Eight, sir."

Loud cracks announced the arrival of more pain. Two stripes of pain landed at the junction of the cheeks and thighs, hurting worse than all the ones on her ass combined. Tears filled her eyes as quickly as wails left her lips. The two excruciating smacks at midthigh took her breath. Their burning dwarfed the sting and ache she had grown used to.

Her body quivered and yanked against the restraints. She panted and gasped for breath she could not catch. Her back arched against the pain, and the collar held her neck in place, forcing her chin into the pad. *I can stop this. I need to stop this. It hurts too much.*

Sensations from her entire body swarmed into her belly, combining and reacting, boiling an orgasm that despite a power she sensed, had not released. *But I want this.*

And then he filled her.

The long, thick, curved cock she knew so well grazed over her G-spot on its way to hammer her cervix. It spread her from opening to top, and he withdrew even before she could squeeze against the wonderful shaft. Three fast thrusts gave her more of the same, the pain in her ass and thighs robbing her hungry pussy of the ability to seek the last straw that would break her orgasm free.

He pulled out, and a softer yet still-painful blow landed on her ass.

"Count, Alyssa."

"Nine." She moaned through gritted teeth. "Ten." She panted two more quick breaths as the painful fire in her ass mixed with the burning desire in her cunt. "Eleven…twelve" She grabbed another quick breath as her abs settled into a slower rhythm. "Thirteen, sir."

He rubbed her cheeks and thighs. His firmer caresses appeared intended to ease the sting but increase the ache. "Do you still feel you have the power, Alyssa?"

She flexed her pussy, trying to open it for him to return. He laughed. She stifled a sob. "Yes."

This blow landed lengthwise along her pussy lips. He clearly softened his stroke, but powerful shocks flew all the way to her head. *My god, the pain. Why does anyone take this?* The pain twisted inside her, finding the burning rapture pooling there and landed on it like gasoline. Her body spasmed but refused to come. *Because the orgasms are gigantic.*

"I meant no, sir. Fourteen, sir. Please fuck me. Let me come."

He thrust into her, the angle ensuring strong pressure on her G-spot and cervix as he accelerated with long, deep strokes. Her orgasm started to escape its confines when he stopped.

"No. Please finish me, sir."

"Who owns this pussy, Alyssa?"

He gave two quick thrusts before she could answer. She grunted and clenched her jaw as her body tensed for its release. He stopped moving. She tried to move against him, but another blow to her ass stopped her. The pain compounded inside, but she needed just a few more strokes. *Please, this one is so huge. Don't let it fade. Let it shatter me. I'll say anything for this one.*

"Fifteen, sir. You own my pussy, sir."

He caressed her ass before giving three more hard thrusts and one that crept in while she whimpered and quivered, only seconds from release.

"Am I better than your husband?"

No. I won't answer that. His cock slid slowly out, pulling her lips, stretching them over every ridge along his thick cock. The orgasm he had built with his skilled hands refused to release, and abated just enough for her to feel her stomach slow its trembling. *No. Don't lose this.*

"Please don't make me answer that."

Another slap on her ass juiced the orgasm to its brim.

"Answer me."

"Sixteen. Yes, sir."

"Yes, sir, what?"

"You're better than my husband."

"Good girl." After another caress where the paddle had landed, he fucked her hard for a minute.

Her body quivered. She spasmed on his cock as it swelled inside her. She tugged against the restraints and ground her hips to feel every inch of him. The orgasm inside filled her entire body. She could almost hear it growling in her ears as it strained to feast on her.

Hayden stopped moving.

So close. Please. She whimpered. "No. Not now."

A hard slap landed on her ass cheek.

"Do you love me?"

"Seventeen. I love my husband, sir."

Another slap preceded a slow grind by the huge cock suppressing her orgasm.

"Don't lie to me."

He pulled out in a slow move, the ridges of his cock rippling her lips until her need to come overcame her brain.

It's all just sex talk. It isn't true. "Eighteen. Yes."

"Come for me, aby."

He fucked hard into her with long strokes, and his hot cum splashed on her cervix perfectly.

Her orgasm consumed her. *It is true. So true.*

❦

Alyssa kept her eyes closed, the soft touches along her hairline a wonderful way to wake up. The tender brushing in the silent room combined with the warm glow still coursing through her body. The warm tenderness pooled in her chest in an emotion previously reserved only for Robert. Wanting to preserve the peace of the moment, she hesitated to speak but decided she needed to whisper to the man generating these feelings. "Thank you."

"You're welcome, Baby."

He called me that as I came. As he destroyed me. The afterglow of the biggest rapture she had ever had ebbed as she realized she would let him call her Baby again. *After that, he earned it.*

She kept her eyes closed and smiled. "How long was I asleep?"

"You mean passed out? Maybe five minutes. Long enough to get you unbuckled and into bed."

"I've never come like that. I want that every day."

He chuckled. "You will probably change your mind as the soreness sets in tonight."

"Maybe. Did the lady in the pictures teach you how to build such a huge orgasm?"

"No. She taught me about the bench. The lady who lived next door when I was growing up taught me about pleasing a woman a long time ago. I'm glad I remembered how."

"I'm glad too. Thank her for me."

"I can't. She died."

Alyssa opened her eyes. "I'm sorry. I didn't mean to—"

He smiled and patted Alyssa's chest. "You didn't know. I miss her. She molded me in ways I didn't understand for years. I am glad to have someone worth sharing her lessons with."

"What do you mean?"

"She was a stay-at-home wife. Her husband traveled a lot for his job. When I was eighteen, she asked my mom if she could hire me for work around the house, so I spent a lot of time there. She decided she could trust me. She seduced me, then offered to teach me about sex."

"This sounds like some kind of fantasy. Are you telling the truth?"

"It's the truth. She was midforties and pretty. I was eighteen and horny. After that one afternoon, we split our time between housework and sex lessons. She taught me everything she knew about pleasing women, then told me to use it for someone I cared about and trusted, because people use sex to hurt."

"Sometimes." *Like when you made me say those things when I needed to come. Even if they are true.*

"Anyway, she taught me a lot. I fell in love with her, at least what a teenager considers love. She died during my first semester at college. Cancer. She had known before I left, but she never said anything. This is the first time I've used that edging technique since that summer. You are the first person I've wanted to use it with, Baby."

Again she swallowed the reflex to prevent his use of Robert's pet name. *He's showing me he cares by calling me that.* "I'm flattered that you care enough to share that with me. That makes the pleasure so much better." *Shit, Alyssa. You said it out loud. You let him call you Baby. Stop lying to yourself. You need to think. A lot.*

Hayden leaned forward to kiss her. This was not the hungry, urgent kiss of a fling but the soft kiss of a lover. He ran his fingers up the side of her head, rubbing the scalp underneath the hair. One thumb grazed the edge of her earlobe, then he pulled away.

He pulled a bottle from the bedside table. "You will want this. Roll on your tummy."

She groaned as she rolled onto her stomach. Lying flat arched her back too much after she'd been bent over the bench for so long.

"Here, use this." Hayden pulled a pillow under her raised hips. When she settled in, he dripped cold lotion over her cheeks. It felt like water on a fire rather than making her jump. He let it sit and cool her burning skin. She sighed, enjoying the relief. He took his time, barely touching her skin at first, and added more before he increased the pressure to rub the lotion into her skin.

She rolled onto her side to face him. She propped her head on one hand. "That felt wonderful. The perfect antidote to the spanking. I loved it."

His hand feathered along her side, creating a glow of soothing warmth between her hip and ribs. He leaned in for another soft kiss. When he pulled back, she leaned in for another, then he delivered one more.

Oh my. Tender and loving. Get out of here, Alyssa. "What a beautiful kiss to leave on. Thank you for doing this for me. I'll always remember it."

This was supposed to be the grand finale to clear your system, not to make memories.

His smile told her he recognized her weakness. "Maybe we can use this again soon."

"I'd love to, but you know I can't. This is the last time I see you." *He did this for me. Nobody else even knew I wanted it. Hell, I didn't know. He broadens me. And nonetheless, you need to be done.*

She rose from the bed.

"Your clothes are in the bathroom over there, unless you want to dress in front of the window upstairs."

She laughed. "Mm, it would be a thrill, but if I do, I'll be too excited to leave." *Taking care of me without my knowing it.*

She stopped for one last kiss before leaving.

"You will need this." He handed her the lotion.

"Thank you."

"I will never hurt you, Baby."

She smiled and left, unable to trust herself to even say goodbye.

❧

Alyssa didn't get far before she needed to pull off the road. Turning into a parking lot, she pulled under some trees and put the car in park.

"The sun makes my eyes water." *Not the sun, Alyssa.* She wiped her eyes until she could see clearly. *A Catholic church. Appropriate. I need to confess, at least to myself.* She dropped her head to the steering wheel and wept until the "Screaming Car Guy" commercial played on the radio and broke through her haze.

"That jerk can even interrupt a good cry." She sat up. The tear tracks down the wheel and the spots where they landed on her jeans let her know it had been a good long one. Alyssa wiped her eyes again, then closed them and leaned back against the headrest.

Today was bad, Alyssa. You had an afternoon of bondage sex with the one man you promised your husband you would cross the street to avoid. Jesus, the things you said.

He owns your pussy.

Better than your husband.

You love him.

Letting him call you Baby.

It was just a heat-of-the-moment thing. He made me say it to get off during sex.

That's not what his face said afterward. He knows, Alyssa. And he's using it to make you risk your marriage.

No. He knows I like the excitement. That's all. Besides, this was the last time.

The kind of excitement that would ensue if Robert knew you were shackled to a bench with Hayden instead of being at work?

Alyssa's stomach dropped like on the first hill of a roller coaster. "I don't want that," she said aloud.

Are you sure? You say you want to stop, but you answer his texts. You don't walk away when you see him in public. He knows. Do you think he shops for antique books? No. He followed you in there because he knew you would react the precise way you did.

Stop this before the consequences crash down on you.

But I want both of them.

Then you should have played within your rules with Robert. Instead, you put your marriage further at risk with every deception. He knows you are emotionally involved, and that should terrify you. Let this be the last time you wanted, and drop Hayden.

Alyssa leaned her forehead on the steering wheel and spoke to the empty car. "I don't want to."

17

FRIDAY, JULY 9, HOME

Alyssa pulled Robert's shirt off and tossed it on the corner chair. Dim light escaping the bedside lamp through the red chiffon laid over it hid the tiny flecks of gray in his hair. The laugh lines around his eyes vanished, but the shadows on his body defined the muscles. He looked twenty-five again. Tonight, she hungered for twenty-five-year-old Robert.

She felt twenty-five again, despite her aching ass. She had fidgeted through Sawyer's birthday dinner, every attempt to find comfort thwarted by today's spanking.

Eighteen spanks for an explosive orgasm. I'll never forget the number.

The kids had noticed. So had Robert. She'd laughed it off, saying she slipped on a grape squished on the kitchen floor at work. She'd accepted the joking about her clumsiness with a smile and a fond memory.

Tonight, at home, she knew she had to connect with Robert.

God, the things I said. They weren't true. Just pillow talk.

Hayden doesn't own my pussy. He's not better than Robert. I don't love him.

But he does.

And he is.

And I said it.

Thoughts wrestled in her head; feelings wrestled in her heart. Every time she saw Hayden, she felt less attached to Robert, and she feared that path.

I've stopped. He's going to be out of my system, especially if I keep reconnecting with Robert. Like we did in the mountains. Like we will tonight.

Having a young, gloriously skilled lover blew her mind every time, and the more she knew him, the more she liked him, the more she wanted him, and the more their sex became making love. *Even today when he applied lotion.* With every meeting, her entire being felt younger, more alive, like she was aging in reverse. And falling in love.

I'll never leave Robert. I'll never want to. I love him too much. He is too much of me.

Having a husband she loved made her safer, more secure, more loved. Making love with him anchored her. Every moment with him felt mature, confident. The gravitas they created together empowered her. She prized her family above everything else. Robert might not be as adventurous or edgy as she wanted, but he knew when she wanted to fuck instead of make love.

The way she wanted to fuck right now.

So prove it. Connect.

She kissed him. "Our kids are so grown up. Why do I feel young?"

"Because we are in here making out like the partygoers

instead of actively chaperoning? I mean, they could drink, or even make out."

His smirk told her the red light was aiding her appearance like it did his. *And maybe hiding my raw ass cheeks.* He wanted to fuck, and he didn't care one bit about the party going on outside their bedroom.

She chuckled. "There are five boys we have known since the fourth grade and their girlfriends, and they are good kids. This is a safe place to celebrate while we stay out of the way."

"Right." Robert nibbled her neck. "And our bedroom is lit only from the bathroom so they can pretend we are asleep while they have a few beers, party, and eventually pair off to make out. So a high school birthday party."

He unsnapped her bra. Her tits usually relaxed after being cooped up all day. Tonight, they ached to be touched like when she was younger. She looked younger. So did he. She felt young. *Let's have fun with that.*

She tousled her hair, letting it jumble around her face as she adopted her character. "We're in college. We shouldn't be at a lame high school party. Thank god we found a free bedroom. Let's fuck." She crooked her finger at him, hoping he would understand the role-play.

"I'm glad we got this room first. Should I wear protection?" Robert laughed.

He got it. Fun. "I'm on the pill. No rubber."

"You're on the pill? At least you didn't say you had your tubes tied when our son was born." He shook his head with a chuckle, then unzipped her skirt. "Okay. We can pretend to be in college again. Do you think Clay's parents will come home tonight, you hot girl I just met at a party?"

"I don't know, you rugged guy I just met at a party. I hope they do, but, you know, not until after. His dad is hot."

"His mom's hot too. But, yeah, like, I hope they stay out until…after."

Alyssa kissed Robert hard, pulling his head to hers. "I'm hotter than Clay's mom. Pull my skirt off and you'll see. I dressed for fun tonight, Babe."

Robert pulled her skirt off, leaving her naked. "No panties. I like the way you think. You are hotter than Clay's mom."

Alyssa removed Robert's pants and gripped his hard cock. "Oh, you are so much hotter than Clay's dad. You are getting lucky tonight, guy I met at the party."

They lay on the bed facing each other, kissing and fondling with the urgency and energy of twenty years earlier.

Robert sucked her nipple into his mouth, flattening it against the ridged palate behind his teeth while he squeezed her ass. Her angry muscle fired sparks through her hips, forcing her breath out with a moan. *That hurts, but tonight the pain turns me on. Hurt me, Babe.*

"We just met. How did you know I like that?"

"Lucky guess." Robert pinched the sides of her clit and jacked it like a small penis. "I bet you like this too."

Alyssa's hips bucked, searching for more pressure against her clit. "Oh, I do. Another lucky guess?"

"You did say I would get lucky tonight. You seem to be lucky too."

"Mm, I am. Keep going."

Robert sucked and bit Alyssa's nipples while he jacked her clit and fingered her wet lips. Alyssa pulled on whichever nipple wasn't in his mouth with one hand and held his head in place with the other. She bucked her hips in time with his fingers as his skillful hands inflated her coming orgasm. She pulled him on top of her and lined his cock up with her opening.

"Don't move. Let me do it." Alyssa raised her hips, drawing

Robert inside as he held his hips above hers, stopping when their skin caught long before his hardness had opened her as deep as she wanted. Her glutes ached with every move. *I don't care how much it hurts; he reclaims me tonight.* She pumped her thighs to fuck up at him, taking his cock deeper, letting it spread her closer to her cervix with each movement.

She pulled at her breasts as she humped onto her husband, letting her breath get shallower as her climax began. She thrust up one final time, her clit ablaze, and ground against his pubic bone as his cock rubbed her cervix. She strained to breathe while she held all her weight on her feet and her neck. Her flowing juice ran down the crack of her ass and up her back, refusing to drip from her body.

When her lungs screamed for air, she collapsed to the bed and inhaled. She grabbed his hips and pulled him down to her. "Now do whatever you want. I got mine, so you do anything. Just come, sexy party guy."

Robert lowered his hips. She guided his cock into her open cunt, and he pushed forward until he bottomed out against her cervix.

"Okay, sexy party girl. You asked for it."

Robert pulled almost all the way out and slammed downward into her, the power driving her aching ass into the bed and exploding fireworks from her entire spasming pussy. He sped up until her rebounds off the mattress resonated as he pounced on her. He held the headboard with one hand and slipped two fingers from the other into her mouth. She sucked his fingers and swirled her tongue around the tips, her taste on them adding to the naughty fantasy.

Robert leaned back, rubbing the head of his cock against Alyssa's G-spot and the sensitive spot beside her cervix, his aim perfect, electrifying her body on every plunge. He pushed her legs open and back, letting him drive deeper, stretching her. With every movement, she clutched at his hardness with her pussy, never wanting him to withdraw but not wanting him to stop moving.

He smirked as her thighs quivered against his hands as he pushed them closer and closer to her shoulders. The pressure built in her cheeks like they would burst apart. When he spread her legs wide and his hip bones hammered her cheeks with every deep plunge inside, fireworks burst behind her eyelids. She fought the scream of pleasure and pain struggling through her lips.

God, I don't know whether to say "waffles" or let him make me come again. So painful. So good. Alyssa chuffed her breath in staccato grunts each time his cock touched the top of her tunnel. The climax exploded, bouncing its waves between her screaming ass and her distended pussy, tightening her abs in long spasms separated by tiny relaxations.

Robert plowed one final time into Alyssa, pinning her against the headboard. The pressure on her head and the spurts on her cervix roiled her. Her thighs strained against Robert's hands, and she tightened her pussy around him. Her breath caught in the spasms flogging her body, slipping out in the short breaks between waves.

When her body relaxed, Robert released her legs to splay open and settled on top of her, resting his weight on his elbows but cuddling her beneath his mass the way she liked after a great session. He kissed her eyelids and cheeks. "I think I love you, hot party girl."

She mustered the strength to wrap her arms around his neck and smiled at him. "I know I love you, hot party guy. You think Clay's parents would mind if we slept in their bed?"

"We're in college. Who cares if they do?"

Alyssa shuddered in a breath as his cock softened and slipped out of her, dropping down onto her anus. "I love that feeling. Who would believe that a soft, wet dick on my ass would be a turn-on, but it is. Thank you for lying here until you slipped out, Babe."

"I love giving you what you like." He rolled off her, and she curled up onto his chest. Robert feathered his fingers in small circles on the small of her back until he began to snore.

"I love you, Babe. Thank you for reclaiming me, even if you didn't know you did."

18

WEDNESDAY, JULY 14, OFFICE

THE PING PULLED Alyssa's attention out of her planning schedule. She was waiting on a message from Susan that she had reached Houston safely for the second summer session. Despite knowing Susan was more than capable, she had worried about her driving across the country by herself. *I'll always worry about them, I suppose.*

She looked down at the screen, and her stomach knotted. Hayden.

"How are you feeling?"

I shouldn't even answer. But a few words would be okay. I don't want to be rude.

Don't be rude to your family.

"I'm fine, thank you. I can't talk. Please understand."

"I understand. You want to pretend that you never said I own your pussy."

"That was just sex talk. I said it to get you off."

"What about that I'm a better lay than your husband?"

Shit. He remembers all of it. "That too. Just talk."

"And when you said you loved me? Do you just throw that around casually during sex?"

She couldn't say no, or it would invalidate all the other things she'd said. She couldn't say yes. She'd meant it when she said it, and she refused to cheapen those words by saying otherwise.

But if I say I meant it, I'll be in his bed by noon.

She didn't want to cry, but tears blurred her vision. She blocked his number and stared out the window until she could see again.

19

THURSDAY, JULY 22, COUNTRY CLUB

Alyssa sipped wine while she waited. She hadn't talked with Jessica since that night in the trees, so she had invited her to dinner. She had requested a table away from other diners, which wasn't an issue on a July Tuesday. Only a few other tables were filled. Jessica texted that she would be a half hour late, so Alyssa stared out the window across the room and enjoyed the peace settling into her chest.

Someone broke her reverie by placing a second glass of wine on the table.

"I didn't order this." She looked up. Her peace fled, leaving a struggle in its place. She wanted to leave but lacked the will to stand. She didn't want to talk but couldn't look away from the man looking down at her. She wanted to send him away but couldn't form the words.

"I see. If you don't want it, may I sit with the most beautiful woman in town and drink it myself?" Hayden sat across from her without waiting for a response.

She had only thought about him once today. She was slowly inching him from her mind, one stifled fantasy at a time. She would have to start over. She would have to do more than that if Jessica didn't arrive soon. She gripped her seat to avoid crossing the table to kiss him.

Her heart swelled because he pursued her. He remained perfect in her eyes, and he wanted her. He wanted her enough to ignore her pleas to stop. His desire for her had started this. That same desire wouldn't let it die. And she loved that.

Yet she loved her husband and wanted to protect her marriage. To do that, Hayden had to stop, because she didn't have the will to stop him.

She tightened her abs, trying in vain to quell the storm in her stomach.

"Hayden, I can't see you like this."

He smiled. "How would you prefer to see me?"

"You know what I meant."

"Yes, I do. You meant that you miss me and wish we could be together."

"Hayden, please. I can't be with you anymore. I wish things were different, but I have no choice. I refuse to destroy my marriage, and being with you will do that. Please don't make this harder on me than it already is."

He nodded and stood. "It's hard on me too. I love you, and you love me. You said so yourself, and you have never denied it. When you are ready to act on that, I'm ready for us to make a wonderful life together."

She watched him go. *Please leave. Don't stop at the bar. Go out.*

She sighed when he walked past the bar and out the front doors. *Small blessings.*

Alyssa drank the rest of her wine. *That took everything I had. A longer conversation would sway me. And if he had touched me, I would have done anything he wanted.*

She sipped from Hayden's untouched glass. She longed for the calm reflection of twenty minutes earlier, but the buzz of the wine only jumbled the thoughts tormenting her brain.

If she doesn't arrive soon, I'll be drunk.

Jessica breezed in a few minutes later. "Sorry I'm late. I got tied up with a patient."

By the time their plates were cleared, Alyssa knew that Jessica had earned a promotion at work, that she and Drew had returned to the copse of trees to finish what Alyssa had interrupted the night of the fireworks, and that five glasses of wine over two hours had left her tipsy.

Jessica leaned across the table. "Okay, Alyssa. You are getting drunk for a reason. What is it?"

Maybe it was the alcohol. Alyssa told the entire story. The cupola house, the sneaking, confessing to Robert—everything rolled off her tongue. Then, with a quieter voice, she covered everything since: the trip to the mountains, failing to avoid Hayden, the meeting in the bookstore, the sex dungeon house. She recounted the things she'd said as Hayden taunted her with a simmering orgasm, and she wept while she verified that what she'd said was true.

"To top it all off, when I'm sitting here tonight, congratulating myself for focusing on things at home, he waltzes up, sits down with a glass of wine, and tells me when I'm ready to act on my love for him, he's ready for me. I managed to tell him to leave, but it was close. My plan was to let wine wash him away, but it hasn't worked yet."

"Alyssa, you know you can't see him. Robert won't abide those feelings. You need to steer clear of this guy, no matter how much you want to do otherwise."

"I know. It's so hard. Why can't I have both? That would make life easy."

Jessica shook her head. "Because you got your husband to agree to an open marriage under the pretense that it's all fun. Surprise, it can be more complicated. This is how your open marriage feels on a bad day."

"How can I fix it?"

"My guess? You either close your marriage and stay with Robert with no outside temptations, or you use your open marriage to let a distraction or three help you forget this realtor and remember how to have fun with your other toys."

"I've thought about it, but nobody catches my eye. They aren't Robert or Hayden and somehow don't measure up. Believe me, I'd love to drown my woes in a hunk or two, but I'm not tempted lately. I'm either making amends to Robert or going from pillar to post over Hayden."

I can't tell you what to do, but I hope you opt for the distractions. Oh, that means we play with Robert, doesn't it?"

Alyssa laughed. "You bad girl, with your designs on my husband."

"No designs. I like getting together with you two, so figure it out before I feel neglected."

"I'll figure it out. One more glass will help." She motioned to the waiter.

"I hope you do, Alyssa. Another glass of wine might not help, but I'll talk with you while you drink it and I'll drive you home."

"Thank you, my favorite neighbor."

20

FRIDAY, JULY 30, HOME

"We can make an offer on those two, then?" Alyssa looked at her husband as she slid into the satin nightgown.

"I think so. The condo downtown will draw young singles, and the little ranch will suit a young family. It's too bad we didn't see one more we liked. Maybe you and Lauren will find one in Wilmington tomorrow. You sure you don't want me to come with you? Leaving at seven to drive four hours to look at houses and drive four hours back is a long day. With three of us, somebody would be fresh for the return drive."

"No. You haven't golfed in three weeks. Go have fun with the guys. It will be a long day, but Lauren says the rental market there is much better."

"I don't know. The last time I sent you house hunting alone with a realtor, you fell in love with him."

His comment stung, but his tone told her he was playing, so

she held her tongue. Even if she wanted to argue, he was right. She rolled her eyes. "I'm going with Lauren, Babe."

"Yes. She's beautiful, and you like women and men. I worry."

"She just came off maternity leave. She won't be ready." Laughing, she crawled into bed and laid her head on Robert's chest. She took a breath and lowered her tone so he would know she was serious. "Besides, we have barely reopened our marriage. I promise to talk before doing anything."

He stroked her head. "I know. I'm only teasing. Sort of."

"I know." She reached for his cock. "You're thinking what I'm thinking."

"What's that?"

"That we need to celebrate finding two houses today." She ducked under the covers to suck his already hard cock into her mouth. After only a few strokes, she pulled the nightgown off and sat across his legs. Keeping eye contact, she scooted her ass forward. "Sit up some and lean back on your hands."

When he was more upright, Alyssa put her calves on his shoulders and raised her hips over his cock. She guided him in as she lowered herself. When her cheeks hit his thighs, she leaned back to rest on her hands.

He's crushing against my front wall. Thank you, Jessica.

Alyssa began grinding, seeking to align his cock across her pleasure centers. She found the angle with a delectable shock in her G-spot, and she let her weight smash it against his head until her belly quivered around the pleasure building inside it. She pushed up and down with her legs and arms, pulling almost off his cock, then plunging down on it, pounding her G-spot on the way to the electric spot beside her cervix.

All her weight pressed her body against the cock standing up inside her. The explosions of pleasure as she dragged across her G-spot and hammered beside her cervix threatened to rob her arms and legs of their strength. She was tempted to allow it.

Robert leaned back against the headboard. He moved one hand to her hips, helping Alyssa move as she fucked him. He positioned his free hand to grind her clit with his thumb as she worked.

That's what I need. I'll explode soon. I'd better. This is hard work.

She watched his body as she rode. His shoulder tightened as he helped her up and down. His pec rippled as he adjusted to keep his thumb on her clit. His thighs pushed against hers as he thrust the little bit he could from underneath.

Those eyes. He watches my face, my body, and where we join all at once. That hungry look. That's what he does best: want me.

Alyssa slammed down onto him and stopped, grinding his cock inside and his thumb outside as her orgasm stole her ability to move beyond the clenching of her pussy around the steel shaft filling it. She gritted her teeth to stifle the scream that threatened to burst from her chest, knowing Clay was up the hall. Her arms failed. She collapsed on the bed, releasing the last of her tension with a low moan. She looked up between her legs at her husband, still hungry for her.

Keep looking like that, Robert. "I can't move, but use me, Babe. Do anything you want, so long as you come inside me."

Robert leered at her body. He moved to his knees, keeping her limp legs across his thighs. As he stood, he lifted her hips and let her legs fall toward her head until she was almost vertical above her shoulders and bent in half. He kept her up by gripping the backs of her thighs and pinning her back against his legs.

Oh fuck. Hayden did this. I can't wait to feel Robert do it.

Her toes touched the bed beside her head, and he drove his cock down, spearing into her until his balls smeared her cum over her flexing anus. She squeezed her pussy around him again as his tip ground around her cervix, calling her next orgasm forward. Again and again, he pulled up, letting her grab a bite of air before dropping down.

His body weight was a hammer forging an orgasm against the anvil of her cervix. Her body weight tightened her throat, the lightheadedness keeping her ecstasy contained while it grew. By the time she felt his cock swelling, her nipples were sparking, her ass was opening and closing under his balls, and her rapture spilled over when he sprayed her insides with a hot load. Her exhausted body quivered as waves of pleasure flowed out of her belly, finding the energy to spasm and relax while he filled her.

Robert laid her legs sideways, spooned behind her, and rubbed her belly.

"That was amazing, Robert. When I said use me to come, I thought you'd pound me. I didn't expect you to destroy me. Thank you."

"I thought you would like that, but I didn't know it would cut off your air so much. Are you okay?"

"Much better than okay. You were masterful. You were gentle in such a brutal position. I loved it. Where did you learn that?"

"Jessica taught me."

"When?"

"Tuesday."

"You fucked her on Tuesday?"

"If I had, I would have told you. We had lunch. I asked her how to give you a little excitement, so she showed me."

"That's some lunch." Alyssa grinned and squeezed his hand against her stomach.

"Not exactly. She showed me some pictures of unique positions. Yes, right there in the restaurant. Where did you learn what you did tonight? That was new too."

"Jessica has been a busy matchmaker. She had lunch with me on Wednesday. She looked so beautiful in those photos."

"That she did. Did she ask you about getting together with her and Drew? She said they would like to play with us. I told her we were going slow right now."

"Maybe that's why she showed me the positions 'to spice things up.' When we play some more, we should repay her."

Robert pulled his face away from her ear. "When? Have you decided you're ready to be more active?"

"No. I haven't thought about it much. Those pictures of her and Drew blew on the coals a bit."

"I'm glad I'm the one stoking your fire for right now."

"Babe, tonight you made me a blast furnace for you and only you. I want the outside excitement, but I want to be safe doing it."

21

SATURDAY, JULY 31, WILMINGTON

"I'm glad we found one so quickly. It's perfect for what you want." Lauren put out her hands as if to show it off.

"Me too. I love the view." Alyssa looked out the bedroom window over the marsh to the river, where two boats followed each other toward the channel.

"You can see the river, but there's no dock to maintain. This is a good rental neighborhood. And it falls just in your price range."

"Yes. You did a great job, Lauren. Thank you for stepping in."

"Glad to do it." She looked at the small diamond watch on her wrist. "It's not yet two o'clock. A friend of mine has a boat at the marina. Want to take a ride to celebrate?"

"Thanks, but I'd prefer to get back. It's a long drive. What about a good lunch, then we go?"

Lauren nodded. "Sure. I know just the place." She sent a text. "We're all set."

149

❧

Alyssa looked out the window by their table across the Intracoastal Waterway. The waitress took their order, and Lauren leaned closer. She needn't have worried. The lunch crowd had thinned to only two other tables on the other side of the room.

"If you don't mind me asking, what happened between you and Hayden? He's a great guy, but Rosalyn had me come back two days early from maternity leave to shop with you."

"Lauren, you didn't need to do that."

"According to Rosalyn, I absolutely did. I thought you guys would hit it off. What went wrong?"

"We've known each other a long time. This is just between us, right?"

"Absolutely. I promise."

Alyssa watched two men tie up a boat at the dock below their window. "We did hit it off. He is a great guy. He helped a lot with that house we flipped. Took care of everything." She looked down. "Even me."

"You slept with him."

"Yes. A lot. No, way too much. It was a torrid two months."

Lauren looked around the restaurant and smiled. "So he's good?"

Alyssa let the corners of her mouth rise just a bit. "Mm-hmm. Too good. I couldn't say no to him, then I fell for him. Almost ruined my marriage."

"How did you work it out?"

She doesn't need the entire truth. "I gave him up cold turkey. I had no other options. Robert talked with Rosalyn about it."

Lauren nodded. "That's why she called me, I guess. How awful, to have to choose between great sex and your marriage."

Hot flames of anger shot up Alyssa's throat and out her

mouth before she could stop them. "I have great sex in my marriage, thank you very much."

Lauren blushed. "I didn't mean to imply you didn't. You did say that Hayden was too good for you to say no. That sounds like he's better than what you get from Robert."

The cold water of her own words cooled the fire inside. Anger gave way to embarrassment. *Save this.* "Not better, just different. And yes, too good to resist. That's why I can't be around him."

Lauren nodded and winked. "If you could see him again, would you?"

"I can't. My marriage can't take it. I'm getting over him, and I need to continue getting over him."

"If there were no consequences, would you?"

"Why do you ask that? There is no such thing as no consequences. I'm free of him, and I intend to keep it that way. I won't see him again, ever."

"How is he so irresistible?" Lauren let the waitress top off their drinks. "The rumor is that he fucked Rosalyn to get hired."

"Isn't she a lesbian?"

Lauren nodded. "Has been for years. I want to understand just how good he is."

"He's good enough to make you consider trashing your marriage. Think a long time before satisfying your curiosity."

Alyssa texted Robert while she waited on Lauren to return from the restroom. "Found one. Here's the link. Coming home soon. Love you."

"Hello, Alyssa."

Alyssa dropped her phone. "Hayden. What are you doing here?"

"You wanted to see me."

A knot formed in her stomach, threatening to throw back the lunch she'd just enjoyed. She didn't want to be near him; there was too much to lose. Anger welled in her chest and raced up her throat. "The hell I do. I can't see you again, ever. Leave before Lauren comes back."

"Lauren isn't coming back. She left a couple of minutes ago. If you want to get home, you need to come with me."

Alyssa looked toward the hostess stand. Through the glass doors, she saw an empty space where Lauren had parked. "What's happening?"

"Your husband needed some time to trust you again, so I was careful where I contacted you. Now here you are, two hundred fifty miles from home, and your only ride is a man who, how did you put it? Made you think a long time about trashing your marriage? That's it. Are you coming with me, or are you taking a four-hour Uber?"

She looked around the restaurant as panic turned her breath to short gasps. He hadn't been in the dining room. "How did you hear what we said?"

"Lauren is a good friend to both of us. She's helping us get together today."

"This was planned?"

"How else could you get what you need?"

"What I need is to go home. I'll call Lauren to come back." She dialed Lauren's number. It went to voice mail. She watched him as he waited. That same self-assured look, something between a smile and a smirk, teased her. She remembered him giving her that same look after ruining her with orgasms. *So many times. All he did was please me. I put my marriage at risk, not him. He didn't do anything I didn't ask for.* She dialed again to the same result three times, each unanswered call pulling her toward resigned acceptance of the situation. "Shit."

"You want to come with me?"

I shouldn't. But if I call Robert, he won't be here for four hours. Uber? Maybe five hundred dollars. He planned this, but I'll only ride back home with him. Nothing can happen while we are driving. I can still be home for dinner. "No. But I don't have a choice. Take me home."

He led her to a boat. "My car is down in Carolina Beach. We'll ride with my friends back there, then I'll take you home."

She needed to be away from him. As angry as she was at the situation, she couldn't deny her attraction or remembering the decadent pleasure of being with him. Her breasts ached to be caressed while her brain screamed "run." Her crumbling defenses wouldn't hold if she boarded that boat.

"Why don't we just Uber there? It's faster."

He grinned at her. "Feel free. I'll be taking the boat. I'm down for a visit with my friends, and I am willing to cut the visit short a day to get you home tonight, but I'm riding back to my car on their boat. By the way, you don't know the address, so enjoy wandering aimlessly through Carolina Beach until I arrive. Your choice."

Talk him out of it. "Why are you doing this? I can't see you again. That won't change."

"You aren't seeing me. You are with Lauren, whose phone is off. You can't say you hate me; you said you love me. You can't resist me. Why not enjoy the time?"

He's a good man. He won't hurt me. Appeal to his morality. "No. I don't hate you. I hate what I become around you."

"You mean happy?" He smirked at her again.

I don't have a good alternative. How long can the boat ride be? I can just sit in the sun away from him, then we will be driving. I'll be fine.

She accompanied him toward the dock. "Please, let's get this over with as fast as possible."

"We'll go quickly. But you might as well enjoy this beautiful day for a boat ride." He shook hands with the two men who stood on deck. "Alyssa, this rugged creature is Eric. We were partners in a real estate office, but he decided to become a charter boat captain. We go way back. This is Kevin, Eric's first mate and the smartest seafarer I've ever met."

Hayden and his friends talked in the cockpit. Alyssa sat in the bow by herself and texted Robert to let him know they were taking a boat ride but would still be home tonight. *No answer. He's having fun playing golf. I wish we could talk. He could keep me occupied. I'll sit here alone for the ride. He hasn't bothered me so far.*

She remained up front alone until the sun and the slow pace drove her to walk back to them. "Why are we going so slow? I need to get home."

Eric turned to her. "We aren't allowed a wake in this narrow channel. Once we get to the waterway, we can open it up a bit. We should be down there in about ninety minutes."

Ninety minutes? Shit. "I see. Would you mind if I went down to the cabins? I'm getting sunburned up there."

He stepped aside, allowing her access to the ladder. "Sure. Go anywhere you like. It isn't very big, and if you get hot, pop the hatch above you to let the air circulate."

Alyssa descended into the stifling bow cabin and opened the hatch at the far end. She sat on the bed, letting the resulting breeze between the doorway and the hatch cool her skin. She had just lain back when she felt lips on her thigh, sending a spark straight to her clit.

"Stop, Hayden."

"Nobody will know. You know you want me." He kissed her other thigh, sending more sparks, hardening her nipples and making her pussy throb and flower open. He stroked her calf while he removed her shoe.

"I'll know. Stop." *Push him away, Alyssa.* She pressed her head back into the bed. Her hands gripped the covers in tight fists. *Or don't. He's so good, remember?*

Hayden continued to shower kisses on her thighs as he massaged the other calf and removed her other shoe. Her thighs fell open when he dropped her leg, and his kisses moved higher. He unbuttoned her shorts.

I can't, but I want this. "Stop, Hayden."

Just once more. Far away from home. In secret. The really last time, then he'll be out of my system. She invalidated her words by tugging the T-shirt hem out of her shorts.

"Take that off for me."

She sat up and pulled off the T-shirt and bra. His lips maintained contact with her thighs.

"Raise your hips."

Her shorts and panties disappeared to the floor. He stood at the edge of the bed, between her open legs, leering at her. She leered back, hungry to watch his show. He pulled off his shirt, then returned his eyes to hers. He unbuckled his shorts and dropped them to the floor.

God, it's magnificent.

Hayden chuckled as Alyssa stared at his cock, memories of its ravishing effects on her body flooding away any thoughts of hurrying home.

He licked her pussy from bottom to top. She grabbed his hair with both hands.

"Just fuck me. I'm soaking for you. We have the boat ride. That's all."

He lifted her ankles to his shoulders and moved forward above her, stretching her hamstrings and tilting her hips up for his use. He tapped the head of his cock on her opening and her clit a few times, the hot sparks forcing a moan from her throat. He pulled back and slid the tip into her. The ridge on the bottom spread her lips near her taint, and the head pressed the rough portion of her G-spot as it worked forward to her cervix.

The curve of his cock ensured the head massaged the line of sensitive spots on her front wall up to her cervix, and its girth stretched her lips with delicious pain. She was indeed ready for him. She had done nothing but lubricate since stepping on the boat, and he slid forward, stretching her tunnel into her body until his balls rested on her tingling asshole.

Hayden rested one hand on the bed above Alyssa's shoulder, bearing his weight and preventing her from sliding as he thrust into her. The other hand caressed and pulled her breasts and nipples in time with his slow thrusts, letting them stretch and leak golden pleasure into the orgasm building in her belly.

Alyssa moved a hand to her clit, wanting but not needing the extra stimulation for a powerful release. Her face flushed hot and her belly tightened as her climax swept through her. Her cries filled the small cabin, drowning out the increased rumble of the engines.

The boat jerked forward, then slowed with a lurch, then jerked forward again as it sped up on a course against the motion of the waves. Hayden timed his thrusts so he bottomed out inside her just as the boat hit the next wave, multiplying the force inside her stretched pussy, the bursts of fullness propelling mournful grunts through her body and out her mouth.

Alyssa's hamstrings were stretched almost as far as her vagina, the ache in the backs of her knees adding to the overwhelming sensations coursing through her body.

Nobody makes me feel this good. God, I'm folded in half, the ride beating me to death, and I can't stop coming.

Her body tensed and she tightened around his cock just as the next wave slammed the boat. She lost her breath. Her mouth opened and shut. She couldn't inhale as the orgasm tightened her body.

Hayden must have noted her red face and stilled. Alyssa gasped in a breath, then another. "Don't stop. Keep pounding. Give me more."

He leaned forward, stretching her yet again, and in a couple of tries, matched his thrusts with the rhythm of the boat. The break forestalled her orgasm, but it recovered on his next stroke. The tapping of his balls on her pucker when his head shoved her cervix deep inside her belly fanned the hot cauldron of fire about to erupt within her. Her chest flushed hot as his cock swelled within her.

Alyssa pinched her clit as her orgasm began. Her ab muscles fluttered as her thighs clamped together, pinning her hand on her pleasure button.

Hayden buried himself in her to spray directly on her cervix, the powerful bursts inflaming her body all the more. Alyssa's hips hunched with the warm eruption inside her. *Love that.* She pulled her nipple, stretching the electric connection between it and her clit to the very tip. She sucked for breath before sagging back into the mattress, spent.

Hayden stayed inside her and lowered her slack legs one at a time. When the bouncing of the boat slid his limp member out of her, he rolled to the side and traced her abs with his fingers. "I'm glad we could get together."

"Me too. Give me more." She palmed his softening cock without opening her eyes.

"You want more? More what?" He dipped his fingers to run along her swollen lips.

"Just more. Fill me."

He inserted two fingers. With his thumb beside her clit, he rolled his hand in circles, rubbing across it and her G-spot at the same time. She gasped in his mouth when he kissed her. He fluttered his tongue against her lips, and she let him enter.

Alyssa sucked his tongue and humped her hips against his magical hand. A third finger stretched her, rekindling an orgasm that simmered under her belly. Her legs straightened and bent. Her toes pointed. When his pinky finger rubbed across her anus, her orgasm moved from her belly to her pussy and began knocking at her door to come out.

Hayden pulled his head back as Alyssa writhed under his ministrations. She pulled at her breasts, and her head pressed back into the mattress as her back arched. Her eyes closed. Her entire body stiffened, trapping his hand between her steely thighs. His hand moved as best it could, extending her pleasure. Her body relaxed with a throaty sigh, and she nodded off.

&

Alyssa climbed onto the deck behind the three men sitting in the stern, talking and watching the sun near the horizon. She felt Hayden's muscular shoulders, then trailed one hand along his back as she moved to sit in his lap.

"This is beautiful, but shouldn't we be at your car by now? I should have been home already."

Hayden patted her thigh. "You said we had the boat ride, so you decide when it ends. It seems we are having a little engine trouble."

"What kind of engine trouble? Why aren't you working on it? Can we call someone?" Alyssa pulled her phone out of her pocket and opened the phone. When she could get no signal, she looked in every direction but didn't see land.

"It's the kind of engine trouble that lets us stay out here

a little while. We are far enough offshore that there is no cell signal." Hayden slid his hand inside her T-shirt to caress her bare back. "Don't worry. We are fine. Tonight is a gift, if you want it."

"A gift?"

"Yes. You told me that you like having multiple men at once. You can have that tonight."

Eric leaned forward. "It has to be quick. I have a charter of college girls at six a.m. I need to get back to meet them. No offense, miss. You are one hot woman, and I'll be happy to fuck you, but that's a good charter."

Hayden waved his hand. "I told you I'd pay the six hundred they offered."

"Man, it isn't just the money. They booked a lot of liquor. They will be naked and ready to fuck by ten in the morning. Six of them. That's good pussy for Kevin and me."

Alyssa leaned forward. "You're very confident."

"They start drinking early. They take a half dose of Dramamine to prevent seasickness. They get warm in the sun, and those bikinis come off. They warm up, and the only dicks available are mine and Kevin's. It happens most of the time, and every time they order a lot of booze."

Alyssa sat on Hayden's lap as the sun set. She watched and thought about what she had done. She looked around. No land. No cell reception. A captain willing to corroborate engine trouble. She could not undo sleeping with Hayden. If she didn't keep this secret, her marriage was over. If those were the stakes, she might as well go all in for the night.

As the sun ducked below the horizon, she turned to Eric. "If Hayden pays the money for the charter, what else do you need to stay here all night and blow off the fare tomorrow?"

"You really want all of us tonight?"

Yes, I do. "It's a rare treat."

"You are asking me to give up a great day of pussy."

"For a great night of pussy."

"All right, how about this? After whatever we do tonight, tomorrow you remain completely naked until we pull into the marina. And every time I get hard, we fuck."

Kevin spoke for the first time. "What about me?"

Eric patted his mate's shoulder. "Kevin too."

Alyssa felt Hayden's cock hardening under her thigh, and his hand slipped around her back to caress her breast. *This will be good. It's after sunset. I wouldn't get home tonight anyway, so enjoy it. I can't wait to feel Hayden and someone else.*

"Hayden and I must leave the marina no later than two o'clock tomorrow. Is that sufficient?"

Eric stroked his chin. "With tonight, that works."

"I'll do it." She kissed Hayden. "But I'm in charge tonight. You set the rules for tomorrow. I set them tonight. Fair enough?"

"Fair enough. What do you want us to do?"

"Make dinner. I'm starving."

The captain and his mate laughed and went to the galley.

"This is the last night, Hayden. Never contact me again."

"I miss you. You love me, remember?"

"I've missed you too. I can't see you though. I said those things during sex, and I meant them then, but they aren't true now. The sex is great, and you are a wonderful man, but I have to choose, and I choose my marriage."

Are you sure?

"Do you? I ask because you didn't resist coming on the boat, or getting undressed, or taking my cock inside you. In fact, you demanded it. And you just negotiated a naked day of sex in exchange for a gang bang tonight. You can understand my confusion."

"I understand it. I'm confused too." *You aren't confused. You are greedy and reckless. You should be home right now.* "What we do together is exciting, even mind-blowing at times. The next few hours will create memories that I'll treasure forever. But when you drop me at my house tomorrow, we're done for good."

He raised his beer. "Then here's to a night to remember."

∾

Fresh seafood and vegetables eaten under the full moon enhanced the tales of the three men's adventures. Beer and salty air had the four of them laughing about inept guys showing off on the boat and drunk girls spending the entire day vomiting over the side. Alyssa left them talking and cleared the plates to the galley sink. She returned with a rag and wiped off the gear locker they had used for a table, the men still telling tales to one another.

Alyssa dropped the rag in the sink as she descended to the bow cabin. She shucked off her T-shirt and shorts, picked up one of the thin pads that passed as a mattress, and climbed the ladder.

The laughter stopped as she stepped into the moonlight.

"Her tan lines are glowing," an enraptured Kevin said to no one in particular.

"White targets," Eric added.

She dropped the pad and knelt. "Y'all are overdressed."

The three men stood and removed their clothes. Kevin was the first one nude, and he stepped in front of Alyssa. She took his entire cock in her mouth. *Small. Everything about him is small. He can go first in my ass.*

As the other men joined them, Alyssa took their cocks in hand and jacked them before turning to suck Eric's cock. *Nice. Straight and a good size. I'll like fucking him too.* She bobbed on him until she could take all of him in, the head sliding into her throat. "You taste almost as good as that fish you cooked."

She turned to suck Hayden and stroked the other two. *That's what I want inside me.* She didn't take all of him in but worked the head, flicking the frenulum with her tongue. Her nipples pulsed at his groans of approval.

With a slurp, she popped off his head and stood. "Put the pad up there." She pointed to the locker where they had eaten. "Let's fuck under the open sky. Hayden, lie down." He did, and she straddled his face, grinding his mouth while she pulled her nipples. The other two men caressed her butt and thighs as Hayden spread her lips with his tongue. She had been wet when she stepped on deck and didn't need the stimulation, but she wanted to give them a quick show.

When she was ready, Alyssa scooted down Hayden's body, reached beneath her, and slid his cock inside.

"Don't go anywhere, boys, you'll both be in me in a minute." She ground her hips, letting the large shaft spread her and working the head up to her cervix. When it touched, she bounced a few times to loosen herself for the event to come.

She pointed to Kevin. "Do you have lube? Go get it and fuck my ass. Wash after."

He scampered belowdecks and returned less than a minute later.

The lube dripped onto her opening and sent a shiver up her spine. "You ready to warm me up after that?"

"I'll warm you up." He worked one, then two, then three fingers inside her with heavy dollops of additional lube. When he pulled his fingers out, she concentrated on holding her ass open, and he lined up behind her.

The small intruder filled her ass and pressed against the underside of Hayden's cock through her thin tissues. "Mm. Perfect. Fuck me slow, guys."

They found a rhythm after a few tries. They filled her concurrently, keeping the head of Kevin's cock squeezing against the underside of Hayden's, creating a moving compression massage inside her. Her belly fluttered above her womb.

"Oh god. Just like that. Okay, bring that cock here." She gripped Eric's cock when he stepped onto the pad straddling Hayden's head. She teased the head with her tongue, licking over it, flicking the sensitive underside, then sucked it all in.

As she bobbed, jolts from her breasts went to her clit. Hayden was holding them with both hands, and as she moved, they stretched, pinched and stinging enough to electrify her pussy. Alyssa lengthened her strokes on Eric's cock as far as her breasts would allow; Hayden's hands held them still.

I love this. Outside. The moon. Three men. So full. So hot. Thank you, Hayden.

Alyssa's neck flushed hot. She buried the cock in her mouth to the root, letting the head into her throat, then pulled until the tip rested on her lips, letting her breasts stretch like they were being pulled from her chest.

The cock in her ass broke rhythm as its owner breathed heavier in her ear, but it pressed on the back of her tunnel, now opposite Hayden's strokes, peaking her pleasure. Hayden's magnificent pleasure tool did what it always did: filled her full, touched the G-spot and cervix on every stroke, and rubbed the end of her clit.

Her mouth, her breasts, her ass, her pussy all sent bolts of lightning to collide in her belly. The roiling there built and spread. It filled her body with a boiling feeling. *This will be a big one.* Alyssa sucked in a breath and plunged back onto the cock before her. When she felt the first shot of cum in her ass, she exploded.

Alyssa's eyes popped open wide. The skin of her neck felt tight against the veins that must have been bulging against it. Her hands dug into Eric's thighs as she pushed back against the two men filling her pelvis. Her body tensed from neck to feet. Her thighs clenched Hayden's sides. She felt her juices flow out in a splash, surely soaking Hayden's balls and the pad below. As the jerking body against her back stilled, she regained control of her own.

She pulled Eric from her mouth. "Are you close?"

"Oh yeah. You are some kind of cocksucker."

"Come in my mouth." She resumed bobbing, this time faster than before her orgasm.

"Here it comes." Eric placed both hands on her head as he erupted in her mouth. She pulled back, letting the fluid pool on and under her tongue, then swallowed once before sucking the final drops from his opening.

Now to ride this stallion. The other men out of her, Alyssa chased another rapid orgasm by bucking her hips, taking Hayden as deeply as she could, then letting his tip rest between her lips before plunging down again. When she let her cervix touch his tip, she rotated her hips to feel him drag across the sensitive tissue around it.

Hayden switched from holding her breasts to rolling her nipples as she bounced. With the other men out of the way, he thrust up into her, meeting her on her downstroke and hammering her mons against his pubic bone, sending sparks through her body.

Kevin had returned from the cabin and sat beside Eric to watch the two lovers tussle. She saw them watching. She liked being watched and would ordinarily make eye contact with them to heighten the thrill, but this was not an ordinary circumstance. This was Hayden and his magnificent cock.

She returned her attention to Hayden below her. Alyssa bounced as if she were driving him into the ground, and Hayden thrust as if he wanted to buck her completely off him. Every collision produced grunts from both, and they both leaned their heads back as their pleasure peaked.

God. Coming again. Alyssa leaned back and looked at the moon overhead while Hayden's back arched as he came. His spurts shocked her cervix, firing her orgasm higher. He groaned and spasmed until the spurts stopped, before sagging into the cushion. Alyssa flopped forward.

As she regained her breath, Alyssa spoke without opening her eyes. "I want more. Who's ready?"

The three men shook their heads. Eric said, "I think it's time you showed her what you can do, Kevin."

"I agree. Lift her off me. Alyssa, lie on your back." Hayden scooted off the cushion when Kevin and Eric lifted Alyssa by her shoulders and thighs. Their strong hands were rough on her skin, but despite the firm grips, they handled her gently and easily as they put her down and rolled her onto her back. *I wonder what he'll do? I can't wait.*

Kevin moved to the end of the locker. Eric and Hayden lifted Alyssa by her thighs and arms to move her ass in front of him. They held her legs to their chests, opening her to Kevin's gaze. Hayden caressed Alyssa's cheek. "This will be a sensation beyond any you have ever had, Alyssa. It may sting at first, but it will feel amazing if you persevere through the initial feeling."

Her belly tightened. This was going to hurt? *Wait a second.* "What is he doing?"

"You'll see. You're going to love it." He caressed the inside of the thigh. She felt comforted rather than aroused by it.

"How do you know?" *Hayden won't let them hurt me. He's here.*

"Everyone does. But if you don't, we can stop."

She looked at Kevin. The hint of a smile turned up the corners of his mouth but in a kind way rather than something menacing. He had been gentle in her ass and had washed after, like she'd asked him to. And she was still super horny. Whatever this was going to be, she wanted to feel it.

"Dazzle me, Mr. Magician. Please."

Kevin's smile widened.

Mischievous eyes.

He held up his black-gloved hand so she could see him cover two fingers with lube. He rubbed it between them and his thumb, then dropped his hand to her open lips. He smeared it across her lips, dipping inside to coat all the edges and surely mixing the lube with the semen deposited there earlier.

That feels good. No stinging, just like getting good foreplay.

After four passes, he repeated the process, adding a third finger to the massage and pressing them inside until his pinky knuckle stopped his forward progress. Her lips stung about the same as when Hayden had first entered her.

Stretched just right. So far, really good.

Again, he coated every side, and Alyssa hissed in a breath when he crossed over her G-spot.

Ooh. More of that, please. "Yes. More."

Kevin raised his hand to let her watch as he lubed four fingers.

"I don't know if I can take all four." *I'm glad he has small hands.*

Hayden smiled at her. "You can. And the thumb."

Kevin formed his fingers into a cone and tucked his thumb inside them, pushed into Alyssa up to the knuckles, then rotated. His knuckles bounced across her clit and the base of her opening. Lightning exploded from her pussy through the rest of her body and back to gather atop her pussy. Her hips jerked, releasing another burst.

"Oh. Do that again."

Kevin rotated again, keeping his fingers in place as she

humped with her hips. He continued to rotate. She continued to buck against him. She was building to an orgasm fast.

"Keep going. That feels so good." She pulled her nipples against the shocks coming through her core, sensitizing them from inside and outside.

Kevin watched her eyes as she headed toward orgasm. The lube he dripped onto her lips no longer shocked her with cold. She was too aroused for it to affect her beyond letting his bony knuckles roll faster across her clit as he spun his hand.

I'm coming again. Alyssa's legs strained against the men holding them up. She squeezed around Kevin's fingers. The ridges of his fingers and the gaps between them played across her taut lips in exquisite detail. The climax was not a large one, but it was good. She lay back to catch her breath. "That was so good. Thank you."

Kevin kept his finger cone inside her as she panted. "I'm glad you liked it, but we are just warming up." He pressed forward with his hand. His knuckles passed the very edges of her lips. The sting she had enjoyed became the stabbing of a knife on every inch along his hand. Her reflexes responded. Only the strong arms of Hayden and Eric prevented her from kicking at Kevin.

Alyssa jerked her head off the mat. "What are you doing?"

"Relax. When my hand is inside you, you will feel pleasure you never thought possible."

"Your hand?" *You're ripping me apart.*

"Yes. Lie back. I'm almost in." His hand flexed vertically to fit her opening, and he popped the knuckles inside.

She screamed as the knives intensified, then sighed as they abated, his knuckles now seated inside her.

The rest of his hand slid in with little resistance.

"How does it feel now?" He rubbed his fingertips over her

cervix, stimulating all the sensitive tissue around it, providing pleasure to harness the pain that lingered under her clit.

"Like you drove your car in there. I've never been this full." *I'm going to burst.*

Kevin stopped rubbing her. "Do you want me to pull out?" He pulled back only until her lips felt his hand widening.

She wanted him to return to stroking her cervix. What a cock did in one place, his fingers did in four. What a cock stretched, his hand went beyond. Her entire pelvis burned with pressure, pleasure, and pain. She needed it to last.

"No, please. Keep doing what you were doing. Please me. Make me come again."

"I will. Several times." He rubbed around her cervix with his fingertips, inching his fingers apart to stretch her further. He applied more lube to his wrist and smeared it along her lips with his other hand. He pistoned forward and back with his hand, surely less than an inch with each movement but powerful inside her overwrought pussy.

God, he's fucking me with his hand. It feels like a football in there, touching and stretching everything. "Yes. Keep going." She gripped the edges of the pad as her body began to quiver.

Kevin increased the length of his strokes to about an inch and a half and folded his fingers into a fist. Her channel felt stretched until it would burst apart.

Didn't think I could get fuller. Coming again. She spasmed around his hand, milking it, pressing against the hard bones that stretched her, reaching the limits of her tolerance while begging for more. Her body arched off the cushion, and she wailed loud enough to reach the shore.

Kevin lengthened his strokes a little but maintained his slow pace. With his other hand, he stroked her clit as she climaxed.

When the spasms passed, she settled into a state just short of orgasm but coherent enough to seek more stimulation. Her hips bucked in time with his thrusts. Her head lolled from side to side.

Her arms flexed, pulling her body toward Kevin's hand. *More.* Her hips moved farther as she stretched, using longer movements, faster.

"So good. Faster."

Kevin smiled as he lengthened his stroke and alternated extending his fingers and re-forming his fist. Each change distended and relaxed her tunnel like she had never felt. Better than she had ever felt. Her cunt tightening on him as she orgasmed again and again, the pauses between them less than two minutes.

After five or six releases, her eyes fluttered shut and her arms went limp. Kevin's hand stilled inside her. The hand holding her thighs relaxed. She must have startled the men when she spoke.

"More."

Hayden and Eric tightened their grip on her legs.

Kevin resumed stroking. "It's what she asked for. One more should do." He maintained a steady pace with limited length. He opened his fingers to focus on the area around her cervix. The pressure and the stretch tore through her. This release shattered her.

Again. Alyssa wailed until she ran out of breath, and what had been a limp body tensed and curled what it could into a ball between the men. Her belly spasmed up and down as she took bites of air. Her toes curled and held until the arches of her feet cramped. Waves of electricity shuttled outward from her pussy, flexing and tensing every muscle, then releasing it to quiver until the next wave. They continued for more than a minute, and Alyssa sagged, totally spent.

Kevin stilled his hand. "I'm going to pull out now. I'll go slow, and you may have another orgasm. Let me know if it hurts too much and I'll slow down."

Alyssa waved her hand up and let it drop. Kevin pulled back until the heel of his hand rested just inside her lips. Then he tugged.

Alyssa grunted and raised her head as the heel of his hand slipped out of her.

Kevin stopped and waited for her. After two deep breaths, she nodded, and he pulled until his knuckles stretched her lips, revisiting the knives from earlier. Alyssa gritted her teeth and let her orgasm revive, hoping the fluid would help him extract his hand. Kevin tugged again, and with the contraction of her pussy, his fingers slid out in a flood of juice and lube.

Hayden and Eric let her tuck her legs to her chest as she rode out her final spasms. As she unfurled, Hayden picked her up.

Kevin ducked to examine her opening. "She looks fine. I don't see any tears or spotting. I believe she enjoyed it."

Hayden chuckled. "That she did." He carried her below to his cabin in the stern.

When he slid next to her under the covers, she rolled to him. "Make love to me. I need one last gentle time. Please." She pulled his arm and rolled onto her back, spreading her legs for him.

Hayden climbed onto her. His cock went easily into her stretched and lubricated pussy. Over the next few minutes, he rocked into her. He caressed her face, her sides, and her legs. He kissed and sucked her breasts. His cockhead barely touched the deepest parts of her, bringing her pleasure but not like he usually did. By the time she enjoyed her last orgasm, she urged him to fuck harder and begged him to fill her. He did, and they fell asleep holding each other.

22

SUNDAY, AUGUST 1, WILMINGTON

"DIDN'T I SAY you were to be naked all day?"

Alyssa turned toward Eric's voice in the galley door. "You did, but I'm not getting naked until I'm done cooking. Hot bacon grease and bare skin don't mix."

Eric pulled a red apron out of a drawer. "Wear this."

About time. I woke up sore and horny. "Watch the bacon." Alyssa shucked off her clothes and dropped the apron over her head, running the strings behind her back and tying them over her belly before taking the spatula back from Eric.

Eric pressed close behind Alyssa. "Didn't I also say that whenever I got hard, we would fuck?" He ran his hands inside the front of the apron to cup her breasts.

"You did. That cock feels good in the cleft of my ass, but if you fuck me into the hot stove, our fun ends pretty fast."

She reached behind her ass to grab his cock. As she leaned

forward, she dipped the cock to line up with her wet folds. "Gently, or you will be double-timing me to the burn unit instead of blowing a load in my mouth. Okay?"

Eric tightened his grip on her breasts. He pulled them as he eased his cock forward, spreading her lips. "I'll hold you up."

He eased in and out of her as she turned the bacon. His hands kept her upright as he gently slid in and out of her. He didn't jar her ass or bump her with his hips. He slid forward and back. The slow grind of it teased her tunnel while stretching her lips, leaving her hungry for more and unable to commit to the hard fuck she wanted.

Alyssa breathed heavier when he pulled his right hand off her breast and traced down her side, tingling every point his fingertip grazed. She hummed when he repeated the trip, grazing his fingertips up to her breast and down to her hip, then beneath the apron to finger her clit. She pushed back against him, driving his cock deeper than he had allowed on his own.

"Chewy bacon this morning." She put the bacon on the plate and turned off the stove. With a small step sideways, she bent further, braced her hands on the counter, and looked over her shoulder. "Finish me."

Eric pinched her nipple and plunged inside her, increasing his pace. His fingers on her clit positioned above and below it, then remained still, letting the motion of her body bounce it between them.

"Yes. Like that. Squeeze my clit a little." Alyssa pushed back against him. *Right there. Rub that G-spot.* She squeezed her walls around his cock, loving its resistance as he filled and retreated. "I need to you to fuck me hard now."

He picked up the pace with long strokes, ramming her ass cheeks as he fucked her. He released her nipple to grip her hip, pulling her against him.

Her breasts swung free against the apron, the friction tickling her distended nipples. Each movement built the storm low in her abdomen. It coiled inside her and grew, penned up above her cervix until he pinched hard on her clit and rubbed her G-spot on one last thrust. Then it broke free, sapping the strength from her legs and making them quiver.

Alyssa braced herself with her hands until her legs settled, just as she felt Eric's cock swelling inside her. She pulled him out, spun, and knelt to take him in her mouth.

Alyssa bobbed her head and stroked with her hand. Before she settled into a rhythm, his salty goo blew into her mouth. Not missing a beat, she pulled back until the tip sat inside her lips and the semen pooled on her tongue. When he stopped spasming, she pulled off and made a show of swallowing the mouthful.

Alyssa stood, turned on the stove, then whisked the bowl of eggs. "Go set the table and wake the others. The eggs will be ready in a minute." She gripped his slick cock. "And don't bother getting dressed either."

☙

Alyssa leaned back in her chair after they ate. She looked at Eric. "How would a normal fishing charter go?"

"Real fishermen, or girls' weekend?" Eric responded.

"Girls' weekend. That's what I'm subbing for."

"We don't start as early, maybe six or six thirty, even seven, so they stay awake on the way out. We hit a couple of the good spots and help the girls catch something while they drink beer. To celebrate a good first stop, we make margaritas or something like that while we go to a dead spot. After a few drinks and some dead fishing, the girls usually want to sunbathe. There's never anybody around, and nobody will know if they get a little naughty and sunbathe nude. We are fucking before lunch."

"Every time?"

"Almost. It only takes one to start the ball rolling. They all want to join in when they hear or see one girl getting fucked." Kevin smiled. "Or fisted."

"I understand that. It was amazing. I've never come so much. But I don't want to do it again today. I'm sore." Alyssa rubbed her crotch and moaned under her breath. "The college girls let you fist them?"

"Some don't. Afraid of getting stretched out. Older ladies, though, they all want it. Every one of them, every time."

"Older ladies?"

Kevin shook his head. "I mean late twenties or older. We had one charter of grandmas. They were crazy but tired out early. The horniest ones are the moms. They all want everything we offer."

"Everything you offer?"

"For bigger groups we add a couple of hands. It can get busy." Kevin untied her apron. "Why don't I show you? All this talk has me hard, and we have a deal."

"Even after I made you breakfast?"

"It was delicious, but our deal was for fucking, remember?"

She knew the deal she had cut. The damage to her marriage had been done. Until she had to face that music, she might as well enjoy today. She intended to come as much as she possibly could. With three men to rotate through, she expected to come a lot.

Alyssa dropped the apron to the deck and walked to the cushions in the bow. She lay down and lifted her legs before spreading them wide. She looked between her splayed tits at Kevin. "I remember. You coming?"

"Not until you do." Kevin knelt on the cushions. He buried his face between her thighs.

His tongue started low and wide, licking up her folds to flick her clit at the top, then back down between her inner and outer lip on the right side, before circling back up the middle and down on the left. He reversed course, traveling up between the puffy lips and down from the clit, spreading her opening with each pass. As she opened to him, he slipped two fingers inside, curling upward, finding her G-spot and pressing. A warm glow filled her lower belly from the gentle pressure.

Right there. "Suck my clit while you rub that."

She pulled his head where she wanted it and tickled the underside of her breast with the other hand. The shock from his first hard suck paled when he nipped her clit with his teeth and pulled. The warm glow in her belly ignited with the spark, and her orgasm was building inside her.

Alyssa yanked at his hair. "Again."

Kevin chuckled around the clit between his teeth and nipped again, then sucked, then nipped, all while pressing against her swelling G-spot with more vigor. Alyssa's legs trembled, and her hips writhed. She fought to control her motions to avoid breaking contact with his talented mouth. Kevin added a finger inside her and sucked and nipped her clit in rapid alternation.

"Yes. Yes. Right there. Don't stop." Alyssa's legs clamped onto Kevin's ears. He increased his pace and pressure, pulling her climax out longer. Alyssa arched her back, pressing her sparking clit into his mouth, driving his fingers hard against her G-spot. As her legs gave out and fell away from his ears, she pulled his head up her body to kiss him, savoring her taste on his lips.

"You are a magician. Thank you. Now I need you inside me."

Kevin gripped his cock and smeared it across her wet opening before plunging in. He sucked her nipples before raising his head and pinning her shoulder to the cushion, holding her in place. His other hand rubbed, pinched, and pulled her breasts and nipples as mercilessly as he was driving his cock into her.

The pain in her tit inflamed her pussy. She felt him more than she should given the size of his dick and the stretching he'd given her last night. Her recent orgasm rekindled.

Smaller but vigorous. Taking advantage of the big O that hasn't subsided yet. He knows his strengths. "Fuck the hell out of me. Harder. Faster."

She pulled at his hips, helping him slam against her thighs. *I'm still sensitive. Come on. I'll come again.*

"Pound me, Kevin, then come all over my tits. You are pulling them and marking them with your fingers; mark them with your cum." She felt his dick swell inside her. *Too soon.*

Kevin pulled out and jacked his cock at her body.

"Show me. I want to see it come." Alyssa hissed as the first pearly white globs flew from the red cockhead, landing in the valley between her tits like hot rain.

"Yes. Paint me." The next few volleys dripped on her belly, with a last drop or two falling onto her shaved lips.

She lifted her head to survey her body. It had been a while for him. The cum was bright white against her tan skin, not the watery fluid you get at the end of a long night of sex.

"Beautiful. What great cum." Alyssa blew a kiss to Kevin. "You made me feel so good. I hope we aren't done yet."

"We're just getting started." He smiled at her, then moved off to the right.

Eric came from her left to kneel between her legs. "My turn." He wagged his hard cock at her before lining up and entering her. He spread her more than Kevin did, and her pussy clenched at him. Her body hung halfway to a second orgasm, and his cock gathered its reins and drove her toward it.

Nice size. Perfect for a second go. "Go easy. He just pounded me."

"The deal is, when I get hard, we fuck, and I don't fuck easy." Eric pulled back until just the tip was inside, then inched into her, then repeated the slow movements, smiling. "I do sometimes fuck slow, if you prefer."

"Mm. I do. For now." Alyssa gripped his shoulders as he continued the slow grind, stretching her lips with the friction, making her feel fuller than she knew he would make her. *Like the change of pace. Pick up where Kevin left off. Make me come.*

Eric rose to his knees and lifted her legs up his body, raising her hips and pressing his straight cock against her front wall, stimulating her G-spot. He increased his speed, letting her body sway as he held her by her legs.

She watched his eyes as her breasts bounced in time with the faster fucking he gave her. "Watch my tits bounce. See that cum on them. I want you to add yours to it."

Her hip joints stretched from the weight, piling discomfort on the pleasure building inside her pussy as he held her up by her thighs. *I love it too. And those forearms, god.* The stretching feeling expanded to her lower ab muscles, making them tense and relax in time with his thrusts filling her just behind them. Alyssa gripped at the vinyl cushions as her climax built. Her breasts warmed as they flushed. Her hardening nipples sent currents through her body to boil the orgasm above her cervix. She jammed her eyes shut and let herself explode.

Eric sped up as her tunnel spasmed around his pistoning cock. Despite an orgasm before breakfast, watching Kevin please this beauty must have revved him up, and he swelled against her walls. He increased his pace, then dropped her legs and jacked his load all over her belly and tits as she bounced down to the cushion, his hot cum adding to the cream left there by Kevin.

"Yes. Cover me."

Alyssa again appraised her sticky body. He watched her rub the shiny fluid into her skin, making a show of coating herself from her tits to her pussy, moaning at him while she did.

She winked at Eric. "Is this good sunscreen?"

"They say it is. I wouldn't know."

"It's my sunscreen today. I'll have to reapply often."

Hayden tapped Eric on the shoulder. "I think she's ready for mine." Eric moved back, taking a seat in the shade beside Kevin to watch.

"Yes, I am. Come here." She lay back and opened her arms to Hayden. She pulled his face to hers, delivering a steamy kiss. Open as she was, the head of his cock notched between her lips without any help from their hands, and he pressed forward, stretching her despite the two cocks preceding him today. The delicious slide toward her cervix continued until he hit home, shooting sparks from her cervix through her body to accumulate in the glowing area between her hip bones.

So full. Not like being fisted, not like Paul, but perfectly full. "Take your time. Make me come."

"I will." He ground into her, rubbing his tip around the hard button.

"You remember who gave you all this. Remember who gave you the unbridled, shameless pleasure."

He pulled out, then slammed back in, hammering her pussy and firing tendrils of pleasure and pain through her body. They tingled where they met her skin on her sides, the insides of her thighs, her breasts. She tensed her muscles around him, searching for even more pleasure.

"Remember who gave you all the men you want." He repeated the slam. Her body repeated the fireworks. Her brain began to fog as she touched the rim of her boiling orgasm, trying to spill it out into her body.

"Fisting. Nonstop fucking." He ground around her cervix again.

"Not your husband." He pulled out and inched in as he

spoke. The change of pace teased her lips, tugging them, pulling sparks from them as her vagina clenched against the emptiness beyond his cock, needing only one more sensation to come.

"I gave you that." He picked up his pace, pounding her to release the rapture she sought. Alyssa's eyes closed and her head lolled while a low moan flowed from deep in her belly.

The pleasure. Yes. More. Alyssa clutched at her breasts as Hayden's cock tortured her insides with pleasure. Her orgasm was like a sprinter on the line, coiled and ready, waiting only for the crack of the starter's pistol.

He bit her breast hard.

Electricity cascaded from her flaming breast like gasoline on the fire inside her. The orgasm in her belly burst out, spasming her legs and abs, driving a wail from her chest. She scrabbled at his arms, trying to pull him deeper with what control remained in her body. Her pussy clamped onto his dick as her fluid splashed down her ass to the cushions.

Her conscious thought ceased. Her body took control. *More.*

He continued his pounding, filling her, not letting her tattered nerves recover. Her brain slipped deeper into the sensations clouding it, and her exhausted body ground out another orgasm. When she came for the third time, he pulled out and sprayed over her body, the huge load landing like a hot shower. When the last of it dripped on her pussy, he left, and she drifted off to sleep.

Alyssa woke to Kevin spreading her ass cheeks to lick her pucker. Warm tingles spread out from where his tongue circled around and over her anus, reaching her pussy and making her want more. *I've woken up to worse. He's good at that.* "How long was I out?"

"Maybe an hour, but I've been hard for twenty minutes, watching your gorgeous ass. I want it again."

I do too. She tilted her hips back, opening for him and thrusting her ass to his face. "A deal's a deal. You're hard. Lube me and let's go."

He licked her a few more times before dripping a healthy dollop of lube between her cheeks and swabbing it inside her ass with two fingers. She heard the liquid sounds of his stroking his cock with his slick fingers, then he inserted himself. He lay on her back, capturing their sweat between them as he inched into her, stilled, rotated to spread her, then inched forward again.

This is good. He knows how to stretch the sides without tearing me up.

Alyssa reached back with both hands to spread her cheeks, letting him penetrate her as far as his smallish dick would allow. Alyssa slid one hand beneath her to pull on her clit as he filled her ass.

His licking got me good and warmed up. He is good even if he's small. She pushed her hips back at him as she ground onto her hand, building an orgasm inside her belly. *And I love the weight of him on my back. I feel secure and like I can't resist, all at the same time.*

Alyssa felt him swell inside her ass. "Cover my back, just like my front. Come on me."

Kevin pushed off her back. His hot cum sprayed onto her lower back and ass, leaving a bigger load than she expected for a second load of the day.

"You have a magnificent ass, Alyssa. I'll hope to see you again." Kevin moved toward the bridge.

She lay on her side, watching him go. Her pussy simmered, unfulfilled. *He is skilled but a bit quick. I need three more minutes.*

"Let's get you out of the sun a bit," Hayden said as he patted her hip from behind her.

Alyssa looked over her shoulder. "That sounds good. I could use a rest."

"Oh, you aren't going to rest." He pulled her by the hand toward the cabin below.

When he pushed her to the bed, she spread her arms. "Make love to me. No foreplay, just get inside me."

He did. Already hard, he knelt between her legs and slid into her as he had so many times. Her vagina clenched at him, and her lips tingled for him, and her breasts ached to be squeezed by him, and she yearned to come for him as she had so many times.

When he folded her legs to her shoulders, he increased his pace, salvaging the incomplete climax Kevin had left her and fanning it to a blaze in her belly. He pounded into her, spilling her orgasm out in a series of spasms. He fucked through it, and her spasms stopped before he stopped deep inside and ground the head of his cock around her cervix.

"Keep going."

Alyssa gripped his arms as they held her legs. She pushed her hips against him as best she could given she was folded in half and pinned beneath his heavy body.

Hit those spots. I love when you do. She chased another orgasm up and down his cock with every thrilling spot he touched. She squeezed her muscles around him. She was too wet to slow his movements, but every vein and ridge shot sparks through her belly as he spread her tunnel. Her climax strained against her belly, ready to escape.

"Come with me. I'm so close. Please come with me."

He grinned. "I'm ready. Here I come, Baby."

He pushed into her as far as he could, then seized her thighs and ground her pelvis, crossing and recrossing her cervix with his cockhead. Her rapture rolled through her body while she cried out. His cock swelled and sprayed jet after jet of cum on her cervix, extending her orgasm with waves of spasms until their juice mingled inside her and spilled down her ass.

She stayed bent as her breathing slowed. She pulled Hayden's head to her own, groaning with the stretch of her hamstrings as she kissed him. "That was perfect, Babe." *No! I didn't call him Babe.* "I loved it, Hayden. You were so good."

"It was my pleasure, Baby."

He called me Baby again. I should have stopped that earlier. He won't have another chance after today.

The sound of engines firing was followed by movement forward. Alyssa hated the thought of heading to shore. "Is it two already?"

"No. Just past noon, but we are a few miles out, and we can't make a wake once we enter the channel."

"Can I lie in your arms a while?"

"You can indeed."

Alyssa dozed on Hayden's chest until Eric opened the cabin door. "When I said stay naked all day, that meant on deck, not hiding in a cabin. Please bring that nude, fuckable body to the cockpit, where I intend to have you one last time."

He left the door open when he left.

Hayden held her hip possessively. "You don't really have to."

"Who says I don't want to? After all, you reminded me how many times that you were giving me this special occasion? Why should I not enjoy your gift to its fullest?"

Alyssa pecked him on the cheek and scampered out of the room with a giggle.

Alyssa found Eric alone in the cockpit. "One nude, fuckable body in the cockpit, as requested."

He laughed. "Have a seat." He patted the bench beside him. "You have been a good sport. And your cooking is great. I'm glad you stayed today."

"Thanks. I'll be sore, but I enjoyed it. So many orgasms. You guys are insatiable. For food too."

"If I can get hard one more time, I'll get you off again."

Alyssa slid off the bench to kneel between Eric and the console. She took his soft dick in her mouth. Swirling the head with her tongue and stroking with her hand, she coaxed life back into it and stood. "Fill my cockpit, Captain." Alyssa braced her hands beside the wheel and jutted her ass back.

Eric slid into her. "Fuck, you feel good."

He turned the wheel, and the boat bumped, hitting the waves as they traveled toward shore. He braced his hands beside hers. "Let the boat do the work."

Their bodies crashed together as the boat bumped across the ocean. In this position, Eric's cock thumped Alyssa's G-spot with every collision. When Alyssa's orgasm started to mass inside her, she grunted with every bump, and Eric pushed the throttle forward to speed up. The boat hit the waves at twice the rate, and Alyssa's head hung down as her orgasm grew. Her arms weakened. Her hips banged against the wheel when Eric banged against her, but her orgasm refused to release. It continued to grow until her belly barely contained it. She arched her back and pushed against him as it broke through her belly and flowed down her thighs, making them tremble.

His cock swelled inside her just as they overtook a boat on their port side. She pulled off and knelt beside him, offering her breasts in her hands. "Come on my face. My tits."

He jacked his cock, and she watched the white spurts leave the slit to fly toward her face. Hot spatters of cum covered the bridge of her nose, her lips, her chest, and the valley between her breasts in thick ropes. The guys in the other boat were waving at her as she looked past Eric over the starboard railing.

He angled the boat for a smoother ride and helped her stand.

"That was a great way to end the weekend. Get dressed. Get a shower if you want. We are pulling into the waterway, and it will be crowded."

"Those guys didn't think it was too crowded."

"Yep. They'll have a story to tell, but it won't be as good as mine."

"You wouldn't."

"I will. But I'll never use your name, Alyssa. What happens on the boat stays on the boat."

⁛

Alyssa got out of the shower and dried off. She slipped on her bra, then took it off and stuffed it in her purse. *Should have used real sunscreen. Sunburned breasts and bras don't mix. Thank god this T-shirt is so soft.* She suffered the panties, knowing they would irritate her sunburned ass less than her canvas shorts. Looking down at her pink feet, she decided to remain barefoot until they reached the dock.

She picked up her phone. *Forty-two texts? Twenty phone calls? Most from Robert.* She scrolled to the top of his unread texts.

Oh god, no.

Her legs failed, and she crumpled onto the bed. Her hands trembled as grief and regret consumed her entirely, leaving her skin to cover only the darkness that was left behind. One tiny pinprick of hope remained where her heart had been moments before. It strengthened her legs and engaged her brain. She ran up the stairs.

"Go faster! I have to get home now."

Eric caught her hand as she reached for the throttle. "Easy. We can't go faster. We'll damage all these boats."

"Then damage them. My son's been in a wreck. I have to get to the hospital."

He put a hand on her shoulder with sufficient strength to comfort without controlling her movement. "Okay. We will get there. Is he going to be all right?"

"I don't know. I haven't read everything or called my husband. I need to get home now."

"You get ready to leave. We're only a few minutes from the dock. Tell Hayden to be ready to hop off."

✍

"How is he?" Alyssa almost cried into the phone when Robert picked up.

"They are discharging him now. Where have you been? I couldn't reach you, and you didn't come home."

Her stomach knotted at what she had to do. "The boat was out of cell range and developed engine trouble. We just got in. It was awful." *There I go, lying again.*

"You didn't get a tow?"

"The captain and first mate worked all night to fix it. They didn't want to call a tow service."

"Whose idea was this ill-fated ride?"

"Lauren has a friend down here who offered it, as a celebration for finding a house."

"She's going to hear from me about her harebrained ideas. In fact, let me talk with her."

Bile surged to the top of her throat. She looked at Hayden in the driver's seat beside her. She was caught, even though Robert didn't know it yet. This conversation needed to occur in person, not over the phone. She faked a cough to think.

"She's on the phone with her husband. He sounds more upset than you are. She knows this ride was a bad idea."

"Okay. Just come home."

Despite her fending off the consequences of her bad decisions, her stomach knotted tighter as her thoughts returned to her son. "Can I talk with Clay?"

"He's with the doctor."

"Can you call me when the doctor leaves?"

"You can talk with him when you get home."

A sob stole her ability to speak for a moment. She inhaled a jittery breath and forced herself to respond. "I'm coming as fast as I can. Love you, Babe."

The connection broke. "Drive faster, Hayden."

23

SUNDAY, AUGUST 1, HOME

HAYDEN'S CAR WAS still rolling when Alyssa jumped out and ran up the lawn. She burst into Clay's room and stopped just short of jumping on her son's bed. She hugged and kissed his head while tears of relief spilled down her cheeks. She caught her breath and looked down at the two casted legs for the first time. Tears flowed again, this time in sympathetic pain for his battered body and guilt that she had failed to be there when he needed her.

"I'm sorry I wasn't here, sweetie. I'm here now. I'll take care of you."

Clay's eyes fluttered open and shut as Alyssa stroked his hair. She looked over her shoulder around the full room, then turned back to her dozing son, kissing his forehead again. "What happened?"

Robert stepped beside her and held her waist. "He and Sawyer were driving back from rowing practice. A truck crossed the center line and hit them almost head-on. Clay took the brunt of it. Broke both his legs below the knee, bruised a few ribs, got some cuts and bruises here and there."

"And Sawyer?"

"Banged up by the seat belt and airbags, but she's okay."

"Yesterday afternoon?"

"Yes. I tried calling and texting you and Lauren. No answer."

She turned to face her husband. "We were out beyond cell range. Signal only reaches about two miles offshore. I wish I had never set foot on that boat."

"We can talk about that later, after our guests leave."

"Leave?" Jessica bellowed, then covered her mouth. "Guests? We are here because Clay needs our expertise and we are close family friends. We are neither guests nor leaving before our work is done."

"That's right," Summer agreed. "We aren't leaving until you don't need us here." She hugged Alyssa. "For me, that's now. I'll come back tomorrow to start therapy on his upper body. He's going to be in the bed for a while, and we will need to keep up his strength for when he starts to walk again."

Alyssa's legs buckled. Summer caught her before she fell. She teared up and hugged her friend. "Walk again?"

"It sounds scarier than it is. Robert can explain later, but it's a normal process for this kind of injury. And I'll help him through every step of the way. Sorry. I didn't intend the pun. Do you want me to stay a while?"

Alyssa stood back and shook her head. "No, thank you for offering. Robert is all the support I need. I'll see you tomorrow."

"I'll go too." Jessica filled Alyssa's arms as Summer stepped toward the door. "I told Robert this, but I'll be by a couple of times a day to check vitals, change bandages, check stitches, and make sure his feet don't swell too much. And anything unusual happens, I'm close by. Just call me." She wiped a tear from Alyssa's cheek. "He's going to be fine. You'll see."

Another hug, and Alyssa was alone with Robert. "How bad is it, really?"

"He won't go to college this semester. The crash broke both bones in both lower legs. The left one was a compound fracture. They decided not to put rods in his legs, but that means he can't bear weight for several weeks. This won't be easy, but we'll make it. Come on, let's let him sleep."

⸜

Alyssa sat beside Clay's bed, stroking his hair, when Robert returned from taking the pizza box to the kitchen.

"He'll be fine, but what about you?"

Alyssa looked at her son's bruised face, fighting the sobs that pushed at the back of her throat even now, two hours after arriving. "I'll be fine when he's fine."

"I know. I was asking about your boat ride."

"I feel so guilty about that. I only wanted to come home, and we got stuck out on the ocean. And I wasn't here when he needed me. When you needed me." She hung her head as tears overwelled her lids.

"Things happen. It must have been a long night. Come with me. I'll run you a bath."

"That sounds nice. Thank you, Babe."

She sat in the bath. Robert sat on the edge of the tub and massaged her eyes, face, and head until Alyssa dozed off.

Robert woke her while the water was still warm. When she stood, he wrapped her in a warm towel.

"You put this in the dryer? Oh, Babe, thank you. It feels wonderful."

"You're welcome. This too."

She stepped out of the tub into the warm robe he handed her.

"How did your sail work?"

Alyssa shook her head. "My sail? What are you talking about?"

"The sail you must have made on the boat. I can't think of another reason your tan lines would be sunburned unless you tied all your clothes to the mast as a makeshift sail."

His tone conveyed no anger. He had spoken softly. His face had remained neutral with a hint of curiosity around the eyes. The image of a sail made of clothes would be absurd, like he wanted to make a shy child feel at ease.

Alyssa was no shy child. He did not make her feel at ease. Instead, his soft comment wrested the strength from her body, buckling her knees and casting her confidence, her will, her very soul, to the floor like shards of glass. She couldn't inhale, but she knew when she did, air would fill the vacuum where all the good parts of her had once resided. He knew what she had done and that she had lied. A steamroller would have crushed her less completely than his one soft comment.

He guided her by the shoulders to sit on the tub surround, then sat beside her with an arm around her back. "Are you ready to tell me the truth about this weekend?"

She inhaled. Despite the steam in the air, her chest burned like when she ran on a cold day, searing the inside of her chest against the vacuum where her heart had been. She stared straight ahead, unable to face the pain she knew would be on his face. "It's not what you think."

"You didn't make a sail?"

"You know we didn't."

"Tell me what you did do."

The empty hole in Alyssa's chest grew, and tears pooled in her eyes. "Lauren and I found a house. We went to lunch and were going to come home. She ditched me, and—" Her lip quivered as the first tears spilled down her cheeks. She clutched at her stomach and sobbed. "—and Hayden showed up."

When she stopped crying, Alyssa held up her hands and shook her head. "I was mad. I told him to leave. I told him I wouldn't see him, but Lauren wouldn't answer the phone and he was my only ride back. He had arrived in his friend's boat, so his car was in a marina down the waterway. I was going to ride to his car and make him bring me home. That's all, honestly."

"You didn't call me. You didn't rent a car."

"I was too mad at them for setting me up to think clearly. I didn't want to ask you to drive four hours to get me, or spend hundreds on an Uber, and I didn't think of renting a car. I got on the boat intending nothing more than coming home."

"It didn't work out that way, I take it?"

Alyssa shook her head. "You know it didn't. He got me belowdecks and promised me one last amazing time together. I let myself believe that."

"How were you there until this afternoon?"

"By the time I woke up after…after…after I gave in to him, it was sunset and we were out at sea. It was beautiful, and I resigned myself to not getting home last night in any event. He offered an orgy with the three of them. He reminded me you would never offer that, so I should take the chance. I was horny. I figured the damage had been done, so I rationalized enough to agree." She propped her elbows on her thighs and buried her face in her hands. "I'm so sorry."

Robert pulled her to sob into his shirt. He rubbed her back and head without speaking. When the sobs turned to silent weeping, he led her to lie on the bed. "I'll be right back."

Alyssa lay on her stomach, still weeping into the pillow. *He loves me more than I deserve. Why do I hurt him?*

The bounce of the mattress broke her train of thought. Robert unzipped the suitcase he had dropped on the bed beside her. "Pack your things, Alyssa."

She rolled away as if the suitcase were a rattlesnake. "No, Robert. I said I was sorry."

"You're sorry? Alyssa, I have humored your open marriage fetish for months. We set up rules to protect ourselves, and I have stood by while you flouted and disregarded all of them without bearing any consequences. I gave you so much freedom that you fell in love with another man, again with no consequences. I had enough faith to accept your promise to never see him again for the good of our family.

"I even pretended to believe that ridiculous story about falling on a grape. Your bruising was too uniform, and your discomfort lasted too long for a fall. I hope you enjoyed the sex dungeon house. That is where you went, wasn't it?"

I thought I hid it better than that. I should have known he knows me too well to hide anything. I should have known a lot of things. Icy sadness filled her guts as she began to understand the depth of his anger. Unable to speak, she nodded.

"Uh-huh. I let it go, thinking it would be some last special time as you got him out of your system, some kind of full-circle closure."

It was supposed to be. He even knew the pitiful lies I told myself.

"And today, you believe that saying 'I'm sorry' will make up for not only lying and seeing him again but also fucking two of his buddies in a twenty-four-hour orgy at the same time our son was in a horrific car accident and needed you? You're smarter than that, Alyssa."

She sat, the weight of his words and the power of his voice robbing her ability to speak. Her thoughts rambled, refusing to connect or formulate a response. She watched her husband as he waited for her to answer. As she sat stunned, she watched his eyes narrow and his lips press into a thin line. Her chance to fight for her place in this house evaporated in their silence.

I've lost.

He rubbed his eyes, then pointed to the suitcase. "You won't hurt our family any longer. Pack your stuff and get out."

Here, at the end, she clung to only one hope. "Clay needs me here to help him. I can't go."

"That didn't matter yesterday."

"That isn't fair. I didn't know."

"Because you were on a boat with your boyfriend. Don't bother arguing."

Beg. "Robert, please. Don't keep me from him."

"You'll go?"

"Yes, though I don't know where."

"You should have figured that out yesterday. Maybe some boat that needs a first mate."

Her last remnants of hope died, crushed under his icy comment. She sighed. "You've made up your mind. I'll go, as long as I can help Clay."

"I know better than to stand between you and the kids. You can visit him, but never come when I'm here. I don't want to see you."

Alyssa choked on a sob, then nodded.

Alyssa rolled the suitcase past Robert's office after leaving Clay's room. She stood in the doorway, knowing better than to enter. "I may need to get more stuff. I don't really know what I packed."

Robert sipped his drink without looking up from the baseball game on the TV. "I know. Get it when you visit Clay."

"Please, Robert. Can we work this out?"

"What will you promise that you haven't already? And what is the over/under on how long you keep those promises? You worked things out yesterday. I hope you like the result. Now go."

24

SUNDAY, AUGUST 1, HAYDEN'S HOUSE

ALYSSA HEARD SLAPPING noises when she opened her car door in Hayden's driveway less than an hour later. She walked through the gate into his backyard and stopped.

Hayden was pounding a woman with long legs and high heels into his patio furniture. Alyssa saw some blonde hair but couldn't see her face because a nude older lady suckled the tall woman's breasts while fingering herself.

"Hayden?"

He looked over his shoulder at her and redoubled his efforts on the woman before him. She groaned and pulled her legs apart with her hands. Milk sprayed from her exposed nipple when she screamed. Hayden pulled out to spray across her body with a roar. The older lady lapped the milk and cum on the blonde's body.

"Hayden?" Alyssa hadn't moved while she had watched the three of them.

He looked over his shoulder and sneered at her. "He finally threw you out? Took him long enough. That's the perfect addition to tonight's fun."

Now I see his flaws. Too late. "What? I thought you cared about me."

The blonde laughed, then raised her head to look at Alyssa. "He doesn't care about anyone. He loves fucking married women. His kink is ruining marriages. He's good at it, too, isn't he?"

"Lauren?"

"Yeah. Sorry about leaving you yesterday, but it was Hayden's condition for fucking me tonight. It's been six weeks since the baby, and I wanted him to be first. Hope you don't mind."

"Mind? Because of what you did, my husband threw me out."

The older lady cackled. "Honey, you ended your marriage. When Robert called me, I knew it was close."

"Rosalyn?"

"How do you think Hayden got the job in the first place? His cock is amazing. I love helping him with the rest of my girls, and a lot of my clients. I get an occasional finder's fee, of sorts."

Only numbness kept Alyssa standing erect. Learning that she'd traded her family for a predator's amusement should have left her in a quivering heap, but she had no strength left to lose. Her bones bore her weight on locked knees. "I was just…a kinky conquest?"

Hayden shook his head. "You aren't that kinky, but it was fun to let you do what you so clearly wanted to do. As soon as you saw my sex dungeon, I knew you were ripe for the taking. Yes, that's my house. I take women there to 'accidentally' find the bondage room. It's a test. You passed. It was so easy to addict you. Now, if you want to get kinky, come drink Lauren's milk and I'll fuck you in the ass." He wagged his dick at her. "Just thinking of it gets me hard."

"What about the older lady who taught you how to be a lover? You described a tender relationship."

He laughed. "She taught me to love breaking a marriage. Hers was my first. She was lonely, and I played on that until her husband finally caught on. I've never equaled my earth-shattering orgasm when she came crying after he threw her out."

"Monster."

"You would think that, wouldn't you? You know what happened instead? Word got around that I broke up their marriage. There wasn't enough time in the day to fuck all the housewives who came looking for what she got. It hasn't stopped. Monster or not, I'm popular."

"And you know why, don't you, Alyssa?" Rosalyn leaned back, splaying her legs so Alyssa could watch her stroke her lips as she spoke.

"He's addictive. Once you have had his dick, you need it again. Hell, I'm only into women and I need it. You need it. Lauren even let him get her pregnant. Yes, that baby is his, and her husband doesn't know." Rosalyn licked her upper lip and glanced at Hayden, then continued.

"I'm almost as excited to find out as he is. When Carlos finds out, Hayden is coming over. When he's high like that, he's amazing. I can't wait to watch him with my wife. She's quite expressive and has never had a dildo his size, much less a real man. She may spontaneously combust. It will be delicious."

Alyssa slumped against a chair.

Hayden turned to her. "Are you going to suck Lauren's tits, or am I going to slide into Rosalyn while you leave? I'm good either way, but decide, because it's time to fuck."

Alyssa shook her head. She heard Rosalyn groan as she exited the gate.

25

SUNDAY, AUGUST 1, EMBASSY SUITES

Alyssa slammed her empty glass on the bar. "One more, Keegan."

"This is really the last one, Alyssa. We're closing."

"It's been a shit weekend. Give me another drink."

Keegan poured a gin and tonic.

Alyssa downed half of it. The first drink had burned in her chest as she swallowed, the liquid sear a welcome change from the emptiness it replaced. The second and third fell silently through the void. Her broken heart consumed even the sensations of the alcohol. If she couldn't feel, she didn't want to think either. Halfway through drink number four, that plan wasn't working. She took another swallow.

"Everything was just fine until I got addicted to his dick."

Keegan saw the businessman at the other end of the bar listening a little too intently. "We're closing, she wasn't talking about your dick, and she's with me, so don't stick around trying to get lucky. That last one's on me, so you can go."

The man grumbled and left. Keegan guided Alyssa to the door and locked it after turning off the lights. "Which room are you in? Let's get you there."

⤚

Keegan escorted Alyssa to her room, steadying her once when she stumbled walking down the hall. Keegan knew she had been right to make the last two drinks light on the gin.

While Keegan locked the door, Alyssa pulled an airplane bottle of vodka from the minibar.

"I've only had four drinks. I'm not nearly drunk enough to get through tonight."

"You'll get through tonight without a bottle. I'll help you."

Alyssa drained half the bottle. "I've ruined my entire life, I have a serious X-rated sunburn, I didn't pack a toothbrush, and I'm living in a hotel. What about that doesn't call for a bottle?"

Keegan stepped close enough to smell the gin on Alyssa's breath and see the blood vessels in her eyes seem to grow redder as she watched. "The part that keeps you from adding a big hangover and some drunk dialing to that list. Sip that bottle, but that's the last one."

Alyssa chugged the rest of the vodka.

Keegan had known she would, stifled a smile, and pulled Alyssa down beside her on the couch. "Okay. Sit here and talk with me."

Alyssa's head and shoulders sagged forward until she caught her face in her hands. Her elbows rested on unsteady knees. She managed a few words as she cried into her hands. "I don't want to talk. I want to die."

Keegan held her, rocking her and rubbing her back. Alyssa buried her face in Keegan's chest and flung her arms around her waist, squeezing tight as if she were afraid of falling. Keegan leaned against the arm of the couch, pulling Alyssa with her.

Keegan held her in silence; no need to whisper in a storm.

Alyssa settled. Her whimpers became infrequent, then stopped. Her tight grip around Keegan's waist relaxed, as if Alyssa had mentally stepped away from the cliff she had feared minutes before. She lifted her feet onto the couch, a small sigh announcing that she had settled more comfortably, despite the tears that still seeped from her eyes.

Keegan stroked her hair as she broke the silence. "I won't let you die. Death is a permanent solution to temporary problems."

Keegan waited, but Alyssa responded only by tightening her grip. Another stroke of the hair brought another break of the silence. "Tell me why you came here. I know it isn't because you want some redheaded lady loving."

Alyssa vibrated as a chuckle penetrated her tears. A couple of deep breaths shuddered out of her. "I have loved two men in my adult life, and I lost both of them in the last few hours."

Keegan wrestled the amazement that urged her to stand. With a deep breath of her own, she kept her tone soft and volume low to keep Alyssa talking. "What happened to Robert?"

Alyssa wiped her eyes. "I killed him tonight. Not literally. I told him where I was this weekend, and it killed everything inside of him, at least the parts that cared about me. The light went out of his eyes. I saw it happen. His tone when he threw me out...I've never heard icy disdain in his voice like when he said I should go."

"Where were you that was so bad?"

"With the only other man I've ever loved."

"You two have an open marriage. Wasn't that okay?"

"No emotional attachments, no interference with the family. I had promised Robert I wouldn't see Hayden again precisely because I was falling in love. Stupid me broke that promise at the absolute worst time. Clay was in the hospital after a wreck, and I was on a boat having an orgy with three guys, including the only person on earth who was off-limits."

Her body shook as she sobbed. Keegan again stroked her hair and back until she settled.

"Alyssa, why?"

Alyssa sniffled and wiped her eyes again. "It's a long story that I can spin to blame other people, but that's a lie. I was there because I thought nobody would get hurt. I was wrong."

Bartending had made Keegan a master therapist. Alyssa's last sentence told her to remain silent and let the admission sink in. When someone recognized they were the cause of their own problems, they would talk in bursts. Rushing that tempo was counterproductive for the conversation and the healing. Keegan counted out a full minute before asking the hard question.

"You chose this Hayden over Robert? How does that happen?"

"Slowly, then all at once. Isn't that the line about how things fall apart? I met this guy and fucked him. I mean really fucked him. A lot. I couldn't get enough. So much that Robert started getting testy, so I hid it because I didn't want to hurt him."

She shook her head. After a couple more jagged breaths, she gripped Keegan's hand on her shoulder. "That's not true. I didn't want to hear him tell me that I was getting attached. I was addicted, and I didn't want him to tell me to stop seeing this guy. He seemed so perfect. He did charity work. He is good at his job. Everyone likes him. He was inventive with sex, and was willing to let me explore kinks, even bondage and orgies. Over time, he seemed like a better man than Robert."

"Why aren't you with him tonight? Surely a great guy would swoop in and save you."

"Another thing I was wrong about. He's not a good man. He's a bastard. He didn't love me. He loved that I was married and that he could fuck me until it ruined my marriage. Destroying marriages gets him off. And I invited him into mine. I didn't know until tonight. I showed up at his house, and he was with two other women. They had quite enjoyed watching my descent."

Keegan felt Alyssa begin to tremble and tightened her grip. She needed to keep Alyssa in the moment. "Oh, Alyssa. If only I had known, I would have warned you. Guys who are too good to be true are hiding something bad. And you can't have repeated sex with someone without developing feelings."

Alyssa spat out a harsh chuckle. "I would have added your warnings to my trash heap. Two friends in town warned me. Two friends in Houston warned me. Even Robert warned me. In my brilliance, I knew better. Right up until I didn't."

"What will you do?"

"Dying keeps coming to mind."

"Stop saying that. Even as a joke."

Alyssa sat up. "Okay. My marriage is over. My affair is over. The guy was my realtor on some investments, so they're over. Clay can't walk, but I can only see him when Robert isn't home. He needs me, but when he learns the whole story, my relationship with him is over. To top it off, my daughter will probably fly from Texas just to slap me until I go blind. I have destroyed everything that matters to me, everything I know to do. When I say I don't know what to do, I mean it."

Keegan was afraid of this. She dreaded what she knew she had to do. She stood and took Alyssa's chin in her hand to force eye contact. "Then I'll tell you." Keegan retrieved Alyssa's suitcase and opened it on the floor in front of her. "Two bottles of aloe on top?"

"I told you I had a bad sunburn."

"You look fine."

"I'm sunburned on my tan lines."

"Ouch. Does it hurt?"

"Nothing like my heart."

Keegan slammed the bottles on the coffee table. "Then strip. Take care of yourself first."

When Alyssa didn't move, Keegan gave a dismissive back-handed wave in her direction. "Go ahead. Do what I say."

Alyssa stood to ease her clothes off, wincing as she unsnapped her bra.

Keegan dug through Alyssa's suitcase until she retrieved a skirt and blouse. "You wear these to work?"

When Alyssa didn't respond, Keegan looked up for a nod. Alyssa's breasts glowed a deep red that was almost purple. "Holy shit, I bet that sunburn does hurt."

Alyssa shrugged. "Sunburn doesn't matter. Yes, those are for work."

"I was going to have you iron these, but instead, stay there and put aloe on your boobs and coochie."

"My coochie?"

"Fine. Your cunt, and all that bright-red skin around it. Cake it on. Leave your butt for later or you'll mess up the couch. I'll iron." She moved to the bedroom to iron Alyssa's skirt and blouse, pulled some panties and a bra out of the case, and laid them along with the freshly ironed clothes on the second bed. She dug around in the suitcase.

"You really didn't pack a toothbrush." She picked up the room phone. "Carla, It's Keegan. I'm helping a friend tonight.

Would you please send up a toothbrush, toothpaste, floss, and a hairbrush? Thanks."

Keegan touched Alyssa's breast, making her wince. "The aloe's dry enough. Go lie on your stomach on the bed. I turned it down for you."

Keegan met Carla at the door and put the toiletries in the bathroom. She sat beside Alyssa on the bed. Her face was away from Keegan, but little jerks in her back confirmed she continued to weep. The tiny hiss when the cold gel first touched the inflamed skin gave Keegan hope that Alyssa remained connected to the world enough to feel something. Maybe a total collapse was avoidable. She had to keep Alyssa focused and sober.

"Here's your plan for tomorrow. Get up at six. I'll set the alarm. Get a shower. Apply aloe. Fix your face and hair while it dries. Get dressed. The bra will hurt, but that blouse is too thin to go without. Go downstairs and eat breakfast, then go to work early. Think only about work until lunch. Eat lunch. Work and think only about work until six. Meet me here, and I will take you to dinner. Do you understand?"

"I need to see Clay."

"Right. Work until eleven, then take an early lunch. Go see Clay and make him his favorite breakfast. Eat with him. Take as long as you need; your boss will understand. If he doesn't, threaten to take twelve weeks family and medical leave. When you have finished eating, clean up and return to work until six."

"You are very certain of my schedule."

Keegan squeezed her shoulder, then patted it. "I gave the same instructions to my mother every day for three years after my dad left."

"Three years?"

"She drank a lot. I saved her. I'm going to save you."

"Wow. You never talked about your childhood. How old were you when he left?"

"Eleven."

Alyssa pushed up to face Keegan. "You gave her instructions like that when you were eleven?"

"No. I gave her the instructions, cooked for her, kept up the house, slept beside her, and made sure she got to work every day."

"You knew to do that when your dad left?"

"I knew to do that when I came home from school and a bottle of pills was dumped on the kitchen table beside a bottle of whiskey. I didn't believe her when she said she wanted to die. I believed her in that moment, and I wouldn't let that happen."

"I was exaggerating when I said I wanted to die."

"She said that too. Sometimes people don't know what they want."

"I know what I want. He threw me out of my house tonight."

"And you may never get to go back."

Alyssa dropped her face into the pillow and whimpered while her body shook with ragged breaths.

Keegan feathered her dry hand across Alyssa's back. "This is going to suck, but I will help you through it."

Alyssa's body settled into low, even breathing. Keegan covered her and snapped a picture of her face on the pillow, then texted it with the message, "She's safe." Keegan turned off the lights.

As she walked to the bedroom door to leave, Alyssa spoke. "Keegan?"

"I thought you were asleep." She returned to the bed.

Alyssa rolled onto her side. "I have no right to ask."

"Ask what, Alyssa?"

Alyssa sniffed. "Never mind. I'll see you tomorrow night."

"Alyssa."

"Would you, I mean, just for tonight, would you sleep beside me like you did for your mom? Having a warm hand to touch when I wake up crying in the dark might help." She waved her hand. "No, you won't get any sleep. It's not your job to pick up my pieces. Go. Get a good night's sleep. Thank you for your—"

Keegan placed two fingers across Alyssa's lips. "Hush, sweetie." She unbuttoned her blouse. "I'll stay. I'll hold you while you cry yourself to sleep, every time." She finished undressing while Alyssa let her tears flow again.

Keegan slid into the bed close to Alyssa, not wanting to hurt the sunburn. Alyssa closed the gap, pressing their bodies together and her head on Keegan's chest. Keegan wrapped both arms around Alyssa and held her close. "I'm here. You're safe. Let it all out."

Alyssa did.

26

MONDAY, AUGUST 2, HOME

"Honey, how would you like—" Alyssa stopped as she opened her son's bedroom door. "Jessica, I didn't expect to see you here."

"Hey, Alyssa. Clay needs around-the-clock support while he is non-weight-bearing, and I'm the nurse on duty today. He can't go to the bathroom, and bedpans are not for the untrained."

"Oh. I was going to make him breakfast." She kissed her sleeping son on the forehead. His bruises were turning a deeper purple. She knew he was healing, but he looked worse, and her chest ached for his pain. And it emptied for her failing him. "How long has he been out?"

"A couple of hours. He gets meds and lunch in about thirty minutes." She pointed to the baby monitor on the nightstand. "Come on. We can cook together."

When the bacon was in the oven, Jessica leaned across the island. "What did you do, Alyssa? Robert wouldn't say, but he

206

was a zombie this morning when I arrived. You weren't here, and your eyes tell me you cried all night."

Alyssa nodded. "I fucked everything up. You remember that perfect guy?"

"The one you couldn't get enough of? The one I warned you about?"

"That's the one. I wasn't supposed to see him anymore, so of course I was having an orgy with him and two friends on a boat when Clay had his accident. There's a long version, but it isn't better." She hung her head. "Robert threw me out."

"Alyssa."

She made eye contact with Jessica. She might not be able to be with her family, but she could do something to help them get through this. "I know your ex cheated on you and how much you were hurt. I understand if you don't want to be my friend. Please keep helping Clay though? And Robert? Please?"

"Of course I will help them. I don't know how badly you messed up to make Robert throw you out, but you aren't like my ex. I care about both of you, and I'll help you any way I can. I get the feeling that letting Robert have sex with me all night won't fix what you've done this time."

Alyssa slumped as the last of her energy evaporated. "No. I broke his heart. I saw it in his face. He's done with me forever."

Jessica hugged her friend. "Maybe. Today is day one. You have time to repair your marriage."

"Repair it? I have to resurrect it. I killed it with cruelty and apathy I didn't know I possessed. There may not even be a body to resurrect."

"I've never seen a couple love each other like you two. Give it some time. Don't screw up again because, to be fair and honest with you, if Robert goes on the market, women will be fighting to snatch him up."

Alyssa's vision blurred through her welling tears. "I don't blame you. He's wonderful."

"I didn't say me."

"You don't have to. I'm a fool, but I'm not blind."

⁊

"Mom! Hey!"

"Hey, sweetie. I thought we could have lunch together." Alyssa and Jessica helped Clay sit up before putting the tray over his lap. Jessica took his vitals and gave him some pills, then excused herself.

"Aren't you supposed to be at work?"

"I'm taking a long lunch today so I can see you. How do you feel?"

The corners of Clay's mouth twitched upward. "Like I got hit by a truck."

Maybe he will be okay. A flicker of happiness rose through her chest to escape in a chuckle. *Maybe I will too.*

"Funny. How much pain are you in, sweetie?"

"Not as much as last night. Why didn't you come when I called for medicine?"

One innocent question emptied her chest to refill it with guilt. "I wasn't here, sweetie. Dad took care of you, didn't he?"

"Where were you? I don't remember seeing you at the hospital either."

Alyssa swallowed the sob that threatened from the back of her throat. She plastered on a fake smile and squeezed his arm. "I didn't make it back before you got home. Those doctors patched you up so quick."

Clay took a bite of waffle. "This is good. What are you making for supper?"

"I don't know what Dad will make."

"You aren't cooking?"

Alyssa put her hand over her mouth to cover her tightening chin and quivering lip. Her vision blurred as tears welled in her eyes, then spilled down her cheeks in hot streaks.

"Mom, what is it?"

She shook her head. "I'm—"

"You're what?"

Alyssa watched through the window as two cardinals jumped from branch to branch four times, unable to speak. *I wonder if cardinals play in the trees outside some shitty one-bedroom apartment I'll end up renting?* She flexed her abs and took a breath before facing Clay again.

"I'm not living here right now, so Dad is cooking."

"Not living here? Why?"

She hadn't intended to have this conversation today, but she wouldn't hide from it. *Be honest. You have lied enough.* "Dad doesn't want me here."

"What did you do? Was it the person you text when you think nobody's looking?"

"You noticed?"

"What did you do?"

"I hurt Dad worse than I thought I could. I don't think we will make it." She sucked down a sob. "But I still love you every bit as much as ever. And I'm still going to take care of you."

"How, if you don't live here?"

"I'll come when I can. I just won't come when Dad is here."

"Don't put yourself out. Just stay with Mr. Text. Ms. Hedgecock and the other nurses can help Dad."

"Sweetie—"

"No, Mom. When you started this open marriage bullshit, you promised it wouldn't affect the family. Just one more lie, right, Mom?" He turned his face away from her. "I'm not hungry anymore. Thanks for the waffle. Don't inconvenience yourself to come back."

The emptiness inside had been a defense mechanism, but she hadn't realized it until Clay's scorn poured over her guilt like gasoline and his focused scrutiny of her behavior lit it like a magnifying glass in the sun. The flames inside her seared her chest and throat as they consumed her heart, leaving a smoldering cinder to remind her what she'd once had. The floor seemed to fall away, and she rested her forehead on the edge of his bed as she struggled to breathe.

When she reached for his arm, he jerked it away. She struggled to her feet and took the tray of half-eaten food with her as she shuffled out of the room.

She closed the door before slumping against the wall with a sob.

When she made it to the kitchen, Jessica gripped her in a hug.

"I'm sorry, Alyssa. Give them time. It will be okay."

"Please take care of my family." Alyssa ran out the front door, unable to draw another breath in her own house.

27

FRIDAY, AUGUST 6, HOME

Alyssa stopped before she opened the door. She knew better than to turn the knob, but in all her years here, she had never rung the doorbell. She had never been so afraid of something she wanted so badly. Her stomach knotted, and her legs quivered, but her hand stayed by her side.

Maybe he's not home yet.

Keegan lifted Alyssa's hand to the button.

"I'll do it, Keegan. I just need a moment to process ringing the bell at my own house."

"Then do it. Don't talk yourself out of it."

Alyssa pressed the doorbell. She stared through the privacy glass to the distorted figure moving toward them. Her chest tightened when he stopped and put his hand to his mouth.

Keegan squeezed her waist. "Be still. Give him a second."

Alyssa exhaled the breath she had been holding when the door swung inward. *He looks tired.*

"Still wearing your ring, and you brought your suitcase. That's a little presumptive. I didn't expect to see you yet."

"More like you never expected to see me again?"

"I knew you would come eventually, maybe next week. Is this where you beg forgiveness? Because I still don't want you near me."

Keegan pressed Robert's chest until he stepped back. "That's why I'm here, Robert. You and I are going to have a nice chat out of the way while Alyssa makes supper for Clay and packs some things she forgot. Now let us in because it is hot as hell out here."

"Shit. Good evening, Keegan. Come in. Alyssa, you don't need to cook. Just get your stuff and leave."

Her heartbeat slowed under Robert's words, and she took a breath to plead her case.

"I won't take long. Can I please just put some spaghetti sauce on to simmer? You two can eat it in a couple of hours. You know how much he likes it, and I'll be done in half an hour. Please, Robert, let me take care of our little boy." She sniffed and blinked, but a tear spilled down her cheek. She looked down. "And you."

Robert's head flushed bright red. "Just get what you need. We don't need you to cook."

Keegan inserted herself again, cooling the room. "Robert, you're going to let her cook. Look at it like ordering out but free and fresh. Show me your basement. Alyssa says you have a pool table, and I love pool. Alyssa, hit the kitchen."

Robert shook his head. "Keegan, you are the only person I'd let get away with this. Come this way. Alyssa, please don't dally."

✍

The sauce was simmering in less than half an hour. Alyssa had stopped to cry only twice. She heard the click of billiard balls when she passed the basement door on the way to Clay's room. She opened his door and stopped.

Sawyer was bent over, kissing Clay while their hands caressed each other. Alyssa backed out of the room, closed the door silently, then knocked and reopened it only an inch. "Sawyer, when you are finished, would you please come to my bedroom? Thank you."

Alyssa lay on Robert's side of the bed beside the open suitcase. *I miss his smell.* She wiped her eyes, then took one of Robert's old shirts out of the closet. She had just packed it when Sawyer knocked on the door. "Come in, Sawyer."

The tall girl strode into the room. "Mrs. Davis, if you want to yell at me, don't. Not after how you hurt him."

"Sawyer, please. Settle down. If I had wanted to yell at you, I would have done it in Clay's room." She pointed to the two chairs by the window. "I wanted to talk. Will you sit with me?"

Sawyer huffed, then sat.

"How is he? He isn't very talkative when I come at lunch every day."

"Are you asking about his broken legs or his broken heart?"

Alyssa gasped as the words stole her breath. Being here left every nerve exposed and raw. Sawyer stomped on all of them.

"Did you plan that one before you came in? If you meant it to hurt, it did."

"You don't think you earned it? He's lying in there having to use a bedpan, and you aren't here because you got a boyfriend. You couldn't have hurt him worse with a chainsaw. I love your son, and anybody who hurts him, his mother included, gets on my shit list."

She shook her hands in front of her chest. "Do you know what I was doing before kissing him? I was holding his head to my chest as he cried. He smelled supper cooking and he wanted his mom to be the one doing it, knowing she couldn't. He's crushed by the disintegration of this family. Despite knowing it's your fault, he wants you home."

"He isn't happy to see me when I come at lunch. He just eats quietly and I leave."

"He isn't happy. He's furious at you and never wants to see you again. For some reason, that doesn't prevent him from wanting his mom when he's in pain. And he is in pain."

"Are his legs still that bad?"

Sawyer stood and bent into Alyssa's face. "He has meds for his goddamn legs. He hurts every minute he's awake because his dumbass mother left, and somehow he thinks he could have prevented it. When he isn't sleeping, he ponders how to fix your mess. He deserves better."

Alyssa stared back into Sawyer's eyes until tears blurred her vision. While Alyssa wept, Sawyer returned to her seat and watched.

Alyssa used some tissues from the nearby table to wipe her tears. "He does deserve better. I'm glad he has you. Thank you for telling me the truth. You are the first person who has, including Clay himself." Alyssa looked away from the angry girl. "How do I fix this?"

"You are asking me how to fix your marriage?"

"No. I'm asking you how I fix Clay. Does he say?"

"He needs you here. I don't know how you work that out, but if you come home, he gets better."

"That's the one thing outside my power to do."

"Until you figure it out, you're on my shit list."

Alyssa chuckled. "I'm sorry. It's just unusual to have a teenager threaten her boyfriend's mom." Alyssa stared at Sawyer. Sawyer looked right back at her. Alyssa had always liked her, but in this moment, what Sawyer commanded was respect. *This might be awkward, but she might appreciate an adult conversation. And I might gain an ally.*

"It's empowering, isn't it?"

"What's empowering?"

"Giving your man pleasure and expecting nothing in return."

"Making out…and stuff?"

She didn't flinch at the topic. She has some backbone. "That's the most common method, but there are others."

Sawyer's eyes narrowed and her head cocked. "I guess. I never thought about it."

"It's affirming when he responds, knowing that you are the one pleasing him, eliciting that reaction, all the while cognizant that you can back off and elongate the moment or speed up and bring him to a big finish. That power is exhilarating."

"Yes. I like that."

"I noticed."

Sawyer flinched backward. "How?"

"You didn't scurry to cover up when I knocked, and you came in here like a woman on fire. You tapped into the power you have over a man and you used it for yourself. Don't stop doing that, even when you use it on me."

Sawyer smiled. "Okay. Why are you telling me this?"

"First, so you will know that I know you make my son happy, and I want you to keep making him happy. I'm pleased that you two are together, even if I'm on your shit list." She pulled a tissue from the box and dabbed Sawyer's chin. "And second, to remind you to fix your lipstick before tapping that power for an adult conversation."

❧

Alyssa stuck her head in the bedroom door. "Clay?"

"Mom, you should learn to knock."

"I thought two broken legs would hamper your activities with Sawyer. I was wrong then, but I knew I was safe this time. I asked her to watch the spaghetti sauce."

"I thought it smelled like spaghetti. Are you staying for dinner?"

The emptiness eroding her insides took another chunk from her gut. "No. I can't. Would you like me to stay? You've barely spoken to me during lunch this week."

He looked out the window. "I want you here, and I'm mad that you aren't, but I'm furious about why. How do you even cheat in an open marriage? Holy god, you did that. Anyway, you found a boyfriend and blew up the family."

Alyssa clenched her jaw to stifle her defensive response, knowing his insight was accurate even as it flayed her soul.

"I don't have a boyfriend. I have you, and Dad, and Susan. You three are all that matter to me. I've just screwed it up."

"I see. He dumped you."

The sob caught her breath before she knew it was there. "There was nothing to dump. I never had a boyfriend."

"The guy you were willing to throw away your entire family for doesn't even rate the term 'boyfriend'? Even better. Dad said 'boyfriend.' It doesn't imply that your wife is a slut like 'fucktoy' does."

"Watch how you speak to me."

He rolled his eyes. "Don't get offended at the word 'slut' if you act like one. I can't understand why I want you to come home. Is this what you meant when you said you were angry with us but you still loved us? Because it sucks."

"That is what I meant, and it does suck." Alyssa turned away as the tears spilled from her eyes.

He deserved the fun of having a child before he had to learn this feeling. Especially about his mother.

The emptiness in her chest became an ache. "I know I've messed up, Clay. What happened between me and your dad was my fault. Maybe I did act like a slut. I am trying to fix it."

She turned back to him. "Please understand that none of it happened because of you, and none of it means that I love you any less, even when you are angry and don't talk. I'll still move heaven and earth when you need me to."

He leaned toward her to speak through gritted teeth. "Don't move heaven and earth. Get your shit straight. Put our family back together." He sagged back against his pillows. "But, Mom, only if you really want to be here. Don't come back to repeat the cycle."

"I do want to be here. I want to make things right. I don't know if I can, but I'm trying."

"Try harder. Time works against you."

"What does that mean?"

"If we get used to your absence, we don't need you to come home."

Guilt collapsed in her chest like an avalanche, unearthing a new fear to feast upon her. "I hope you never get used to my absence, no matter where you are."

"Not me. Dad."

"How is he?"

"You should ask him, not me."

"He won't talk to me."

"All the more reason."

"Please, Clay. Is he okay?"

"Mom, he threw his cheating wife out of the house. His son is an invalid. He's not okay. If you want more detail, talk with him."

She had hurt Robert with what she did with Hayden. Now she hurt him by not being allowed to help with Clay. And she hurt him by not comforting him while he struggled. Every second she didn't repair her marriage was something else she needed to apologize for.

And she couldn't, not yet. Maybe never.

She'd expected discomfort when she decided to come here, but she'd also expected to feel happy at least once. So far, the best she could do was long for the relative bliss of mere discomfort. She could barely breathe because of the aching void that had replaced everything inside her skin. Alyssa counted to ten to recover the voice her sadness had stolen.

"Will you help him feel better?"

"No, Mom. Clean up your own mess."

"I will. I mean, talk with him. Let him know you love him, and get better fast. That will make me feel better as well, by the way."

He smiled for the first time since she'd walked in the room. She stared, cementing the memory.

"I lie in bed as hard as I can every day, Mom. Don't worry, Dad knows I'll listen when he wants to talk."

"I'd be surprised if he did, but maybe. Mainly just get better."

"Supper would give me energy to heal."

Alyssa looked at her watch. "We've been talking longer than I thought. It's almost ready. I can't stay. Can I send Sawyer with a plate for you?"

"Sure."

"She's a good one. She cares about you a lot. Do you care about her?"

"Mom. This is embarrassing."

"You don't have to answer. I know." She stroked his hair. "I'm sorry I hurt you. If you need me, you only have to text or call. I'll drop anything. I will probably see you again Monday at lunch. Will that work?"

"Yeah. I'm still furious with you, but I look forward to lunch."

⁓

Alyssa called out as she descended the stairs into the quiet basement. "Robert? Are you down here?"

"Yes. On the couch."

Alyssa froze. Robert sat on the couch, his pants around his ankles. Keegan knelt between his legs, her head bobbing. Alyssa had seen them together before but always in fun. Seeing it now battered her crumbling psyche.

Her breath caught in her throat. Her chin quivered. Tears welled in her eyes. "I'll go," she choked out.

"Please, stay. This is what you planned, isn't it? To have Keegan distract me so you could get some extra time with Clay?"

Keegan pulled off his cock. "Robert, you said this was the only way you would give her time."

"I did. You love us and want to help Alyssa get back home, even if only for a while. So, when you brought me down here, I knew the plan. I simply took the opportunity to be with an amazing lover in lieu of my absentee wife. Am I wrong, Alyssa?"

Alyssa wanted to look away but couldn't. She shook her head.

Robert guided Keegan back to his cock. "Speak up, Alyssa. I'm watching Keegan's head, not yours."

"You're right. Keegan was going to buy me some time, but I never expected—" She covered her mouth with both hands, stifling a sob. "Thanks, Keegan. Can you give me a minute to talk to Robert?"

"Stay where you are, Keegan. Alyssa, I said I didn't want to see you. It was your plan to use Keegan to distract me. Maybe you only planned on her playing pool, but I chose the bonus plan. Because she's so good at this, I'll listen to you while Keegan distracts me. You formulated yet another winning plan. Why scrap it?"

Alyssa wiped her eyes, clearing the tears only to have new ones flow. Her conversation with Sawyer replayed in her head. The power Keegan should have instead flowed through Robert to punish Alyssa. He stared at her, his pleasure escaping his lips in long hums while he guided Keegan's head with both hands. *It's never as simple as you think, is it?*

"Please stop, Robert."

"It's only sex, Alyssa. No attachment. You wanted this in our marriage. Why are you upset?"

"Will I reclaim you after?"

"You know you won't."

"That's—" She sucked in a ragged breath, flinching beneath his words as she would a bullwhip. "That's why. You aren't mine now."

"You have been his for weeks."

Alyssa sobbed and sank to her knees to sit on her feet on the floor. "Not true."

"Absolutely true. You left me when you lied about who you were sleeping with and how often. You left me when you developed feelings for him. And you left me when you couldn't keep your promises after we had worked through those two issues. You stopped being my wife when you became a slut for him, after which I could never truly reclaim you."

He had seen through her all along. He had let her go through the motions of being a wife when he knew she wasn't. She had flaunted the cancerous part of her relationship even as she sought to hide the relationship itself. As he revealed his thoughts, she wanted to flee. As she understood the depth of his understanding of what she had done, she collapsed with a groan.

Keegan pulled off his cock again. "I'll stay here so you two can talk, but I won't help you hurt her."

"Keegan, you agreed to hurt her when you agreed to be here tonight. If she wants to talk, she won't like what she hears. You stay there, or you are both welcome to leave, together. Alyssa, do you want to talk?"

She fought to respond. Sobs in her throat consumed her words. She raised her head enough to nod.

"She wants to talk, Keegan, so if you are in, back to work. You are doing very well, by the way." He waited while she sighed and reengaged. "What is on your mind, Alyssa?"

Alyssa sat up, keeping her face in her hands while she fought the cries still welling up from her chest. When the sobs ended, she looked at the ceiling while her breath settled. She wiped her eyes while her body calmed enough to speak. "Can I come home, Robert?"

"No, Alyssa. I can't tolerate your presence. Why do you ask?"

"Clay needs me, and I can help you with him."

"You come every day. The nurses can handle the rest."

"How much longer before I can come home?"

"You mean can you ever come home? Not interested, Alyssa."

She slumped as his icy voice removed even the emptiness from inside her. "I'll need to get an apartment. Can I take some furniture if I need to, please?"

"Maybe. I won't let you inconvenience the family further, so it depends on what you want. I'm sure Hayden can help you find a nice furnished apartment you can afford. He might let you pay the rent on your back."

Alyssa rose to her knees, the tiny spark of indignation like an inferno inside her empty shell. "Damn it, Robert, it's hard to be serious when you are insulting me and getting a blow job."

Robert cupped Keegan's chin. "Thank you, Keegan. You can wait for her upstairs. She got the point."

"It's about damn time." Keegan kissed them both on their heads. "You guys talk like you still want to love each other. I'll be upstairs when you are done."

Alyssa returned to sitting on her heels, wrung out from the emotional visit. "Keegan, you don't need to wait. I'll get an Uber. Thank you for everything."

Keegan nodded and headed upstairs.

Alyssa looked at Robert. "Robert, you were in on this?"

He nodded. "Keegan loves us; I don't know why. She kept watch over you and let me know you were safe. I guess she kept watch over me too. I knew you were coming tonight. She wouldn't put it off. She said we needed it."

"All that with the blow job, and talking so rough?"

He shook his erection. "I can't disguise enjoying the blow job. You brought Keegan hoping she would soften me up. Not a chance. Did you feel how deeply a spouse's disregard cuts your heart? What I did is a pale shadow of what you did to me though. As for the talk, perhaps the harsh words reinforce their truth."

"I can't come home?"

"No. Get an apartment. I've thought about it. I can't imagine ever letting you come home after what you did. Keep seeing Clay like you have. He wants to see you. I don't."

"Robert, I'll do anything to make it up to you."

"That's what you said before, twice. Then you made a promise to me. A promise you broke when it became inconvenient. Until I can trust you, I don't want to be married to you."

"How can I earn your trust back?"

"I don't know that you can."

She knew that tone. Finality. She had never been its victim before.

Alyssa dropped her face to her hands as the tears returned. "I won't have sex with anyone else, ever again. Just you. I promise. I only love you. I'll always only love you. Just please, please give me one last chance."

"You got the last chance a month ago. I don't envision being married at the end of this. Separation of a year is required for a divorce in North Carolina. Let's keep the clock ticking."

"So I have a year."

"Alyssa, I don't want to hurt you, but I won't let you hurt me. A divorce is the best way to achieve that."

She didn't feel the minuscule spark of hope that shaped her words. "I have a year to change your mind."

"The law requires we separate for a year. It doesn't require that I listen to anything you have to say."

"I will win you back, Babe."

"You are welcome to try. And don't call me Babe."

28

FRIDAY, AUGUST 6, NEIGHBORHOOD PARK

IT'S OVER. HIS eyes were dead.

But he had Keegan watching out for me. He still cares a little. Maybe he doesn't want to answer questions if anything bad happens.

Keegan's blow job…ugh, that hurt. He was telling me that other women will be in his bed. In our bed. Replacing his absentee wife. He might as well have turned on a neon sign.

He told me not to call him Babe. That's the worst part. That hurt more than watching Keegan, knowing I wouldn't be next. Twenty-three years calling him Babe, and he corrected me like I had called him Bobby at a first meeting.

I let Hayden call me Baby. Another way I hurt Robert, and he doesn't even know it.

Heavy steps in the gravel toward the road pulled Alyssa from her thoughts. The darkness hid the walker.

Footsteps? Maybe coming here was a bad idea. Sitting under the only streetlight in the park advertises that I'm alone. Shit.

Alyssa wiped her eyes, then looked around and over both shoulders.

"Alyssa?"

The footsteps grew louder on the gravel closer to the picnic tables.

"Don't be afraid. It's just me."

A man wearing a black T-shirt and khaki shorts stepped inside the circle of light and stopped, his face in shadow.

"Who are you?"

He stepped a little closer, stopped, and tilted his face up into the light. "The Usurper. Can you see me now?"

Alyssa relaxed. "I see you. Hello, Drew. You're visiting the park late tonight."

"I always take a walk around the neighborhood before going to bed. Old army habit. I don't usually see you out here."

"No. I came here to think. This place has been good to me over the years."

"Oh. I'll leave you to it." He stepped toward the street.

Alyssa watched him turn. As she eased back into her internal conversation, she remembered the last time her marriage had been in trouble. She'd gotten the help she needed right in this park when she trusted a stranger. Maybe she should again.

"Wait." Alyssa gestured to the bench beside her. "Actually, I could use a little company, if you want to stay."

"Sure." He straddled the other end of the bench, facing her without speaking.

Alyssa pondered the last couple of hours while staring at her hands, the table, and the gravel around them. Her utter failure with Robert twice welled tears in her eyes to roll down her cheeks, hot on her skin even in the summer heat. She rested her chin in her hand to keep it from slamming onto the table when the despair swallowed even the remaining strength in her neck.

Worthlessness is exhausting. At least it's a feeling.

Without looking she knew Drew had not left the picnic table. He had sat with her for more than half an hour as she replayed the dumpster fire she had made of her life. When she realized that he thought she was worth sitting with while her mind wandered, she looked at Drew. "Thank you."

"You're welcome. Do you feel better?"

"Yes. But no. How did you know?"

"Sometimes people want only to feel quietly included, without having to do the work of conversing. You had that look."

"That broken woman in need of a friend look?"

"Something like that. Ready to talk about it?"

"Not yet. Can I ask you a personal question?"

He nodded.

"Why didn't you take your shot with me when I joined you and Jessica?"

"Exactly what I told you. My ex cheated on me."

"Did you give her a second chance?"

"A second, and a third. I loved Holly, and I believed she would stop."

"I guess she didn't. What made you decide to leave her?"

"I didn't leave her. She died."

"I'm sorry. She must have been faithful at the end. Was she sick?"

"She was killed in a car accident. She was fucking him while they drove. A bridge abutment ended their affair." Drew took a breath and looked toward the woods. "I can never think of her without seeing her body on that slab, so horribly broken between his body and the steering wheel that she lay bent. She died hurting me again." He wiped his eyes.

"Oh, Drew. I'm sorry for asking."

"Don't be. I don't speak of it often, but in a way, it made me a better person. I won't ever help someone cheat on her husband again."

"Again?"

A sad smile flashed on his face as he nodded. "That's the lesson in it all. She was married when we met, and she cheated on him with me. I thought she chose me because I was better. I realized too late that she was simply an unfaithful person. So now I refuse to help a woman cheat on her husband, ever."

Drew wouldn't touch a married woman. Hayden hunted them. Why hadn't she seen it? Her self-esteem somehow found a new subbasement in the depths it had sunk to tonight. She was cruel and stupid. *Maybe not.*

"Isn't that the woman's decision to make?"

"She can decide how to treat her marriage, but I decide if I get involved."

"Yet you talked with Robert about me."

"I warned him. Our conversation surprised me."

"Surprised? Or intrigued?"

"Both. Especially now that Jessica tells me you and Robert are having trouble."

If I had any feelings left, his insight would hurt them. "We are. I was just thinking about it."

"Thought so. You don't need to say more."

She sighed. "After what you shared, I kind of owe it to you."

"You owe me nothing. If it helps, talk, and I'll listen. If not, I'll sit quietly while you think."

"I want to talk, if you can stay a little longer."

He nodded.

"You know we have—well, had—an open marriage with some important rules. I lied, I hid my activities, and I fell in love with a man, breaking all those rules. I was unfaithful in an open marriage, if you can believe that. When Robert forgave me, I did it again. I didn't intend to cheat again, but I knew the consequences of what I was doing. I threw my whole life away."

"This guy knew about your open marriage?"

"No. It turns out that he sleeps with married women specifically intending to destroy their marriages. It turns him on. I fell for everything. He was quite pleased with himself when I arrived at his house after Robert threw me out."

"You aren't with him either?"

"No. I didn't realize what a toxic sleaze he was until that terrible night. I'll never see him again, either, and it will still be too soon. He was celebrating with two other women when I arrived."

"You got a dose of your own medicine?"

Alyssa nodded while she fought crying. She wiped her eyes with the back of her hand. "I got another one tonight. I'm taking lots of my own medicine lately."

"What happened tonight?"

"I talked with Robert. I asked to come home. He didn't consider it for a second, and my friend blew him while he told me, just to prove the point."

"Some friend."

"She is one of our shared partners. She and I planned that she would occupy Robert while I spent time with Clay, but he turned that on us and took it beyond what we planned. I guess I knew it was a possibility, but seeing it hurt."

"Maybe not your best plan. The situation sounds like revenge, not true discussion."

"It started that way, but when we talked alone, he was resolute. His stony face hurt me deeper than anything I've ever experienced."

"What did you learn?"

"How stupid I am. How important my marriage is to me, and that I threw it away for nothing. That I'm the bad guy. That my life is over."

"That last one scares me. What are you thinking, Alyssa?"

"I'm not suicidal. I just meant everything in my life is gone."

"It's not gone. You can make things better until you stop breathing. Figure it out. Start by not hurting your family anymore. You may not save your marriage, but they don't deserve a last memory of you like I have of Holly."

"You must think I'm a heartless bitch. Why be nice to me?"

His jaw tightened. "Holly wasn't a heartless bitch. I loved her."

"I'm sorry. The way you talked…"

"She hurt me, just like you hurt your family. I would have tried to salvage something if she had lived. I'm trying to help you and Robert have the chance we didn't get."

"I don't see the ice in your eyes that I saw in his."

"You would have then. She tried to make it up to me, every time. Time helps. Effort helps more. Change helps the most. Find what you need to fix within yourself, fix it, and let them see you fix it. Maybe you will have a chance."

"How?"

"Only you have that answer."

Alyssa turned to let a tear roll down her cheek.

"Come on. I'll drive you home. You don't want to wait for an Uber out here."

"I won't be much company."

"I never talk in an Uber either. I'll let you think."

"Or cry?"

"Or cry."

29

SATURDAY, AUGUST 7, EMBASSY SUITES

OH SHIT. THIS won't be good.

Alyssa took a breath as she pulled her eye from the peephole. She took another before unlocking and opening the door.

Her daughter flew to her as soon as the door opened enough to squeeze through, crushing her in a tight hug.

Alyssa had been braced for an attack. Susan's embrace skirted emotional defenses prepared for something worse, and Alyssa's empty heart guzzled the love flowing around them. It warmed her like coffee on a cold day, flowing from her neck down into her belly, radiating outward as she absorbed every precious droplet.

She gripped Susan as if she were a tall tree in a flood, afraid to let go and risk falling back into the raging failure of her relationships. After two minutes of this miracle, the emotional shock ebbed, and thoughts returned.

"Susan? What are you doing here?"

Susan pulled back without releasing her grip. Her eyes were wide and her mouth hung open in amazement. "Clay was in a wreck. You and Dad are splitting up. The whole family is in trouble, and you ask why I'm here? Come on, Mom. I had to come."

Maybe we were good parents after all. "I am so glad to see you, though this isn't the meeting I expected."

"Thought I'd slap you again?"

"Worse. I'm afraid you'll tell me to fuck off and disappear."

"Mom, I'm here to help. If you two don't fix this, I might never see you again. At least, not as part of our undivided family. Yes, I'm so damn mad at you that I want to slap you over and over. But that won't help. Sit down. Let's talk."

It was Alyssa's turn to rush to Susan and squeeze her tight. She wept into the hair she had stroked so many times when their roles had been reversed. The warm hands rubbing her back steadied her as the sobs buckled her. Susan's whispers caressed the jagged emotions inside, smoothing their edges, cooling them so Alyssa dared to feel them again without fearing they would slash and consume her soul.

When they made it to the couch, Susan's shirt was dotted with dark wet spots. "Oh, honey, I messed up your shirt. I'm sorry."

Susan's pursed lips and scrunched eyebrows scolded Alyssa's triviality. A tingle passed across her butt as if she were a child about to be spanked.

"Worry about your marriage." Susan's face softened. "What happened?"

"You aren't surprised. Why?"

"Beth warned me when you came to Houston that you might

make a mistake. You were sneak-texting a lot when I was home between sessions, doing that little smile and twisting your hair like you used to do when Dad called. I've prepared for this since June, but that doesn't mean I like it."

Everyone knew except me. How stupid was I? "Beth told you?"

"She said something the morning I picked you up, and we've been talking since then. We're friends. She said to tell you that she's, and I quote, 'goddamn angry' you ignored her warning. Despite being mad, she sends her support. She would have come, but the plane tickets are too expensive."

"Are you friends with her like I am?"

"You mean lovers? No. We're friends." She pointed at Alyssa. "Let's get to it. What happened?"

"I ruined everything."

"Knew that. How?"

"I had amazing sex with our realtor. That's okay; I was mainly staying within our open marriage rules."

"Mainly?"

"I fudged on talking with Dad on time, and I didn't disclose everything we did. That wasn't the problem, but it established a pattern I didn't recognize until too late."

Deep in her abdomen, emptiness gnawed at the love Susan had buried it with moments ago. A deep breath settled her to continue.

"I couldn't put amazing sex with him out of my mind but ignored that danger. I saw him frequently, and Dad got concerned. In my arrogance, I broke the rules we designed to protect ourselves and saw Hayden often and in secret. I developed feelings and eventually fell in love. Your dad called me on it, and I promised never to see Hayden again."

"So why move out?"

"Last weekend, I broke my promise."

"Intentionally? When Clay had his wreck? Jesus, Mother."

"The wreck happened while I was gone. I didn't know about that until we came back into cell range on Sunday. My one shred of defense is that I didn't intend to see him. I was set up, but I played along eagerly enough. I assumed nobody would get hurt over one last time. I was arrogant, stupid, cruel, and wrong about everything."

Exhausted from the introspection her confession required and withered under Susan's disappointment, Alyssa leaned forward to rest her elbows on her knees.

"Dad's kinder to you than you are to yourself. He just says you lied to him."

"Even in pain, he protects us. He doesn't want to turn you against me. He's far angrier with me, I assure you."

"It's more than that. He loves you and misses you. He sits in the front room at night after we go to bed. I found him there this morning asleep like he nodded off staring at the photos."

"How long have you been home, sweetie?"

"Since Tuesday."

"And you didn't—I was there every day, and you weren't—" An ache welled in her chest, rose up her throat, and quivered her chin. Her vision blurred.

"Tuesday was the first flight I could get. Did you think I'd sit at school while the family imploded? I wasn't ready to see you. I'm here to help, but I'm so angry."

She put her hand on Alyssa's knee. "This morning settled my emotions. Be glad we didn't meet earlier in the week."

Alyssa sputtered out a chuckle. "Probably so. Thank you for coming at all." She took Susan's hand in both of her own. "How do I help him? He doesn't want me near him. He doesn't trust me and says it's too painful. You talked with him. What does he say?"

"There's no magic trick here, Mom. You earn his trust."

"He doesn't entrust me with anything now. I have no way to prove I'm trustworthy."

Susan stood and walked to the window. She stared out for a minute before speaking. "What does Dad say about trusting people?"

"In the end, you can trust them to act in their own self-interest at the time of the decision. Any other expectation is unfair."

"Do you believe he thinks you are different from everyone else?"

"Do you mean not focused on my own self-interest?"

"More like, does he think your self-interests are aligned? Aligned so that your self-interest is protecting the family's best interests? Maybe even your marriage's best interests over the family's?"

Again, Susan skirted the end of Alyssa's defenses. The understanding she had overlooked swamped her brain and drained down her throat like a cold flood to pool in her gut.

"Oh shit."

Susan turned from the window to lean over Alyssa. "Oh shit is right, Mom. That's what you took from him. You took away your common purpose, your alignment, your partnership. He doesn't know what you want now, but he knows it isn't him. That's why he sits in the front room at night not sleeping."

"I never meant to do that."

"For an accident, you devastated him like you planned it, Mom. Now help him. Either leave him alone to heal, or show him you are worth taking back. Do it before he gets worse."

Alyssa smiled through a tear. "You always were Daddy's girl."

"I still am. I love you, and I'm helping you, but I'm fighting for him. His best chance is if you come back. But only if you come back as his wife, not some unpredictable nympho who is waiting for another chance to break his heart. If you do that again, god help you."

"I understand. I don't know what to do, but I won't let you down."

"You will if you can't figure it out, Mom."

✦

Alyssa climbed onto a stool at the deserted end of the bar and waved for the bartender.

"I thought you'd come by." Keegan took Alyssa's hand across the bar. "Do you want a drink, or just to talk?"

"Gin and tonic. And a friendly ear when you can."

Keegan brought the drink. "We didn't get to talk last night. Are you all right?"

"Yes."

"I shouldn't have kept blowing Robert after you arrived, but he insisted."

"He insisted?"

"Mm-hmm. When we planned for me to occupy him, I think we both knew what might happen. He wanted you to see, I think to make a point."

"Keegan, I knew what our plan was, and how it might go awry. I deserved it. I'm sure he enjoyed it."

"God, so did I. Sorry. That slipped out."

"You enjoyed it?"

"I got pretty revved up."

Alyssa shook her head. "It's fine. It was hard to watch, especially while he spoke so coldly. That aside, consider it a thank-you for helping me spend time at home."

"Did you two talk after I left?"

"Some. He doesn't want me around."

"Yes, he does. He needs to realize it, and you need to help him do that. What else did he say?"

"We're through. I can't come home. He wanted your sex and his words to hurt me. He wants a divorce."

"And what are you going to do about it?"

"Get an apartment."

"No. What are you going to do about Robert?"

"I need to show him that I still care more about our marriage than anything else. Maybe that earns me another chance."

"Alyssa, I ask this because I love both of you. Don't be offended. You have been playing around with your marriage for months. Are you sure you care more about your marriage than anything else?"

Alyssa drank the rest of her drink in one gulp. It burned her throat before disappearing into the void that continuously emptied her body of all sensation.

"You doubt me too? Susan doubts me. Clay doubts me. Robert sure as hell does. Have I been such a train wreck?"

"I met you after you and Robert opened your marriage, so I can't say a train wreck. You lack impulse control. Maybe what you want most is the freedom to act on your impulses. If so, let Robert go. Decide what you want, deep down in your core, Alyssa. Then go for it with everything you have. I will help you either way. I'll help Robert either way, too, just so you know."

Alyssa sighed. "You are the second one of my friends to tell me she wants my husband if I don't."

"Alyssa, I didn't—"

"It's okay, Keegan, I know what you think of him. I know how great he is. I know what a catch he is. Of the three of us, I'm the only one who knows exactly what kind of husband he is. I intend to keep him."

30

THURSDAY, AUGUST 19, CONVENTION CENTER

Alyssa watched from the side of the stage as the speaker addressed the crowd from the podium. Nausea threatened her with every breath. She had not been this nervous since she was a child. Today had to be perfect, and she would not have a friendly audience.

"That finishes the items on the agenda for this meeting. Thank you all for coming to this first large meeting since the pandemic. We had a great two days. There is one item that we need to add to the agenda."

Robert's boss, Matt Burney, held up his hands as the hundred people in the room groaned.

"I know. It's cruel to add an item at the end of a two-day meeting, especially right before the bar opens. We didn't get to honor our 2020 employee of the year because of the meeting prohibitions, and we have a great chance to do that today. We have a guest speaker to introduce him, then you can congratulate him in the cocktail hour. Without further ado, here is Alyssa Davis to introduce her husband, our 2020 employee of the year, Robert Davis."

Alyssa strode to the podium while the audience clapped, intent on projecting the confidence she lacked. She made eye contact with Robert, whose mouth hung open. She waved, then adjusted the microphone.

"Surprise, Robert. Matt made me promise not to tell you I was coming. Folks, it's hard to be between bankers and the bar…"

The audience provided the requisite polite laughter.

"Please indulge me a moment to give you a glimpse into Robert's life during 2020. Working during a lockdown challenged everyone, and Robert was no exception. I feel like I know many of you, as often as you have been in our house through conference calls and Zoom meetings."

More polite laughter.

"Those were all scheduled during the workday. What many of you will remember is how frequently he answered the phone late at night and early in the morning. As COVID ramped up, and the PPP program volume inundated all of you, Robert would often stay on the phone until midnight and answer his next phone call before six a.m. He made himself available seven days a week, almost around the clock."

Alyssa let the murmur of agreement rumble through the crowd and strengthen her, corralling the butterflies inside.

"Those days put bags under his eyes. He put on weight. He had headaches. He was tired, yet he couldn't sleep. His patience was thin some days, thinner on others. When I urged him to put the phone down, to answer the emails later, to take care of himself, he refused. He would say, 'Alyssa, the people at the other end of the line are working just as hard as I am. Their customers are stressed, and the people who call me take the brunt of those customers' anger. If I make them wait to make my life easier, I make their lives harder. I won't do that. They deserve better.' That's why he's your employee of the year."

She smiled as the audience again agreed.

"I'm going to tell you why he is so much more. He went through 2020 under all the stress I just described. In between the time he spent with all of you, he made time to prepare our daughter for her first year at college, move her there, and talk her through the injustice of college under draconian COVID restrictions. He made the time to play basketball every day with our son, whose social outlets were similarly limited to Xbox online. He made time to help a neighbor who lost his wife and others whose supplies ran out. He understood the toll that lockdowns took on all of us, and he cared for us. He cares for the people around him more than anyone I've ever met."

Alyssa made eye contact with Robert, the microphone conveying to the audience the words she intended for him.

"Even with all of that going on, he took care of me. When I worried about our daughter being far away in the middle of a pandemic, he listened and used that calm voice, you know the one, to settle my fears. When there was little to do at my job at the restaurant group, he found tasks we could do together every morning to give me a reason to get out of bed. We took a walk and talked every day at lunch, rain or shine. The time together, the meaningful, adult conversations, the attention he gave even while he spread himself thin for everyone else…"

Alyssa swallowed, willing herself to finish before emotions overcame her.

"And a million other things he did for me during that tough year kept me feeling sane, secure, and loved."

Alyssa wiped her eye again and took a deep breath. "He's the best man I've ever known. He's the man I love more than the entire world. He's your employee of the year. I love you, Robert. Come up and get your award."

Robert reached her and gave a quick hug. "I didn't know this was happening. You could have canceled."

She smiled at him as tears fought to escape her eyes. "Wouldn't miss it. Congratulations."

Robert got to the podium. "Now you know how I made it through 2020. I had a great lady backing me. Thank you, everyone. This award reflects *your* hard work, despite the lovely words Alyssa shared about me."

He held up the acrylic tombstone. "This will be a treasured addition to my home office. I'll leave it here during the cocktail hour. We'll find a Sharpie, and it would mean a lot if you would sign your names to it so I can remember your help when the memories fade."

He looked at Matt, who nodded.

"Now I think the bar is open."

❧

"Nice speech."

Alyssa turned toward the voice behind her in the concourse. "Drew? What are you doing here?"

"My company provides security for the convention center. I'm defending the bank's open bar from attendees at three other events." He nodded down the hallway. "I saw you get escorted through the back, and thought I'd listen. You said some kind things."

"It was less than he deserves. He ran himself ragged for his people last year."

"I meant what he did for your family. Too many wives would have complained that he worked too much and left it at that. You shared what he did at home and how you felt about it. Everyone in that room knows how much you admire and love your husband."

"Everyone but the man himself."

"Jessica said you still aren't at home."

She shook her head. "I'm working on it."

"Today probably helped."

"You think so?"

"You showed up when you could have canceled, then bragged on him to his peers and his boss with sincerity no one could question. You gave him such a look. It would have melted my heart if I were him."

"That wasn't the plan. I didn't have a plan. I just talked about Robert."

"I know. That honest love is a big positive for you two. It's rarer than you think, and you two have it."

"You and I have only talked a few times. How can you know that?"

"I was in military intelligence, so I am adept at reading people. I've talked with Robert a couple of times, too, and Jessica tells me what she talks about with both of you."

"You must talk with her a lot. Are you becoming a thing?"

"A thing?"

Alyssa rolled her eyes. "Are you doing more than hooking up in the woods during the fireworks?"

He laughed. "We are. Sometimes we hook up in the woods and make our own fireworks. Seriously, we enjoy spending time together. We'll see where it goes."

"I'm pulling for you. She's a great friend, and a wonderful lover. Your stories are similar, so maybe you are a good match."

A ray of hope reached her through the crowd. Her heart raced and leaped into her throat to force a grin so wide it almost hurt her cheeks. *I'll take this pain any day.*

"If you'll excuse me, I need to rescue my husband."

"You have a signal?"

"How did you know?"

"Military intelligence, remember? You haven't taken your eyes off him, and nobody new joined him, so my guess is a signal."

"I can neither confirm nor deny your assumption." She patted his shoulder and meandered through the crowd.

∽

"Robert, what time is it?" Alyssa asked as she touched Robert's left arm and smiled at his assistant, who was touching his right.

He bent his right arm to look at his watch, disengaging from the woman. "Five fifteen."

"Surely not." She pulled his right hand closer so she could see. "Huh. So it is. Our appointment with the physical therapy company is at six. You might want to start saying your goodbyes."

"I will. Thanks for keeping me on track. Excuse me, folks." Robert turned, and the other three men in the circle began to talk among themselves.

As Robert walked off, the woman filled his spot beside Alyssa. "Nice speech, coming from an ex."

"You are misinformed, Nancy. Matt wouldn't have had me come speak if we weren't married."

"Matt is a bit oblivious. You may be married, but he's unhappy. Combined with the rumors I hear..."

"What rumors?"

"The ones about you frequenting hotel bars during the week."

"My friend is a bartender. She's busy, so I visit her there."

"And the ones about you having a boyfriend?"

"Not true at all."

"And the fact that Robert looks tired all the time?"

"Clay's recovery is hard on all of us. We don't sleep as much as we would like. We are still very married."

Alyssa leaned closer. "Nancy, you are a nice lady when you aren't on the make for my husband. Robert thinks very highly of your work and likes you personally. Don't mess up by getting him involved in your workplace romances. He'd never endanger his career that way, and I'd never share him with you."

"I don't know what you mean."

Alyssa made eye contact with Nancy and lowered her voice while still smiling. "I know how to flirt too. Batting your eyes, laughing louder at his jokes than everyone else does, touching his arm, bumping his hip with yours…classic moves, and they send the right signals."

Nancy made to draw back, but Alyssa held her upper arm. She wasn't finished. Robert had summoned her for a reason.

"It's okay, I understand how attractive he is. He'd be flattered by a woman as sexy as you coming on to him, if he weren't quite so married and so worried about HR. Oh, you are sexy. But he wants no part of your reputation, whether he's married to me or not."

"You seemed so soft and sappy onstage today."

"I am. For him. I can be for you as well, as long as you keep doing top-notch, professional work for Robert, and stop there."

"Why doesn't he tell me this himself?"

"Because we are a team. I protect him, he protects me."

Robert stepped beside Alyssa. "And anything Alyssa says about me is the absolute truth. Believe it as if I said it."

Nancy gasped as she looked up at him. "Robert, Alyssa misunderstood. I was just being friendly."

Alyssa smiled. "Excellent. We now have an understanding. You will keep everything one hundred percent professional, as I asked, and nobody will have the opportunity to mistake friendly for flirty. I mean it, Nancy. You are a nice lady when you aren't going after my husband, and I like you. Let's stay friends."

Nancy closed her eyes and sighed. "Robert, I don't want this to hurt our working relationship. I heard you two were getting divorced."

He shook his head. "Not anytime soon. Did you hear her speech? Did that sound like a divorce in process?"

Alyssa's legs weakened. She fought the hope that kindled in her chest, knowing it would hurt worse when she left to go home to the hotel. *He doesn't want to make it official in public. Maybe he wants to give me another chance. Probably not. Don't get your hopes up. It hurts when he dashes them with an icy word.*

"It sounded like she loves you very much. So does this conversation. I apologize that I was misinformed. Congratulations on the award, and your strong marriage. See you tomorrow." Nancy downed her drink as she stepped away.

He offered Alyssa his arm. "I'll walk you to your car. Thank you for rescuing me. It took you long enough."

"When you signaled the first time, I wasn't sure it was for me."

"Who else would it be for?"

"You don't want to even see me, remember?"

He sighed. "I remember, and I still don't want you at home. I'm glad to see you today though. I don't remember a yellow sundress. Especially one this flattering."

He likes that I came. Maybe he'll soften. "I justified buying it for the presentation, but I wanted to look good for you."

"You went straight past good to breathtaking."

He held the door so she could step out into the heat before him. She slipped her hand back into the crook of his arm.

"Thanks for what you said. You saw the purpose of my little chores. I'm glad they meant as much to you as they did to me. But you really could have canceled. People will talk about your speech when we do get divorced."

There it is. The iceberg to sink me. She stiffened her back to bear the fresh disappointment without slumping. "I don't care what people think, and I would never skip a chance to talk about you. I meant every word. You are the man I love with all my heart. You mean more to me than anything else in the world. If you will let me demonstrate those truths, maybe we can fix this."

"Alyssa, I believe you love me. I love you too. That's what makes not trusting you so damn hard. I don't trust you to keep our marriage safe. As much as I want to bring you home and pretend everything is fine, I can't. You will eventually recidivate, and I'll pay the price."

"I will earn your trust back, Robert. I'll show you that the most important thing in my life is our marriage. I…I…lost that for a while. Thank you for the reminder of how much losing that focus hurts. I won't forget it again."

"That's what you said before. Like me, you taught my lesson with pain, making it impossible to forget. Here's your car. Thanks again for the loving introduction."

31

SATURDAY, AUGUST 28, ALYSSA'S APARTMENT

Alyssa stepped aside so Robert could enter her apartment. He slid by, carrying her jewelry box with both hands.

"Thank you for bringing this over, Robert. It's time to rotate the jewelry I wear to the office." *That shirt accents his shoulder and chest muscles. Damn, he looks good.*

"I was headed this direction to play golf anyway. Maybe this will help you feel more at home."

"That hurt, Robert."

"I didn't mean for it to. Sorry. Where do you want this?"

"Oh, Robert, I knew you'd ask to get into my bedroom." Alyssa grinned, then stopped when she saw him frown. "Through the living room, the door on the left. Put it on the vanity." She followed him to her bedroom.

"Right there. Thank you."

She put her hand on her hip and cocked it out.

"Would you like a cup of coffee? I just made some. It's the Hawaiian coffee you like."

"Alyssa, I appreciate the effort. My favorite coffee…I smell your amazing biscuits too." He waved his hand at her outfit. "And you are wearing the 'ready for action' tank top and shorts."

"They've never failed."

"And I notice my picture on the nightstand. Is it that selfie I took?"

"It is. You really loved me that day. Though you were furious, you gave me my last chance."

"I should have learned my lesson."

"You were willing to forgive me that day. Maybe you will want to forgive me again. Until then, I see your picture every morning when I wake up. It isn't like being home, but it's what I have."

"You should find something else. When you bring a man here, he won't want me watching you two go at it."

The verbal gut punch buckled her knees, and she fought doubling over. *He doesn't know. Time to tell him.* "I'll never bring another man here or anywhere else. Only you can come into my bed ever again."

"You are in for a long wait, Alyssa."

"Even wearing this outfit? It's your favorite for a reason."

She lifted the hem of the tank top to reveal her belly button and the short-shorts riding low on her hips. *Come on. I see that look.*

"Do you at least want to get a little before you play golf? You know this top and these little shorts can be off in two seconds. You used to tell me you play better after we relieve some stress together."

"No, Alyssa. We are separated and moving toward a divorce. I won't muddy the waters by making love with you."

He moved toward the door. She turned sideways to let him pass, and felt his erection rub her as he squeezed by.

"Your erection wants to stay."

"It wants to stay very badly. It wants every orgasm that outfit promises. My broken heart tells me to go. Bye, Alyssa." He walked toward the kitchen to leave.

"Bye, Babe. Love you."

"Love you, too, Baby." He stopped as he said it but didn't turn to face her. "Shit. Call me Robert, and don't do that again." He walked out as Alyssa fell onto her bed.

&

All that crying, and I'm still horny. Jesus.

Alyssa rubbed her breasts on top of the thin tank top, urging her nipples to harden.

Robert never waited to get this off.

She jerked it over her head and cupped one breast while pinching the other nipple. Her fingers tightened and twisted just enough to ache, twisting back the other direction before she felt pain.

Robert never hurts me.

She pinched and twisted the other nipple and traced light circles down her sides, pausing to electrify the sensitive crease between abs and obliques. When her pinky finger grazed the waistband of her shorts, she raised her hips and jerked them off.

No more foreplay, Robert. Fuck me.

Alyssa locked eyes with the picture on her nightstand.

Please, Babe. I need it.

Two fingers curled inside and upward to press her G-spot. Her viselike grip on her clit sent waves through her belly as she jacked it at twice the pace she fucked herself. Sparks flew through her body, gathering low in her belly to build an orgasm.

There you go, Babe. Look me in the eyes and make love to me. Make me come around you.

"I don't want to see you."

Alyssa jerked as what Robert had said that fateful night shattered her fantasy. Two deep breaths later, she looked at his picture, and her hands resumed their motions. The flutter returned to her belly.

"Just get your stuff and leave."

"No. Don't say that, Robert." Alyssa closed her eyes and kept masturbating, fighting her own memory in search of a release with Robert in view.

"You stopped being my wife when you became a slut for him."

"I don't trust you to keep our marriage safe."

Alyssa sat up and looked at her hands, wet and still on the bed between her legs. Maybe right now wasn't the best time to get off thinking of Robert. She flicked her clit, reveling in the jolt it sent through her.

I still need to get off.

She picked up her phone and walked to the living room. From the couch, she cast her phone to her TV and selected a video she had not watched in a while. She recognized her back and ass, and the three men using her. Her hands returned to her wet, hungry pussy.

The man fondling her hanging tits on-screen talked to the camera. "Every city we're in, man. Women find out what Dave is packing, and they do anything to get it."

Alyssa spread her fingers inside to stretch the parts of her channel she could. She flicked her clit with a blurry hand as the sounds of the video filled the room. She recognized her recorded moans muffled by the cock in her mouth. She didn't blink. Her breath came in accelerating gasps.

The tall man fucking her from behind addressed the camera. "Few of them are like this one. She couldn't move, almost passed out from sex, she was covered in cum so she couldn't even see, and all she said was 'more.'"

Yes. More. For the first time, she put four fingers inside.

Almost like that huge cock.

Alyssa's orgasm boiled inside, pushing against her body's limits as it sought release. Her nipples pointed at the ceiling as Alyssa's ass slid forward, her view of the TV now framed by a breast on each side jiggling in time with her arm movements.

"God, yes. Here I come."

"Don't call me Babe."

"Not now. No. No."

Alyssa's hands stopped. The orgasm that had neared its peak dissipated like a ripple in the ocean. Alyssa watched the man use her head with two hands in her hair, and for the first time, the memory left her clit unimpressed.

32

THURSDAY, SEPTEMBER 2, COUNTRY CLUB

Alyssa smiled as she approached Summer's table. "I'm sorry for putting you off. Dinner is the least I can do to thank you for helping Clay."

"I'm glad you finally joined me," Summer said as they hugged. "You need to get out, and we need to talk. Before I forget, speaking of getting out, the fitness center physical therapists are participating in a Habitat build day on Saturday."

"Labor Day weekend?"

"It's all we could get. Attendance is understandably low, and we therapists are bringing our significant others. Would you take Bryce's place with me?"

Habitat. Hayden's favorite charitable organization. She refused to risk seeing him.

"Did your team fill all the slots?"

"You would fill the last opening."

Alyssa smiled, glad to have an opportunity to do something with a friend. Depression had left her content to sleep in and sit by the pool, but lately she missed the activity of home. If she couldn't do that, she could help build a house.

"Now that you have me at dinner, you're full speed getting me out of the apartment. Sure, I'll join you. I haven't felt like doing much lately."

"I remember the lethargy. I'm only a few months ahead of you on the divorce path, remember? Even though I tossed Bryce out, I know the feeling of suddenly being alone."

Alyssa looked away, unable to look Summer in the eye.

"Sorry. I didn't mean—"

"It's okay. I know what you meant. Thanks for thinking of me."

"I'm thinking of both of you. Robert looks more haggard than I've ever seen him. You don't return calls or texts for days, and I felt your muscles tense up when I hugged you. You two need to figure this out."

"I'm trying. He wants nothing to do with me. I broke his spirit in a way I didn't think I could. Has he talked about it with you?"

"A little. He wants his wife back, but he won't take the risk again. He needs the right nudge, I think."

"Maybe with a bulldozer. Last week, I spoke about him at a work function. I flattered him and pledged my love in front of his entire department. Nothing. This morning I had him bring something to the apartment before golf. I made his favorite breakfast, wore his favorite 'fuck me' outfit, and flat-out offered to just give him some. He told me his broken heart made him leave. I'm running out of ideas, and we've been separated a month."

"I'm sorry, Alyssa. Maybe he'll get horny and have sex with you like I did with Bryce. You can go from there."

"I had him horny today, but not enough to get him into bed. He wants no part of me. Maybe he will pick up someone else. Someone who can't hurt him."

She looked away from Summer again. Summer would probably want Robert like Jessica and Keegan did. She'd wanted him before the separation. Their similar personalities had made them close friends. *Summer would never hurt Robert, and he knows that.*

"Have you scratched that itch since you moved out?"

The change of direction jolted Alyssa out of her thoughts with a laugh.

"I have not scratched that itch, as you so delicately put it. Today I was worked up and tried to. I even watched one of my favorite videos for inspiration, but I couldn't finish. I don't feel right somehow."

Summer leaned forward and lowered her voice. "Would you like me to help you with it?"

"I would ordinarily jump at the chance, but I want to figure this out. I'm sure it has to do with being apart from Robert."

"Probably. If you change your mind, call me. My itch needs scratching, too, and we could help each other. Get ready. He's coming this way."

"What?"

"Your husband is walking this way."

Shit. I didn't expect to see him here. Why would he come over?
"Did you invite him?"

"No, but he's headed this way. Take a breath."

Don't mess up.

"Hello, ladies. I'm glad you two finally got together." Robert stood beside the table between them.

"Yes, your wife finally answered my texts."

Robert winced, then retained his smile. "She's had a rough time lately. Thanks for taking her out."

"Babe, it's unlike you to be at the club on a Thursday." Alyssa ran her fingers along the back of his hand. "Is everything okay?"

"Everything is fine. Clay's tired of my cooking, so I'm picking up something different. And please don't call me Babe."

A tiny reprimand. Alyssa looked at the table before smiling up at him. "I could come cook. It's no trouble. And I've left you a few suppers ready to go when I visit Clay at lunch."

"I know, and they were delicious as always, but no, thank you. We must learn to love my cooking. You two have fun. Summer, are you coming for therapy tomorrow?"

"I am. We will have him walking again in no time."

"I know you will. See you then. You two enjoy the evening." Robert went to the bar. The bartender set a drink in front of him.

"He needs me to be home," Alyssa said, almost to herself.

Summer squeezed Alyssa's hand. "You will be, Alyssa. Keep trying."

Dread gripped Alyssa's struggling heart, sending an instant of dizziness to her head. "Oh shit."

"What?"

"Cassandra Pennington just sat down beside my husband. She's talking with him."

"Is something wrong with that?"

"Summer, she's flirting with him. The last time we saw that woman here, she insulted us and walked through like she owned the place."

"Alyssa, could you simply be sensitive from that encounter?"

"She's a cold bitch with everyone. But she's laughing with him and touching his arm." She gasped. "And his leg."

Summer took a sip of wine and reached to hold Alyssa's hand.

"It's okay, she's only flirting. Robert will have his food in a minute and leave, and nothing will come from it. Be calm."

Alyssa's heart broke the icy grip around it with a move of Robert's hand. She laughed. "I'll be right back. I need to talk to Robert a minute."

"Alyssa, don't."

"Relax, Summer. He asked for help."

When Alyssa arrived at the bar, she put her hand on Robert's shoulder and kissed his cheek. "Babe, did you get Clay a chocolate torte? I promised him one for completing his first week bearing weight."

Robert winked at her. "I didn't, but I'll add one. He's earned it. You could have brought it when you come home."

"I would, but we may be a while. Summer and I have a lot to catch up on."

She looked at the blonde who had leaned back in her chair and fallen silent. "Good evening, Cassandra. Waiting on your husband?"

The cold grin that spread Cassandra's lips chilled Alyssa. "No, I'm talking with yours, since you aren't with him."

"Yes, Robert is giving us some girl time."

"No. I meant that you changed your home contact address with HR. Robert said your family have been in the same house for years, but you seem to have moved."

Alyssa gripped Robert's shoulder to steady herself. *Bitch.* "You looked at my HR records?"

"Certainly not. That would violate any number of privacy laws. I was reviewing the emergency preparedness plan, which includes the home contact addresses. Yours caught my eye because it had an apartment number. I knew that couldn't be correct."

She had tried to be discreet about the change. *Who knew she would review the preparedness plan?* "Hm. I'll have to check on that. I've had the same home for years. That hasn't changed."

"I'll check on it also. We need to know everyone's living arrangements." Cassandra smiled and nodded toward the door. "My friend arrived. Have a good night, Robert." Cassandra held his arm as she descended from the stool.

Alyssa leaned to Robert's ear. "I don't mind chasing women away when you don't want to be rude, but if it keeps happening, I'm moving back home to make it believable."

"Thanks for coming over. She was quite interested in our marriage. And I think she was flirting with me."

"She was, trust me." She squeezed his shoulder. "Robert, I may no longer have a say in who you are with, but please, when you start to move on, please don't get with Cassandra Pennington."

"I won't. She's married. And not my type."

"I mean it. Even if Brock divorces her, or is hit by a bolt of lightning, stay away from her. She's a bad person. And since when is a tall, beautiful, sophisticated woman not your type? I know what you like."

"She is indeed tall, beautiful, and sophisticated. You could add hot and sexy. She was a professional model, so all of that almost goes without saying. But she's not trustworthy, kind, or respectful. That's my type."

His words buckled her knees. She braced herself on the bar and his shoulder to avoid falling. "That hurts, Robert."

"I was talking only about her, though those attributes have failed you lately. If it makes you feel better, even now I'd take you over Cassandra. You lose control. She seems intentional with her deceptions."

"You say the sweetest things. Now that you are safe from

the beautiful blonde temptress, I'm going back to Summer." She pecked him on the cheek. "For Clay. And our observers."

Across the room, Frank and Patricia Martin sat at a table on the elevated rim around the central dining area. They watched both Cassandra and Alyssa steal glances at Robert while he waited for his food. Frank squeezed Patricia's hand and chuckled when Alyssa noticed Cassandra staring at Robert and glared at her until they made eye contact for three tense seconds.

Frank nodded toward the dining area. "Those two are the future, my dear. This will be interesting."

"Perhaps. I'm still considering your idea. I haven't decided it is the right path."

He smiled. "But you will."

33

FRIDAY, SEPTEMBER 3, HOME

ALYSSA PARKED BEHIND Summer's car. *I'll make Clay's lunch while she finishes his therapy.*

In the kitchen, she pulled the ingredients for Clay's favorite monster sandwich out of the refrigerator and put them on the counter.

As she moved to preheat the oven, Robert's boots on the laundry room floor reminded her: *I need boots for Habitat tomorrow.* She retrieved hers from the laundry room and took them to her car.

She walked back into the kitchen. *I'll need thick socks.*

She walked to the bedroom for socks.

She stopped two steps inside the door. "Robert?"

He lifted his head off the pillow and looked toward her, his mouth open but silent.

The blonde curls on his chest moved as well. A familiar hand tucked the hair behind an ear, then pulled the sheet over her bare chest.

"Summer?"

Robert sat up. "Alyssa, what are you doing here?"

Seeing them together released a flood within her. Alyssa knew their marriage had been open before they separated. He had every right to sleep with whomever he wanted. The dam of intellectual acknowledgment crumbled under a wave of eviscerating agony released by seeing herself replaced in her own bed. Tears spilled down her cheeks. "Don't get up."

As she shuffled to the door, she stopped beside the dresser. She removed her wedding and engagement rings and placed them on its dark surface. She traced the circles with her fingertip once, then drifted to her car, noticing nothing until she entered her apartment.

34

FRIDAY, SEPTEMBER 3, ALYSSA'S APARTMENT

Alyssa sat on her couch, sobbing until she vomited onto her shirt. Her body, sore from the heaving, gasping for breath between wails, lacked the strength to get up. The yellow liquid pooled on her skirt. She stared as her vision cleared and the bile soaked into her clothes.

I don't remember coming here. I only remember them.

She pulled several Kleenex from the box on the end table. She wiped her eyes, cleared the acid from her nose and mouth, and dropped the tissues into the pool in her lap. Each time she looked at the tan line on her ring finger, the blow to her heart made her breath shudder.

The cooling liquid on her chest broke her trance.

These are done. Even without the vomit, I never want to remember the last time I wore them.

Without standing, she removed her blouse, dropping it into her lap. She unzipped the skirt, slid it off, then walked the entire wad of clothes to the trash can. She looked down her body and added her bra and panties to the can. She kicked the black heels off and tossed them too. *Ugh, the smell.*

The pool caught Alyssa's attention as she walked back from the dumpster. Dressed only in a pink T-shirt and black running shorts, she dove in, swam across the pool, then chose a shaded chaise in the corner. *Let the fresh air clear my head, and the water cover my crying.* She looked at her wet clothes. *Didn't think about my nipples showing. At least there's nobody here.*

You did it, Alyssa. You ended your marriage. Yes, he brought Summer to bed, but you gave him the chance. Her thumb flicked the bare spot where her wedding rings had resided for twenty-two years, for the first time realizing the fidget she exhibited during thought.

It's an open marriage. He can have who he wants in bed without breaking it. Except he didn't. The only woman he slept with without me was Summer, that first time, when she was upset. Everyone else was someone we shared together.

The epiphany swallowed her brain in an instant.

He never wanted the open marriage.

Realization manifested in her body. She realized she was holding her breath and forced herself to breathe. She clasped her hands in her lap to stop their trembling, then moved them over her stomach, hoping the pressure would settle her growing nausea. She couldn't bear the sight of the white line on her left ring finger. She hid it under her right hand.

For the first time in months, she wondered why Robert had let her take such a risk.

He wanted me to be happy. And he was willing to open up so he could keep at least a part of me.

No. That isn't him. He agreed so he could protect me from the consequences. And I thwarted his efforts every time he tried. Well, I finally got the better of The Great Robert Davis. A win for me…

Pondering the beginnings opened her to new analysis of all that followed. Analysis opened the door to blame.

Summer. That cunt. Last night, she said she wanted to help. Today, she fucks Robert. She planned this. She's been fucking him all along, I bet. Maybe even behind my back, since that first time in March. She probably told Robert about Hayden. I trusted her, and she used it to steal my husband! Miserable bitch. Goddamn. She's even taking care of Clay. I'm not there, and she's trying to take my place. Not just my place in Robert's bed, but my place in my own house, with my children. She's replacing me, and I fucking thanked her for it last night. She probably texts with Susan too. She's ruining my life. Why didn't I see it?

Alyssa stared across the pool and sighed, letting the flash of idiocy flow out with her breath.

Because she didn't do anything, Alyssa. Robert would have told you if she had. Summer even warned you not to get attached when you told her about Hayden. She cares about you and Robert. She probably slept with him because he needed it, like he did for her. Everybody said how hard he's taking this. She is helping him. She's helping him because you hurt him so badly.

Her legs sagged down to the chaise as the strength left them.

She's helping Clay because she's a trained physical therapist, not to become his mom. If she's talked with Susan, it would be as a friend, and that's a good thing. She's helping your family because you can't. You aren't allowed. Robert doesn't want you. He's moved on.

She pulled her hands onto her chest, as if they could protect her heart from the blow her brain was formulating.

To Summer, who is indeed taking your place. Because Robert wants her to.

A sob escaped her mouth before her hands could catch it as she covered her face. Alyssa wept, finally understanding that no one could protect you from yourself.

"Lady, are you all right?"

Alyssa raised her head to see a young woman standing beside her. She wiped her eyes and nodded. "Yeah."

The woman stared at her. "You sure? You're in wet clothes, sobbing in a chair."

Alyssa moved her arm across her breasts.

"It's okay. Nobody here but me. I have tits too." She focused on Alyssa's hand. "Ah. Getting divorced?"

Alyssa nodded. "Looks that way. I just realized he's serious."

"That's too bad. It happened to me before. The best thing you can do is move on. Find another man who makes you feel good. You know, better than the current guy makes you feel, if you know what I mean. As good as you look, you'll have options."

Alyssa shook her head, unwilling to consider the possibility. "It's too soon for that."

"Maybe. You decide. When the new guy makes your eyes roll back in your head and your whole body stops working, you will start to feel better. It worked for me."

"I'll think about it. Thanks." Alyssa lowered her gaze from the woman's face to stare across the pool again.

The woman took a chair in the sun. Alyssa watched the sunlight dance across the ripples when the woman took a dip, then watched the surface return to its glass-like stillness.

Maybe she's right. A big orgasm might do the trick, and I can't seem to force one. I know who to call. And why.

35

FRIDAY, SEPTEMBER 3, DOWNTOWN

Alyssa gritted her teeth and sent the text she had spent minutes writing and rewriting. "Can I come over? I need to talk."

"You have been in the driveway for ten minutes. Come on in, but you will be dressed only in your underwear."

Her belly tightened, nervous about being seen. Her nipples tingled, excited about the same thing.

"It's quarter to five on a busy street. I can't do that."

"You can and you will. Look within yourself. You crave the excitement."

"Are you alone?"

"No. You can join us. In your underwear."

"Who is there?"

"You can see when you come in."

"I can't be on display to people I don't know."

"Yes, you can."

"I'm not wearing underwear."

"Nude it is."

"Please don't make me do that."

"You want my cock. If you acknowledge it by being nude when you cross my threshold, I'll give you all you want, for as long as you want."

"It's twenty yards to the door. Too many people can see."

"Drop the dress on the front porch. I will open the door in thirty seconds, if you want to come in. Final offer. Final text."

Her pussy throbbed. She needed to come. Being nude on the street, more than one lover inside, Hayden's gilded tool… She wanted to obey. *He always hurts you, Alyssa.*

Alyssa drove her head against the headrest. She closed her eyes and groaned. *Remember what you need and why. You need to feel good again. He hurts me with pleasure. I need the pleasure.*

After a deep breath, she opened the car door.

Before she could ring the bell, the door swung inward. Hayden, wearing only a robe, filled the opening.

"Take it off."

Alyssa looked behind her, then slipped the thin straps off her shoulders and let the low-cut floral dress fall to the porch. She stepped out of it, then squatted to pick it up.

"Leave it there. Come in. You can leave the heels on." He stepped aside.

She squirted through the opening, then turned to face him as he closed the door. "Was that necessary? We both know I came here to fuck. Did you have to embarrass me?"

He smirked. "You don't have to stay. The last couple of times we met, you left in a rush. Your dress will take longer to put on than it did to take off. By three a.m., maybe nobody will see you leave."

She stepped to him, putting one hand on his chest and one around his cock through the thin robe. "I did my part. Now you do yours."

"Sure, Alyssa." He squeezed her ass cheeks with both hands before nudging her toward the living room. "You remember Lauren."

Alyssa licked her lips at the nude woman stretched along the entire length of the wide couch. "You're a frequent visitor."

"I can't get enough. Just like you." Lauren eyed Alyssa up and down. "I see why he likes you."

"Likewise. You don't look like a new mom."

Lauren cupped her breasts and offered them to Alyssa.

"I taste like one though. Come have some milk. I'm full." She giggled and pointed to the shot glasses and vodka on the coffee table. "Maybe it's a White Russian."

"Yes, Alyssa. My previous offer stands: Drink Lauren's milk and I'll fuck your ass."

"I want you in my pussy. I came here to come. Make me come."

She bent over Lauren and latched onto a nipple. As she sucked, she spread her feet and opened her wet lips with two fingers. After a couple of sucks, Lauren's milk flowed. *Sweet. Warm. No wonder babies suck so hard.* She sucked harder as Hayden's cockhead split her opening. She moaned onto the hard breast as she stretched around his invading cock. *Yes. Fill me. Make me come.*

He squeezed her hip bones as his cock pushed deeper inside her. Her breath hitched between swallows of milk. Alyssa pushed back as Hayden pulled out and then returned, each time a little deeper, each time stretching her walls and lips with delicious pain and pressure. When he tapped the electric spot beside her cervix, Alyssa positioned Lauren's hand on her breast, encouraging her to play with the nipple, then dropped her own hand to her clit. *Time to come. Please.*

Hayden dove into her faster. Lauren pinched and twisted her nipple at the same pace. Alyssa flicked her clit, desperate for release. Alyssa's pussy stretched over his girth, it stretched with his length, and her body gripped the steely hardness instead of relaxing. Hayden's balls tapped the back of her hand.

Yes. So good. Stretch me. Fill me.

Lauren had a breast in each hand, one cupping the entire orb and stroking its underside, the other pinching and pulling a nipple, firing shocks of pain deep in her body to stoke her building orgasm. *That feels so good.* Alyssa teased the nipple in her mouth as the flow of milk slowed.

Lauren wove her hand into Alyssa's hair and directed her with a tug. "Now this one. Suck it dry."

Alyssa latched and felt her pussy clench as the milk flowed into her mouth. *This is hotter than letting a man come in my mouth.*

Hayden had released one of Alyssa's hips and was rubbing her asshole with his wet thumb. As her sphincter opened, he slipped it inside and pressed against his cock through the membranes.

Yes. I'm getting close. It's a big one. Everywhere she was touched shot a string of electricity. They met low in her belly, and the flutter started there.

"Harder. Faster. More. I'm close."

The three of them quickened yet again. The flutter became a flock of birds, raking her insides with feathers from her arms to her thighs. They focused on the churning spot low in her belly, and Alyssa held her breath.

Alyssa closed her eyes. *Thank god. I'm going to come.*

"Alyssa, what are you doing here?"

Inside her body, the birds retreated from her belly. The strings of electricity thinned and lost connection, crackling in shorter strands that meandered from their origins.

Shit. Not now. Focus, Alyssa. Come. Come for your own good. And his.

"Faster. Harder."

Alyssa sucked harder to get the slowing milk to flow. Hayden's cock swelled inside her, stretching her to her fullest and announcing his impending climax.

Yes. Come on my cervix. I'll come then.

His jizz exploded onto her cervix in hot bursts. *Yes. Keep coming.* Alyssa pushed back against him, embedding the huge, curved cock inside her, pressing and griding all the spots he hit so well. She closed her eyes to let her orgasm come.

He wants her, not me.

Her climax shriveled with every spurt of his cum that painted her insides.

I failed. I can't move on. It doesn't matter.

Alyssa swallowed a last mouthful of milk and stopped sucking Lauren's breast. A bit more trickled out as she removed her head from the blonde's wet, inflamed chest. Alyssa stopped flicking her clit, flexing and stretching her cramped hand. When Hayden's spurts ceased inside her, he removed his thumb and cock.

He slapped her ass, the loud crack echoing in the room, but the pain and pleasure she'd used to enjoy never came. She was numb.

"I knew you'd come back. They all do. It's a magic cock, and I know how to use it. You loved those orgasms I just gave you, and we have all night. We'll celebrate your divorce. I fucking love it."

Alyssa moved to the couch beside Lauren, who shifted to let

her sit. She looked straight ahead, registering nothing against the shock of what had happened.

I didn't come. He used to make me come just by getting inside me all the way. I had him inside, his thumb in my ass, her pulling my nipples, and me rubbing my clit until it went numb, and I couldn't come. I thought about Robert. I wanted to come so bad, but I thought about Robert with Summer. I thought about being alone.

Alyssa let her breathing slow and closed her eyes.

I only hurt the people I love.

She opened them to see Hayden stroking his cock in front of her.

"Get me ready for round two."

Alyssa looked from his cock, up his body, to his wide smile, and then to his eyes.

He doesn't smile with his eyes. That look. Malice? Bitterness? No. Resentment. He resents married women. Why didn't I see it before?

Because you couldn't get your eyes off his cock, Alyssa. You were looking for sexual pleasure. You found it. At what cost? And that big, curved, orgasm-multiplying cock that you trashed your marriage for couldn't even give you one little orgasm today. Why do you think that is?

Because now I know. I wish I had done it differently.

Alyssa stood. "I'll pass on round two."

"You're leaving? You never turned me down before. Nobody makes you come like I do."

"You used to make me come a lot, but today, you didn't even manage once. Don't worry, your dick didn't shrink, just your appeal. They all see it eventually, don't they? These women you ruin?"

She nodded at Lauren, still sitting on the couch.

"She'll see it too. When I looked past your magnificent cock, past that million-dollar smile, to your eyes, I saw you. And you aren't worth my time. I knew that when I came here, but I had to do this. It's done, and so am I."

She stepped around Hayden and walked to the door.

"Aren't you forgetting? You're naked, and it's rush hour out there."

She nodded with a smile. "And the entire town driving by. Even that wouldn't keep me from leaving here and never coming back. I hope they get pictures."

Alyssa opened the door, picked up her dress, and walked to the car. She hardly noticed the honking horns as she slid the dress over her head before driving away.

36

FRIDAY, SEPTEMBER 3, PARK BY THE LAKE

ALYSSA LOOKED TOWARD the footsteps coming closer across the gravel.

"I keep finding you here. Are you okay?" Drew shined the flashlight on his face and stepped closer to the picnic table.

"I don't know. I'm thinking in the park, so maybe I'm still working on it and haven't changed one bit."

"I bet you have. Want to talk about it?"

She nodded. Drew sat on the bench beside her.

"I listened to you and everyone else who cares about me. I closed my marriage. Well, I stopped seeing anyone else, since I don't have a marriage anymore. I focused on Robert. I let him see how much I care about him. You saw the speech at his work meeting. I cooked food for him when I was at the house and he wasn't. I told him that I only needed one more chance. Despite all that, I took my wedding rings off today."

"Sounds like you were making progress. Why take them off today?"

"I put them on the bedroom dresser as I watched him sit up in bed. My friend had to sit up with him."

"Same friend as before? You said you expected that."

Alyssa shook her head. "Different friend. This wasn't Robert using my own plan against me. This was Robert moving on. He had only been with another woman without me once, early on. He didn't care for the open marriage, though he enjoyed it when we invited a partner to bed. He wouldn't have slept with someone else until he was ready to move on. I ran out of time."

"I'm sorry. What will you do?"

"That's what I'm considering. I still don't know."

"Okay." He turned on the bench and leaned back against the table with his elbows propping his arms to the side.

Alyssa stared at the moon as it crept above the trees until the entire thin crescent revealed its bowl shape. "It's empty. Like me."

Drew turned his head. "What?"

Alyssa shook her head. "Just thinking out loud. The moon is empty, like I am."

"Yes. You are just like it tonight."

"Thanks."

Drew smiled and straddled the bench to face her.

"The moon is no more empty than you are. Both of you are there, whole, impactful. Like the moon, sometimes we can't see it. Nonetheless, it's always there, changing the tides, protecting us from asteroids, stabilizing our lives. Right now, most of you is in the dark, but you make a positive impact on the people around you, even Robert. Keep going around Earth until you can see yourself in a better light."

"Thanks for the pep talk, but it's hard to believe I'm doing anything right."

"You are. Trust yourself to be a good person. Keep being the kind, substantial woman you are. You will come out shining again."

"We'll see. Can I ask you a question?"

He nodded.

"Did you and your wife ever separate because of her infidelity?"

He recoiled, then leaned forward. "I wasn't expecting that. No, we never separated. Holly always swore she would never cheat again, and that she wanted to be with me, but everything was always about her. She phrased things using 'I' frequently, like you do, and always told me 'I want to be with you.' I believed her, partly because I wanted to, and partly because she had always jumped directly from relationship to relationship. She understood that need, so she never considered humanely ending ours. She wouldn't take the risk of living on her own."

"I'm sorry. Maybe it would have been better."

"I try not to think of it that way. I just try to remember the good times. Then I see her broken body. I could have been spared that memory." He closed his eyes.

"I shouldn't have asked. Thank you for being honest with me." Alyssa stood. "Thank you for helping me think. Can I give you a ride to your house? It's late."

"No. I think I'm going to sit here a while."

"Okay." Alyssa sat back down and watched the moon.

37

SATURDAY, SEPTEMBER 4, ALYSSA'S APARTMENT

ALYSSA STARED AT the rectangle of light the streetlight cast on the bedroom floor. She hadn't bothered to close the blinds when she shuffled to bed earlier. Her numbed brain had not noticed it was open. She had changed clothes lit only by the glow from outside and crawled into bed out of habit. She had known sleep would not come, so she leaned against the headboard to rehash her thoughts for the millionth time.

This is the right thing to do. If I want to atone to Robert, I am out of options.

Drew's words lingered in her head. She needed to be a good person. After a couple of hours sitting at the table, she knew how.

This is an act of desperation. You can't undo this once it's done.

Allow yourself time to make progress. Maybe what you saw isn't really what happened.

It would hurt. She would have to force herself to do it. But maybe, when it was all over, Robert could be happy again.

No, it was. I know my husband, and I know my friend, so I know what happened and why. He wasn't trying to make a point. He didn't know I'd come early for lunch. He wants her. She wants him. She always has. Who wouldn't?

Her chest filled with a cold terror. Her words would cause irreversible actions. Her life would never be good again, but redemption might be some consolation.

Don't be rash. This won't look good for you.

She laughed into the silent room. Appearances no longer mattered.

I left my rings on the dresser. It looks like I gave up. This will be a surprise. I can't look worse, even if this goes badly.

She flicked her ring finger with her thumb, the lack of rings not deterring her old habit while she replayed every reaction she could imagine yet again. Some were good for Robert. None were good for her.

It will go badly, Alyssa. Take more time to fix things.

She looked at the clock. Two forty-six a.m. She remembered what she'd seen only a few hours earlier. She remembered the sound of the front door closing as she'd fled their house. Resolve settled into her spine, thawing the ice in her chest. It felt right and hurt so bad, but she could do what she needed to do.

I'm out of time. I can't fix things, even with my best efforts.

She stared at the pile of wadded tissues on the bed, then pulled the collar of her nightshirt to dab her eyes.

And I'm done crying. It's time to act, to do the right thing. No matter how it ends, I'm doing the right thing. I'll handle the consequences afterward.

They will be severe, Alyssa.
I know.
She sent a text. "I may need your help tomorrow night."
"Let me know when and where."
She lay down but didn't sleep.

38

SATURDAY, SEPTEMBER 4, CONSTRUCTION SITE

"ALYSSA, I DIDN'T think you would make it." Summer smiled but kept her distance from Alyssa.

"I said I would come, and I'm working hard at keeping my word. I didn't sleep much, but I'm here to help."

"Thank you, but don't feel you have to."

"Summer, I'm staying."

"Okay." The petite blonde looked around, then looked up at her friend. "About yesterday—"

"Later. It's a beautiful morning. Let's just work on the house, okay?"

The two women hung siding together all morning. The conversation revolved around the work, but some more personal tangents eased the mood. Summer tried to initiate conversation about their interaction the day before a few times, but Alyssa deflected. As lunchtime approached, they had almost finished the shady side of the house.

"Alyssa, I really want to talk about yesterday."

Alyssa swung her hammer hard at the nail in her left hand, punctuating every word.

"I." Wham.

"Said." Wham.

"Later." Crunch.

"Ah, god. Fuck. Shit. That hurts."

Alyssa looked at her finger. It pointed sideways, and she swooned. Summer caught her waist before she could fall off the scaffold.

39

SATURDAY, SEPTEMBER 4, EMERGENCY ROOM

"WE'RE GOING TO be a while. Do you feel up to talking now?" Summer pointed to Alyssa's hand, cradled on a bag of ice in her lap.

Alyssa looked around, then winced when her shrug jostled her damaged finger.

"Might as well. I intended to have some more private, uninterrupted time, but we'll probably be here a while. This corner is about as private as we're going to get. I have a lot to say, and once I get started, I may not stop. Do you want to go first?"

Summer nodded. "I'm sorry about yesterday. I showed up to give Clay his PT. He was sleeping. Robert was there instead of the nurse, so we talked. He's sad, and he doubts himself. I reassured him that he's going to be okay, and we kissed. We just stumbled into bed from there."

She touched Alyssa's arm, making her wince. "Oops. Sorry."

Alyssa shook her head. "It's okay."

"I swear, I didn't mean for anything to happen. I've been trying to help you two get back together. He seemed to need it. And I really didn't mean for you to see us. God, I don't want to hurt you. We're friends. At least, we were, and we still can be, if you'll have me."

Summer leaned closer, making eye contact. "I promise I'm not trying to take your husband away. I care too much about both of you to cause trouble. Please believe me, I was only trying to help Robert."

Alyssa stared back at Summer and gave a wan smile. "I believe you, Summer. I would forgive you, but there is nothing to apologize for, and therefore nothing to forgive."

"I slept with your husband."

"No. You consoled a friend who needed it. Who needed you."

She reached her right hand to Summer, who took it.

"I hurt Robert. I broke my marriage in a way that can't be repaired. Robert knew that, but I didn't. I tried to fix it. I tried to make Robert see that I would do anything if he could accept my love again. I tried to recover my husband. I didn't see that I only imprisoned him in the wreckage I created." The sadness in her chest bubbled up. Her chin quivered, and she turned away.

Alyssa turned back after she fought back the tears. "Every time I made him see the good in me, he fell into the trap of loving me but not trusting me. Worse, he was afraid of being with me. He never said it, but he was. He was afraid every time we spoke. He dreaded opening his heart and having me rip it apart like I have been doing."

Alyssa counted to five. She needed to finish this before the tears came.

"That is why he is sad and unsure of himself. The one relationship that has steadied him for decades is trying to crush him, and he is afraid of that very relationship that made him happy for years. My efforts to keep him are killing him."

She smiled at Summer, who nodded but didn't speak.

"That's why Robert slept with you. He is careful. He didn't just fall into bed with anyone to feel better; he let you make him feel better because he knows you are a good person who wouldn't hurt him. He knows that from our years of friendship. He knows it from our time at the end of your bad marriage, and he knows it from your helping both Robert and Clay these last few weeks. You have always been a good friend. You love us, and we love you."

Summer's mouth hung open, but her eyes remained focused on Alyssa's. She remained silent.

"I have been a horrible wife. I have been a bad mother. I've broken the very people who mean the most to me. I've done it because I focused on what tempted me, rather than what's best for me. What was best for me was my family, and I made bad choices. I won't do that any longer."

Alyssa used the hem of her shirt to wipe her eyes. "Summer, when Robert slept with you yesterday, he was inviting you into his life, into his family's life. He trusts you not to hurt him, and he's doing that when he's at his most vulnerable."

She scrunched up her face and swallowed a sob. "I'm not going to ask you to move in or marry him or do anything you don't want to do. I am going to ask you to love him, love my kids when you see them, and be better to him than I was. You're good for him. You two have always clicked. You've been good friends for years, and he will want more. I think you will want more too.

That's okay. No, it's good, if that is what you want. You can make him happy again."

Summer backed away with a stunned expression. Alyssa had gone too far.

"Shit. I don't want to dump all that pressure on you. Can I say it this way? Robert is going to want to form a relationship with you. If that is what you want, will you be as good to him as you always have been? Will you please love him, and give him a reason to trust people again? Will you let me step away and stop hurting him, knowing that he is starting a new and wonderful journey with a wonderful and loving partner? All I want in this world is for Robert to be happy."

Alyssa held Summer's gaze. Each woman squeezed the other's hand. Alyssa nodded as tears flowed down her cheeks.

"Mrs. Davis? You can come back now," the orderly called from the door.

"Can my friend come with me?"

"Sorry, ma'am. No extra people in the ER. COVID restrictions."

Alyssa turned to Summer. "We'll talk when I get back."

"Do you have someone to drive you home? That hand won't work until the numbing wears off, and then it will be sore." The volunteer pushed Alyssa's wheelchair into the waiting room.

"Yes, my friend was sitting in that back corner." Alyssa pointed, then covered her mouth. *Robert?* "Oh. Over there. The two people sitting together."

Robert and Summer stepped toward Alyssa as she approached.

Summer reached her first. "What's wrong? You walked inside."

The volunteer answered. "Standard procedure. Everyone who

receives anesthesia gets wheeled out. Her legs work just as well as when she came in." He put his hand on her shoulder. "Are you all right, miss? Are you safe to get home?"

Alyssa smiled up at the volunteer. "I couldn't be in better hands. Thank you."

She stood and let Robert and Summer offer words of concern and inspect the brace running from her forearm to the tips of her first two fingers.

"It looked awful, and it hurt like hell, but the doctor popped it back in place and braced it. I'll be fine in three to six weeks. I didn't expect you to be here, Robert. Summer had me well in hand, so to speak."

Robert's mouth fell open. "When Summer called and said you were in the hospital, I didn't want you here without family. Of course I came."

"It's only a dislocated finger, but thank you." She smiled and added, "Unless you wanted to be here as next of kin."

They chuckled, then he shook his head. "No dying today. Come on. Let's get you home."

Alyssa patted his shoulder. "Summer can take me. You've been inconvenienced enough."

Summer wrapped her arm around Alyssa's waist, avoiding the damaged hand. "Go with him. Talk. Really talk. I'll see you later." With one last squeeze of Alyssa's waist, she left.

"The car is this way." Robert pointed down one of the aisles. "If you keep it elevated, it will throb less."

"The doctor said that too."

Robert slid his forearm under hers and lifted her hand so gently that Alyssa only felt the pressure relax as blood flowed out of the damaged fingers. "Let me give your arm a rest as we walk. You'll get tired of holding it up soon enough."

As they pulled out of the parking deck, Alyssa asked, "Could we pick up the painkillers on the way to my apartment, please?"

Robert nodded. "Alyssa, about yesterday…"

"Can we talk about it at my apartment? I think that would be better, if you can stay a bit."

40

SATURDAY, SEPTEMBER 4, ALYSSA'S APARTMENT

A LARGE GLASS of water half-empty in front of her, Alyssa sat on the end of the couch and looked at Robert sitting in a chair, the end table between them. She took a deep breath and let it out. She needed this conversation to happen, but her belly ached from dread. Another deep breath was all the delay she would allow herself. She started to speak, and Robert interrupted her.

"About yesterday. I didn't intend for anything to happen. Summer came for Clay's therapy. We talked while he slept. She elicited some emotions I didn't intend, and it went from there. I sure didn't intend to have you see us in bed. We are separated, but I don't want to hurt you."

Alyssa nodded, grateful for the easy start. "I know. It was an accident, and it hurt, but not as badly as I hurt you so many times. Although you didn't intend for anything to happen, your opening up to Summer was no accident. You two have been friends for years. She turned to you when Bryce destroyed their marriage. That was no accident either."

Robert sat back, clearly surprised. "You think she planned it?"

Alyssa smiled as a tear spilled from her eye. "Not at all. You two are alike. So kind. You care for your friends more than most people. You enjoy the same competitive activities, but in a friendly way. You both loved your spouses to a fault, even when they hurt you. And you both need that stable, deep, loving relationship to face the hard world. You two are a natural support group."

"Okay, we are alike. What are you saying?"

Alyssa took another deep breath. Once she began this speech, she couldn't stop. She planned to destroy any hope of reconciliation by hurting him as only she could. Her stomach pushed bile to the top of her throat, and a sob floated on top of it, threatening her ability to speak. She held up her hand in a silent plea for time while she counted to ten and swallowed.

"I've been a bad wife to you, Robert. I was a bad wife when I went on a quest for more exciting sex, and I made it worse when I developed feelings and lied about it. But none of that was as bad as what I'm doing to you now."

"What are you doing now?"

"I'm torturing you. I see it in your face every time we are together. It's there right now. When I try to make you love me again, when I try to come back into your life, you want me to, but you don't want me to. I've hurt you so badly that you fear me. You can't trust me. You walk on eggshells around me, trying to avoid the next time I break your heart. The hell I forge inside you must be excruciating. I'm sorry for that. I'm sorry for everything."

"Alyssa, that isn't—"

"Let me finish, please. And don't deny it to make me feel better. I've known you for twenty-four years, through good times and bad, and I know when you are hurting. This time is the worst I've ever seen. I guess that's fitting."

He nodded.

"I've thought a lot over the past few weeks, but the jumble in my head and my heart started to fit together yesterday. You didn't accidentally end up in bed with Summer. Not consciously, and you wouldn't plan to go to bed with anyone yet, probably not for a while. Subconsciously, though, you know you two make a good match. You were emotional, she was there, and good things happened."

Tears flowed down her cheeks, but her breathing remained steady as she spoke, unwilling to stop for fear of not restarting.

"Robert, I am through hurting you. Seeing your pain crushes me worse this time because my own selfishness stokes it. I wish we could return to the loving marriage we had, but I destroyed that marriage, and every effort I make to rekindle it causes you pain."

She sniffed the tears flowing from her nose and continued.

"You need a loving partner to help you heal and put our history behind you. You deserve a life filled with joy and happiness, not dread and mistrust. Had I understood earlier, I would have stopped then. Now that I do understand, I won't continue."

This is so hard. Keep going. He deserves this.

"Robert, be with Summer, if that's what you want. She's a good woman, kind and beautiful. She cares about you as much as I do, I'm certain of it. Maybe she can help you face the world with the same kind, trusting heart that I stole from you."

He opened his mouth to speak.

She held up her hand. "I know. It's too soon. Start slowly.

Spend time together. Let her turn your thoughts from the bad to the good. Start looking forward to seeing her instead of dreading seeing me. Let her put a smile on your face every day."

She forced a smile to show the sincerity of her words despite the tears dripping on her chest.

"I'll stop trying to get back into your heart. You'll only see me accidentally when I see Clay, and only until he goes to school in January. I won't contest the divorce. I'll do all those things so you will move forward to be happy."

A jittery breath threatened to stop her. *Keep going.*

"Yesterday crystalized everything for me. What I want most is for you to be happy, to be rid of the misery I cause you. For you to have that, I have to stop hurting you. I told Summer the same thing at the hospital. Please, let me walk away and stop hurting you, and go find the happiness you deserve."

"Alyssa, don't—"

Now finish it. Put the nail in the coffin.

"You'll never take me back, Robert. You're too smart, too fair-minded. I confess my love. I confess my understanding that you will be happier with another woman. I confess that I only want you to stop hurting on my account. All those things destroy me inside, but they are true. I'd rather live alone forever than continue hurting you, so I'll confess one last thing."

She took a deep breath and focused her blurred vision on his face, maybe for the last time.

"Yesterday afternoon, I came back here to think. A woman at the pool suggested that the best way to get over a man was to find another one. I decided I want to move on. It was a weak moment, but I went to see Hayden."

Robert stood, shook his head, and walked out.

Alyssa leaned her head into the cushions and cried.

❧

Alyssa opened the door and pulled Keegan close to weep on her shoulder in the doorway. When Alyssa stopped crying, they stepped inside enough to close the door.

"I did it, Keegan. I gave him my blessing, then I sent him away so he'll never come back. It's horrible."

"What did you do?"

"I told him to move on, to get away from me and the pain I cause. He clearly didn't want to, so I hurt him, one last time, so badly he'll never want me again. I told him I slept with Hayden."

"After trying so hard, you nuked everything? You still had a chance. Why did you tell him that?"

"So he would be angry enough to let go."

"You lied to him?"

Alyssa slumped. "No. I saw Hayden. If I had to force Robert away, it had to be authentic. I visited Hayden after I decided to let Robert go."

"Do you want to be with Hayden after what he did?"

"No. To be fair, I unintentionally trashed my marriage as much as he did intentionally. I hoped he could make me orgasm, which I haven't done since Robert threw me out, but that plan failed too. Something good came from it. I saw his true person in his eyes. I wish I had seen it sooner."

"You slept with Hayden, intentionally, to drive Robert away, just in case he didn't go on his own?"

"Yes. Robert always ponders 'what if.' He has been cold, and his eyes are dead, but at the same time, deep down, he refuses to give up on us. The hardest thing I've ever done was meet that sleazebag, but I did it to end Robert's suffering. He'll hate me forever, but now he can move on without feeling guilty. I'm just the bitch who broke his…his heart."

She sobbed into Keegan's shoulder. Keegan guided her to the couch and held her until she stilled. "Alyssa, come on. It's been a rough day. Let's get you out of those dirty clothes and into the shower. Wash some of your pain away."

"Can you help me cover this? I can't get it wet." She held up the brace.

With Alyssa's hand in a plastic bag, Keegan needed to help undress Alyssa without bumping the damaged hand. Keegan surprised Alyssa by pulling her own shirt over her head.

"What are you doing?"

"Getting in with you. You won't get that sweat and funk out of your hair with only one hand. I'm going to get you clean. You can manage on your own later, but tonight, you get clean."

Keegan washed Alyssa's hair, scratching out the grit on her scalp and separating the hair to get it clean, then running her fingers through it under the water, taking her time rinsing it. She put in the conditioner, then soaped and scrubbed her body with a sudsy cloth before removing the foam using her hands in the water, wiping down from shoulders to feet. Though this had been a thorough, utilitarian shower, Alyssa felt warm, relaxed, and glad to let the suds drain away some of today's pain.

Keegan looked up. "Not to kick a girl while she's down, but you're prickly. Give me your razor."

Keegan shaved Alyssa's armpits, then moved to her legs, taking her time while making it evident that she had shaved someone else's body before. She nudged Alyssa's thighs apart. "This too."

"You can leave that. It isn't going to get much use."

"No. You are getting the full spa treatment. Spread those legs." She soaped Alyssa's lips, then tugged them tight as she passed the razor over them.

Alyssa exhaled the breath she had been holding, then held

another. She steadied her body with her hand against the shower wall, nervous that the razor in her crotch was not in her hand.

Keegan slowed and spoke. "Since I have your attention, I want an honest answer. Did you really decide to let Robert go before you saw Hayden?"

Alyssa swallowed and looked down at Keegan focused on her work. "I did. He deserves better."

"Are you certain wanting to get rid of Robert wasn't an excuse to visit that cock artist? I'm not badgering you, but you've invented all kinds of pretenses to see him. He's your kryptonite, Alyssa."

Alyssa shook her head. "Not this time. Yes, I wanted an orgasm. I've been so frustrated that way. But, no, I decided to see Hayden precisely because Robert could never forgive me for it. He could move on without any reservations."

"You sure that's all?"

"Well, I confirmed I was done with Hayden. I felt nothing but contempt for him. He couldn't make me come, not even with all his tricks, so I don't want even his cock again. And he cemented his status as a piece of shit as a person. Truthfully, my main goal was to drive Robert away."

"For someone who wanted to reconcile, you scorched your marriage."

"Robert has to choose to cast me aside. I want him to be happy, even if he's with someone else. He isn't happy with me any longer." She teared up again. "It hurts, Keegan. I guess I deserve it, but it hurts so much."

Keegan stood and wrapped Alyssa in her arms. "I know. The right thing often does."

41

SUNDAY, SEPTEMBER 5, ALYSSA'S APARTMENT

ALYSSA HELD HER hand over her mouth as she spoke into the phone. "Susan, sweetie, do you have a few minutes?"

"Sure. What's that noise in the background?"

"I'm at the pool. I needed to get out of the apartment a bit."

"So you called to tell me you trashed your marriage from the fucking pool? What, you think I won't make a scene because there are people around you? I'm on the phone, Mom. I can scream at you all I want. You should have thought this through, but you aren't thinking these days, are you?"

"Actually, I'm thinking better than I have in months. I'm here so I don't make a scene after you tell me to go to hell. I didn't think you would know yet."

"Somebody has to check on Dad every day. Since you fucked up, that's me. We talked last night. Why did you give up?"

"I was hurting your dad by trying to reconcile. I wouldn't continue hurting him. I let him go."

"Why hurt him by rubbing your boyfriend in his face? Goddamn, Mom. That's cold."

I hate lying to her, but she'll tell him if I tell her the truth. All the pain will go for nothing. "I was being honest. If it was to be the last time we spoke other than through attorneys, I wanted to be honest with everything. He needed to know that I couldn't give Hayden up."

"Fuck that, Mom. You didn't have to say anything. You never had to reconcile with Dad. You could have shuffled him off on Summer and fucked your boy toy forever if that's what you wanted. You didn't have to spit in his face on your way out."

"I didn't intend it that way." Alyssa was grateful for the numbness that had woken her this morning. It swallowed the unspeakable pain this conversation should cause.

"You stupid bitch. How did you think he would take it? My mother didn't have it in her to be that cruel, not even to someone she hates."

"I know."

"You know? Fuck. Here's something to know. When you did that to him, you killed my mother. The miserable woman on the phone isn't my mother, she's the bitch who ruined my family. I'll never speak to you again. If you come near me, I'll make you wish you hadn't. Never contact me again."

The line went dead. Even the numbness couldn't swallow all this pain at once. Alyssa cried behind her sunglasses a while.

As expected. I knew I'd lose her when I gave him up. I hate this, but I have to do it. Maybe one day I'll get the chance to explain the truth.

Keeping her hand dry, she climbed into the pool, bent, and screamed into the water before emerging, taking a breath, and doing it again.

At least the water hides my tears.

❧

"I'm glad you're wearing a bikini today."

Alyssa turned her head to see a young woman settling into the chair beside her. She smiled. "Yes. It works better than wet clothes. Thanks for the advice last week."

"Did it work?"

"Sort of. Not like you suggested."

The young woman leaned closer. "Did you find a great fuck?"

"One of the best I've ever had."

"And did you have a huge orgasm?"

"Not even close."

"Then it wasn't that good."

"Oh, it was. This guy is a master, and he had help. They stimulated all my spots."

"But no big O?"

"It wasn't the right guy."

The young woman rolled her eyes. "Let me guess. It wasn't your husband, so you were too hung up to enjoy it. I thought you said it worked."

"You're partially right, and it did work. I'll never get back with my husband."

"That doesn't make sense. You won't get back with him, but another guy doesn't ring your bell?"

"Right. I couldn't be happier. Nor more miserable. It's costing me my entire family." Alyssa took a swig of her beer.

"And you're happy about that. Whatever works for you. Sounds nuts."

"Maybe I'm nuts, but I hope one day you find people you love enough to drive away. Even a short ride can be glorious while it lasts. It's excruciating for them to push me away, but I can't hurt them anymore. They will be just fine. That's everything I could ever want."

"You must be some kind of masochist. When you are ready to get back on the horse for real, I hope you are better at it."

"I'll never get back on that horse again. He's gone."

42

TUESDAY, SEPTEMBER 7, ALYSSA'S OFFICE

Alyssa knocked on Frank's open office door. "I'm sorry for being late this morning, Frank. It was a rough weekend, and I am moving slow today." She held up her damaged hand. "If I had known you wanted to see me, I would have been here earlier."

"It's fine, Alyssa. No need to apologize. Meeting now is fine with me." He gestured for her to join them in the sitting area.

Frank's wife, Patricia, nodded beside him on the couch in his office. "Absolutely, dear. I understand."

Frank leaned forward. "It hasn't been just a rough weekend, has it, Alyssa? You have had a rough month or so, haven't you? You get your work done, but you are here less. You have made some minor mistakes. You have bags under your eyes. Your hair is a little off. Clay was in a wreck, but it is more than that, isn't

296

it? I have seen you and Robert in public, but not together. Is everything all right, Alyssa?"

She felt like a child about to be punished. Her stomach tightened, and she shifted in her chair to protect her rear end. *I thought I was normal here, at least. No point in denying it.* "Things have been tough. Clay's physical therapy is progressing, and he will heal. Robert and I, well, you noticed that we weren't together in public. I've made some changes, and you will see the old me at the office very soon. I just need to focus."

"I think I can help you with that." He leaned back on the sofa. "I won't be around forever, and neither will Patricia. The company needs a better succession plan than we have. I've watched you the last couple of years. You are good at what you do, and you are excellent with the people you work for, work with, and supervise. People respond to you."

"They are good people."

"True, but I see the impact you have on them. They like working with you. They work harder for you than for their own supervisors, even those who report to me. I want to tap into that power and give you an opportunity. I want you to become my protégé."

Alyssa's stomach relaxed. A warm flicker of pride kindled in her chest. *I thought he was going to reprimand me. I'm due a good day. Maybe this is it.* "I'm flattered. What would that mean?"

Patricia laughed. "My dear, he wants you to take his place when he retires. That's what it would mean. You would become CEO."

Her stomach retightened. She only ran the training kitchens. Several people reported directly to Frank who would surely be angry about being passed over. She felt confident making decisions, but the whole company would take more knowledge and savvy. "That is a lot to process. You have plenty of years left. Why start this now?"

"So I can retire in three years and spend those good years doing something besides running restaurants."

"What about the people already in line?"

Frank shook his head. "They are good people, very good at their own specialties, and I don't want to lose a single one of them. But they don't have the ability to see the entire picture, nor do they get the most from their people. The CEO must understand the strategy, then get everyone involved, both inside and outside the company, to follow it as if it were their own idea. I see that ability in you. Given what is occurring at home, maybe this provides a welcome distraction?"

A distraction that could fill the void in my life. It won't replace my family, but it could fill the time so I don't miss them as frequently. "A new challenge at work could help me recover my footing. What would becoming your protégé entail?"

"I envision a three-year process. You will begin by shadowing me. You'll sit with me during some of my office work, join some meetings, and travel with me on some business trips. You will do the same with Patricia, who runs more of the company than people realize. When you are ready, you will replace Patricia as president, and I'll name you as my successor-in-waiting."

"Won't people think that I'm being groomed as soon as I stop running the training kitchens?"

He grinned. "Good insight. They will. Thus, you will continue to run them. You will create your own succession plan and let your successor assume your responsibilities as you assume mine. Your successor will step in when you become president."

"I'm shocked and honored, Frank. It's a lot to consider right now. Can I have time to think about it?"

He chuckled. "I would have rescinded the offer had you

accepted on the spot. Please take time to think. Talk about it with your family, maybe some limited confidants you can trust, but please keep this secret. This process only works if you can learn while people are straight with you. Why don't you get back to me on Monday?"

⁕

Alyssa reread the text for the tenth time. *The timing on this could have been better, like a week ago or thirty years from now.* "For my entire adult life, you have guided and advised me. There's an opportunity at work. I'd like your thoughts while I consider my decision. I don't have the right to ask, and it's fine if you tell me to go to hell, but I will ask anyway. Can I please talk with you about it?"

Just send it. The worst he can do is say no.

Or intentionally give me bad advice.

He wouldn't do that. He's too good a man.

Even though you have hurt him in the worst ways? The last time intentionally? He might relish some payback.

He might. It's a chance I'm willing to take.

She hit send and turned to the next three months of her kitchen schedule. She finished November before her phone pinged with a text.

"Does the opportunity involve you moving away? If so, take it."

Expecting a snarky reply didn't prevent it from aching in her chest.

"It doesn't entail a move. I understand. Sorry to have bothered you."

"Does it impact the kids?"

"I will spend more time at the office and travel more. I expect more money, but unsure how much. I guess your lawyer can demand more child support and alimony."

"I don't want any money."

"I know. Bad joke. Attorneys often need to justify their fees though."

Alyssa put her phone in her pocket when no reply came. As she closed her computer for the day, a ping announced a text.

"I'll help you one last time. Come to the house Friday at 6:00."

43

FRIDAY, SEPTEMBER 10, HOME

Alyssa straightened her blouse and skirt. She wanted Robert to see her as a potential CEO if he'd never again see her as his wife. She refused to walk in unannounced again, despite having kept her key. A cold hand gripped her heart as she raised her finger to the doorbell. It squeezed and twisted when she saw the fuzzy outline of a short blonde woman through the privacy glass.

"Hey, Alyssa. Robert said you would be visiting. Come in." Summer smiled and stepped out of the doorway to let Alyssa in. "I'd hug you, but I'm dripping sweat. He's so big."

He's big? Her clothes look thrown on. God, I interrupted them fucking again. Alyssa put her hand over her mouth. "I didn't mean to interrupt. If now isn't a good time…"

"Nonsense." Her eyes went wide. "Oh. You thought… No, Alyssa. I'm working with Clay. Robert is in his office."

Even Alyssa's racing heart trailed her brain as it recovered from what she had assumed. Desperate to fill the pause, she let words tumble out. "Is he okay?"

"Clay or Robert?"

"Robert. Both. You are sweaty and in workout clothes, I assumed I had interrupted."

Summer smiled. "No, but thanks for noticing. Clay is getting stronger. He misses you."

The measured response let Alyssa recover her train of thought. "I miss him too. He told me not to come this week. I guess Robert told him we were through."

"He must have. Clay's upset that you quit."

The thought of giving up churned her stomach. Her love for her family, and the terrible thing it had made her do, compounded her nausea.

"I'm sure. It was the right thing to do. Please tell him I love him and I'll talk with him soon. I haven't changed my mind since the hospital. How has Robert been since then?

Summer shook her head. "Robert can choose to tell you how he is."

Oh god. What did I do? "Summer, what does that mean? Is he all right?"

Summer patted Alyssa's shoulder and gave a half smile with sad eyes. "It means go to the office and find out."

✀

Alyssa stuck her head in Robert's office, unwilling to walk in unannounced and afraid of seeing a man she'd broken. "Robert?"

Robert didn't look up from his computer. He sat straight. He looked strong and focused, if a bit annoyed. "Come in. Close the door."

"I intended to." She sat in the chair facing his desk. He didn't look up. *He's gritting his teeth. I guess it's justified.* She sat, his familiar look warning her not to interrupt his thoughts, watching and waiting for him to look toward her. She counted to sixty, then one hundred. "Never mind. You don't want me here. I'll figure it out myself." She rose.

He clicked the mouse, and the printer behind him whirred to life. With a sigh, his tight lips and gritted teeth relaxed as he shifted his attention to her.

"I agreed to talk. Sit down and tell me what's happening. I have another topic after, so you first."

Alyssa recounted Frank's offer, highlighting the travel and time commitments. They discussed the intracompany politics, the expected turnover, her comfort with the change from a tactical role to a strategic one, and the fact that she would become a more public figure.

Alyssa leaned forward. She wanted to be close to talk about the family impact. She wanted to read his emotions in every movement. And she missed his scent.

"It would take me away from the kids, not that either one wants to see me. They talk with you. What will they think?"

"Susan is in Houston, and she's done with you. She won't care."

Alyssa knew how Susan felt. Hearing Robert articulate it so succinctly tightened the cold grip around her heart anyway. "She told me I killed her mother. I know how she feels. Maybe one day we can talk."

"Clay will eventually want you around, probably before he goes to school. He will be fine with the job, unless you don't see him over breaks or on holidays. It will be worse if you miss because of your boyfriend than your job. To salvage a relationship with him, make the time when he's home. You have struggled with that lately."

"I ruined everything. I'm sorry, for what it's worth."

"It isn't worth much. Twenty-four years, a marriage, two kids, other family and friends, all thrown away. An apology? Regret? Insignificant versus what you made the rest of us sacrifice." He leaned back in the chair. "Take the job. It will occupy the time you used to spend on your family."

Alyssa swallowed a sob. "I deserved that. Maybe one day, they will talk to me. Thank you for your insight." Empty inside save for profound sadness inching its way up from her chest, she wanted to continue what might be her last conversation with the one man she loved. She swallowed another sob and clasped her hands on the desk to still their trembling.

"What was it you wanted to talk with me about?"

Robert pulled the document off the printer and slid it across the desk. "It's a legal separation agreement. It isn't required for the divorce, but it defines the date of our separation as August first and establishes fifty-fifty financial agreements around our joint debts, the kids' college expenses, and other obligations while we are separated. It sets some boundaries around when you can visit and what type of contact you and I have until the divorce. It also creates penalties for any dishonesty or fraud in our communication."

Her abs tightened and her back stiffened as panic set in. *No. Don't take the kids.* "You said you wouldn't keep me from the kids. What kind of limits?"

"I'm not keeping you from the kids, they are, though not in this document. The agreement limits visitation to when you have been invited by one or both children, when there is a medical emergency or other necessity that I cannot meet, or when you have previously cleared the visit with me. And it places our bedroom strictly off-limits."

Her body relaxed. *I can live with those.*

"I don't want to repeat that episode any more than you do.

I'll stay out unless the medical emergency requires the first aid kit. Good enough? What are the penalties for dishonesty?"

"Five thousand dollars per verifiable occurrence, netted between occurrences on each side, to be kept in an escrow account with a third attorney."

Alyssa nodded. "Any other surprises?"

"No. Have your attorney read it."

"I told you I won't contest the divorce, and I caused the dishonesty penalties. Give me a pen. I'll sign this." She signed her copy and his.

"I hope you brought your checkbook."

"Why?"

Robert pulled a large envelope from his desk and slid it to her. "Open it."

Shame disguised as vertigo struck her as she looked at the pictures. Close-ups showed tears on her cheeks through the window of her car. Wider shots showed her car in Hayden's driveway and her walking to his front door, scowling with every step. At least twenty shots chronicled every moment of her stripping her dress off, dropping it at his door, and stepping inside nude.

Anger swept through her body. Heat rolled up her face along with the blood as she blushed. For an instant, she readied herself to storm out, furious he'd had her surveilled after they separated.

She froze in her seat. Deep sadness anchored her with an icy weight settling low in her belly and growing. These images would have hurt Robert worse than they hurt her.

"Robert, why?"

He slid a second envelope to her. "Now these."

Alyssa teared up but scanned the photos of her opening Hayden's door, picking up her dress, and walking to her car, the same scowl on her face as when she had entered. Two close-ups showed what was clearly semen dripping down her thigh as she walked. The last four showed close-ups of her mouth open, throat engorged, tears on her cheeks, and body still nude in her car before she slipped the dress over her head and drove away.

He knew she had not lied to him about seeing Hayden. She signed the agreement, so what did he hope to gain by showing her this?

"Robert, why do you have these? This occurred during our separation. It isn't useful in the divorce, which I'm not contesting in any event."

He pulled the photo of her walking into Hayden's door and the one of her exiting. "Look at the time stamps."

Alyssa wiped her eyes before looking in the lower corners of the photos. "They look about right. What about them?"

"Twenty minutes."

"Okay?"

"You were in and out in twenty minutes. You went for a 'moving on' fuck with the guy who owned you, and you were out in twenty minutes. And mad as hell the whole time."

He picked up the clearest picture of her screaming in her car.

"I've never seen you this upset, not in all the years I've known you. And every time you used our open marriage arrangement, the worst emotion you ever had was disappointment from a lover who underperformed. Yet here you are, after being with your favorite, screaming? Not the Alyssa I know. Tell me the truth."

She took a breath to cover how his accurate assessment rattled her. *I can't let him continue. I'll hurt him again. Sell this.*

She waved a hand dismissively and cocked her head to the side, trying to look nonchalant and self-centered. "I'm a different person. You know, the one who trades everything she loves for a good lay. The one who lies to the people closest to her. The one who gets thrown out of her house and exiled by her children. I'm clearly not stable."

She picked up the close shot of her semen-dripping cunt. "You see the evidence. I didn't lie to you."

"I don't think you could, or would, except about the why. Be honest."

He deserves better than me. "I wanted him. That's all."

"Let me tell you what I think, then. I think you were honest with me about how much you wanted to repair our marriage. I think you were honest with every word you spoke at that meeting. I think you were honest when you said you realized that you were hurting me with your efforts. Hell, I even believe you were honest when you told me that Summer would be better for me than you, and you wanted me to move on."

She looked him in the eye. *Believe me, Babe.* "I was. All of that was true then, and it's true now."

"The pain you saw in my face when we saw each other, you interpreted as fear and mistrust. You thought I didn't trust you, even though you know I trust people to do what is best for themselves at the time."

"How could you trust me after all I had done? You made it plain you didn't trust me. I know you too. I know pain when I see it."

"I was in pain. My wife had left me for another man."

I never left. "You threw me out, remember?"

"Because you fell in love with him. That's when you left me. I merely formalized the living arrangements."

His words cowed her, stealing her breath and dismantling the defiance that had stiffened her spine. She slumped forward and looked at the desk. After two deep breaths she could again speak.

"Fair enough."

"I saw everything you were doing to work back in. I couldn't accept your efforts. You fantasized that everything could be fixed, and it couldn't. It made me sad to see you work so hard at recovering yourself without any possible reward."

"Why didn't you stop me?"

"I told you every chance I got that we wouldn't reconcile. You were unfazed. I turned you down in your apartment, but you kept trying. You watched for my signals with Nancy and Cassandra, and I told you we were done, but you continued. This is where I get a little confused. Had you decided to stop trying before or after you saw Summer and me in bed?"

He's right so far. Confirm it so he believes he is better off without you.

"I was headed that way, but seeing you with her got me there in a hurry. I had lost any chance to come home unless I became a monster determined to wrench your heart every day. I realized that you two are good together, and that she is the kind of person who could help you heal. So I told you both that very thing."

"And you told me you went to Hayden. You didn't need to do that, and it doesn't look like you enjoyed it."

"No. The man is a sleaze. I can't take enough showers to get his slime off me." *Shit. Shouldn't have said that.*

"You didn't say why, but here is my guess. You did it to push me so far and so hard that I would never take you back. You wanted me to move on and be happy, so you burned every bridge between us with one final insult. You hated it, but you did it anyway. You were willing not only to give up our marriage but to make sure there was no way either of us could ever return to it. How am I doing so far?"

She tried to recover. "I'm not that thoughtful. By then, I just wanted to come. I haven't since we separated. He's good at making me come."

"Uh-huh." He held up the picture of her screaming again.

"This is not your satisfied orgasm face. Be honest with me or write me a check. You were trying to end things for good."

Alyssa hung her head. *He always could read me. Accept it. Be honest.* "Yes."

"After all you had done, why?"

A seed of something lodged in her chest. It had spikes that ripped at her, but warmed and soothed her like warm towels from the dryer. Her chest tightened around it, soaking up both feelings after weeks of nothing. The seed grew, poking and tearing at her ribs while soothing them at the same time. Her breath caught when the pain tore at her skin from the inside like she would explode, only for her to feel the warmth helping her withstand the pain.

I love him so much it hurts. I can bear the pain of him leaving if he is happy. Tell him, and let him go.

"You *were* better off without me. I had to let you go, and I knew you wouldn't until it was your choice. The pain of being apart is bearable because you can be better off. I love making you happy, even if I end up in the rubble of everything I destroyed. I intentionally obliterated all other options so you can go with a clear conscience."

"You tried. Like all of your wild plans during this separation, it backfired. It backfired because you are who you are, no matter how you try to be something different. You tried to be heartless and cruel, but that isn't in your nature. Nobody who knows you believed you were trying to hurt me, especially not me. Your trump card revealed your entire hand."

Her vision blurred as tears welled in her eyes. She waved a hand and spoke as her chin quivered. "Well, I'm just failing at everything. I can't maintain my marriage without destroying it, and I can't destroy it without repairing it."

"You didn't have the right partner."

"I didn't have a partner. I don't understand."

"Alyssa, you are repairing the broken trust over the past few weeks. You have restored your priorities to where they were before your trip to Houston. You aren't seeing other people, even though you can. You have put the family first despite the pain it causes you. I don't want you to bear that pain, and I don't want us to give up on a great marriage."

This couldn't be true. She had stabbed at his most vulnerable emotions to drive him away where she could never hurt him again, but he was offering to stay. His face didn't show pain; his head wasn't red. He was being sincere. *Surely he doesn't mean we can reconcile.*

For an instant, she dared to hope. The warmth in her chest spread through her body without tearing at her skin.

"Robert, what are you saying?"

Robert pulled her wedding and engagement rings from the drawer of his desk. He held them up to her. "Do you want these back? If you do, then you can come home, subject to some conditions."

Alyssa leaned forward, flailing to wipe the tears from her eyes so she could see clearly the magic he held in his fingers. Her heart pounded in her throat. She struggled to keep from leaping across the desk into his lap. *Whatever they are, I agree.*

"I want to come home. What are your conditions?"

"First, we close our marriage. The only exception is if we both decide to share a person together. No outside partners, no arrangements, just us."

That's easy. "Done. You are all I want. Thank you for letting me explore, but the cost is too high. Never again."

"Second, tell the kids why you did what you did. The whole story about splitting up and trying to drive me away. They need to know you are more stable than you appeared so they will want to stay a family."

God, he's even helping me with the hard parts. "I want that too. I didn't tell Susan because I didn't want her to tell you. You may have to help me get her to answer the phone."

"Third, thank Keegan and Drew for keeping an eye on you."

"Did they do it on their own, or did you employ them?"

"They volunteered. Keegan that first night. Drew after you first encountered him at the park."

"They both helped me think through all this. Did you put them up to that? Did he take the pictures at Hayden's? You couldn't have been there."

"I didn't put them up to anything. He did take the surveillance photos. He's good at it."

"After I watched him on the Fourth, it's fair he saw me naked."

"Everyone in that intersection saw you naked, and it's a good view. I expect he retained copies."

"I'll thank them. I would even without your condition." A cackle burst from her throat. "Maybe I'll autograph his copies of the photos. Any other conditions? I'm ready to accept your offer." She smiled and looked into his eyes.

He didn't smile.

This must be the hard one. I'll do it, whatever it is.

His eyes narrowed. "Last condition. You submit to punishment."

"Submit to punishment? What does that mean?"

"You need to learn that your actions have consequences. A defined punishment may help you remember that."

"Robert, the last month alone cemented that lesson with pain I couldn't have imagined. What could be worse than that?"

"That was horrible for both of us. I believe a distinct, painful punishment for you alone is in order."

Her chest tightened as she watched him. His stony face mimicked his look when he'd thrown her out a month ago. His mind was made up. Leaden dread pulled her stomach to the floor.

What did I do to him? You destroyed him, and the reassembled pieces are different, harder.

This was unlike him. He had never been vengeful. And he had never, ever hurt her. She watched for the tinge of a smile, a wink, anything to indicate he was teasing, but saw nothing but impassive patience as he waited for her response.

He's not vengeful; he's fair. And he's a really good teacher. He only punished the children when they did something dangerous. Trust him.

I did something dangerous. Extending the separation is the only punishment I won't accept. He can keep my phone, drive me to and from work, whatever he wants, I'll do.

"I said I would accept your conditions. I meant it. Impose any punishment except extending our separation. I can't bear that any longer. What do you want?"

He shook his head. "Later. Extending the separation is not your punishment."

Slow down a moment. You're almost home. Find out how close you came to losing it forever.

"How close were we, really, to never getting back together?"

He sighed. "A hair's breadth, maybe closer, but you already knew that. You hurt me, Alyssa. You made it quite clear that you wanted someone else over me, over the family. I wanted to see you happy, but I couldn't bear your changes. You went from the kind, loyal, trustworthy woman I married to a lying, conniving harlot with no regard for the consequences, for her or anyone else. Our marriage had died, and only amputating the dead parts would keep the rot from killing us both. Keegan and Jessica prevented me from acting too quickly. You owe them."

Alyssa settled back in her chair to avoid swaying as his assessment stunned her. *Way too close.* "I know Keegan kept an eye on me. What did Jessica do?"

"Aside from getting Drew to watch you also? She was here every day, regardless of the work schedule. She came under the pretense of checking on Clay, but she always came when I was here, and often when you were here. Every day, some days more subtly than others, she reminded me that you were, at your core, a good woman who loved me very much. She kept me alert for you to get better."

"Get better?"

"That's the way she put it. She said this episode was like an illness. It had to run its course, and with luck, you would survive it."

"Survive it?" *I mentioned dying to Keegan. I was worse than I thought.*

"Yep. She worried you would break, mentally, at least."

"And you kept me at bay?"

"At bay, yet always under watchful eyes. It killed me to worry about you, but if you didn't change, I couldn't let you implode inside the family. Those first couple of weeks were scary. And Jessica kept me in the right frame of mind."

The thought of making people think she would die stiffened her shoulders. They relaxed just as quickly, like a jet executing a touch-and-go on a runway. *I was horrible to him, but he still kept me safe. What a fool I was.* "I'll thank her too. I owe a lot of people, including you."

Tears spilled from her eyes in hot streaks down her cheeks. She cried while she watched him. Elation and relief battled within her racing heart while warm comfort calmed her ragged breath.

When she settled, she wiped her eyes with the back of her hand and chuckled. "I'm so happy."

Time to make up. We need to feel like we're in love again. Let's recover our favorite ground. "I agreed to all your conditions, but I have conditions of my own."

"You do? I'm willing to listen, but you don't have much standing to negotiate."

"First, you have to tell me you love me like you did the very first time."

He smiled. "It's been a long time since you pulled that one out. Okay, here goes. I love you, Alyssa. You are my drug, and I'm hopelessly addicted."

She giggled, but her stomach quivered. Her nipples tingled. She wanted him, and that was his best line, whether he knew it or not.

"It was corny then, and it's corny now, but I love it. And I love you, Robert. Second, I've missed you calling me Baby. Please, call me Baby again."

"That's an easy one, Baby."

Her entire body flamed up. She had made too many mistakes with Hayden, and letting that piece of shit call her Baby was one of the worst. That name was reserved for Robert.

"Ooh. I got all tingly. It's been too long. You met my conditions. Can I come home?"

He opened his arms. "Come here, Baby."

Alyssa burst around the desk and piled onto his lap. She hugged his neck with both arms, pinning his face to her chest while kissing the top of his head.

This is all I need. Oh, I love those arms squeezing my waist. I'm home. Oh god, I'm home.

Alyssa pulled back, looked Robert in the eye, and kissed him, lingering on his lips before parting her lips and fluttering her tongue over his, asking to come inside. He opened his mouth. They fell into a familiar pattern of thrust-and-parry, built over years of make-out sessions.

Robert pulled back and down, nipping along her jawline to her throat, where he sucked on the muscle, sending a spark through her neck into her chest.

Alyssa put her hand on his forehead and pushed back. "Stop. Before we go any further, make me your wife again. Please, Babe, put those rings on my finger."

He brought the fingertip to his lips, planting a kiss there before sliding the two rings onto her finger and settling them into the groove they had created over the years.

Alyssa held her hand in front of her, admiring the rings with an awe she hadn't known since Robert asked her to marry him twenty-three years earlier. The built-in shelves caught her eye. She pointed to a collage of four of the pictures Robert had shown her earlier. The tears, her nude walking in, her nude walking out, and her screaming in the car told the story of her visit to Hayden that day. "You had those framed?"

"That was the day you decided you loved me again. Those are hard to view, but they say more about your love than any others. Even more than the pregnant bikini pictures. They will hang in here."

"Babe, how did you know I would even come back?"

"It didn't matter. You showed how much you loved me that day regardless of what we decided tonight. I would have that picture framed either way. Plus, if you didn't come back, it would be the only way I got to see that great ass of yours again."

"Funny. You will put it in a drawer when anybody comes over."

"It's where only I can see it, but yes, it's only for me, nobody else gets access to it."

"Just like me, Babe." She stood and extended her hand to him. "I'm ready to be home for good. If the last step is my punishment, let's get started. What do I have to do?"

"Let's go to the basement."

⁊

Alyssa followed Robert down the stairs and through a door in the billiard room to the unfinished portion of the basement. *What's in Robert's workshop? Tools. Is he going to smash my phone?*

She froze. Toward the end of the room, a rack made of steel pipes sat in the center of the floor under one of the can lights. It looked almost like a clothes rack or a wide ladder with rungs missing. Hinges and pins created multiple lockable joints. Attached to several locations, she recognized leather cuffs like Hayden had used to attach her to the gymnast's vault at the bondage house.

He's going to lock me up down here. It will be uncomfortable, but I'll be home.

A small card table had been set up in the corner. Three leather paddles and some small metal items lay on the velvet.

No. He's going to spank me.

Her nipples tingled. *Please, Robert, give me eighteen. This will be the best pain I've ever had, even if it hurts. This is punishment. He may be harsher than Hayden was. If it brings me home, that's okay.*

"Please, Babe. I'm sorry, and I'll never forget that my actions have consequences. Don't hurt me."

"Alyssa, this is a condition of you coming home. I will not injure you, but this will hurt, likely to your limit, the same way your actions over the past few months have hurt me. We will stop at any time when you say 'poodle.' That will end our session. If you stop early, however, you go home to your apartment. We do not reconcile until you have been sufficiently punished. Do you understand?"

She nodded. "I understand." *If those are the stakes, you can spank me until I bleed. I'll never say "poodle."*

"Let's begin. Alyssa, strip."

I'll give you a show. She swayed her hips as she reached behind her back to unzip her skirt.

"No, Alyssa. You aren't seducing me. Just take off your clothes to be punished."

He's in charge. The queasy stomach that feared Robert would go too far fluttered as he commanded her. She wanted to be his again, and she loved when he took control. She stopped dancing and removed her heels. The cold concrete floor reminded her of the last bondage room she'd visited. Her pussy throbbed. *Hayden stunned me. Robert will devastate me because I want him more.*

After dropping her blouse atop the skirt puddled at her ankles, Alyssa stood still, facing Robert. *Make me get naked.*

"All of it."

She bit her lower lip to hide her smile. Her pussy ached to be filled, quivering low in her belly. She unhooked her bra and let it slide off her arms as she shoved her panties below her knees and dropped them. "I'm ready."

Robert pulled her to the rack. He buckled padded leather belts behind her back, pinning her against one bar across her stomach and another high on her chest, the cold metal sending chills down her legs and up her spine. He attached soft leather cuffs to her wrists, buckling them tight enough to restrain but maintaining circulation. Then he lifted her arms above her head to buckle them into leather cuffs along the side of the rack. With her pulled erect in this way, her back arched.

My ass is sticking out for him to spank it.

Robert stepped to the card table. When he returned, he held up two shiny metal clips with steel marbles hanging from them.

"These are nipple clamps. They are designed to pinch your

nipples, causing pain and numbness. The small balls add weight, intensifying the effect. They can be adjusted using the screw to balance staying on and preventing injury. I'm going to attach them. Let me know if the pain is too much."

The pinch shot through her breast. Her nipple sparked, sending electricity through her body. *That hurts. I'll take it.*

"That hurts, but I can bear it. Please, no tighter."

"Just a little tighter."

He pulled the clip, and his fingers brushed her breast as he turned the screw. The pinch tightened to a dull throb, until she twisted to pull away, lighting a fire in her nipple as the weight jiggled and swayed.

Robert held the other clip in front of her eyes. "Now this one."

The same pinch and stretch shot through her, this time uniting with the shocks still coursing from the first nipple and returning stronger. She groaned. *Damn sensitive nipples.*

He smiled at her. "Those look good. Your nipples are turning a beautiful purple. How do they feel?"

"Like they are being bitten off slowly."

He nodded. "Perfect. Now your feet."

She felt his breath on the backs of her legs as he buckled her ankles into larger versions of the cuffs on her wrists. The carabiners clicked in the quiet room, attaching her cuffs to the rack.

Robert went to the card table in the corner, then returned to Alyssa. He showed her a leather strap in a loop and attached to a handle. He slapped it against his palm. The crack made Alyssa jump. Her nipples screamed at her as the weights swayed, the pain of the stretch clawing on her skin.

That was louder than what Hayden used. It's going to hurt. And make me come even harder.

"Robert, that scares me."

"It makes a loud slap. I admit, it stung more than I thought it would. The first side hits, then the back portion lands to add to the impact. It's an interesting implement. As you have guessed, I'm going to spank you. You have behaved like a spoiled child, so you will be spanked like one. I am unsure if you will hate it or love it. Either way, you will remember tonight, I'm sure."

Then make me love it. "Whichever it is, do it until you are satisfied that I've learned my lesson."

"I will. Let's get you in position."

He moved to the side of the rack. After some metallic clicks, Alyssa braced to be bent over, but she breathed again when Robert crossed in front of her. With two clicks from the other side, her body bent at the waist as the rack bounced forward. The swift move and sudden stop yanked at her nipples, and she wailed.

The clamps jerked, and she thought they were wrenching her nipples off. The new angle tugged from the underside of her breast, a new pinch from the ache she had grown used to from the top. Sparks met in her chest and probed inside her body until they found the top of her pussy. With a deep breath, she started to convert the burning into pleasure.

Nice touch, Robert. If you'll fuck me, too, I could lose my mind. Please…please…

Robert knelt beside her and raised her head by her hair. "We will begin now."

She heard the crack before she felt the hot pain on her ass. She jumped, and her nipples pulled her attention to them from her ass. Another slap followed before Robert caressed both her cheeks, the warmth soothing the pain. His hand perfectly fit her cheek, as it always had, and Alyssa celebrated with a moan after missing that feeling for weeks. Warmth from his palm seeped through her ass to tingle her pussy lips.

So good.

Robert removed his hand. "Two spanks, Baby. Barely any red marks. You haven't learned your lesson yet."

Four loud slaps rained on her ass. She twisted as much as she could, the noise indicating that these hard blows needed to be dispersed.

Six spanks.

Robert caressed her cheeks, stoking the fire building inside her pussy. He ran his fingertip along her slit.

"You are wet. Do you like this?"

Alyssa raised her head to look over her shoulder. "Yes. I like it."

"Let's see if I can change your mind."

Two loud smacks landed at the junction of her cheeks and thighs, followed by two more on her thighs. She wailed as harsher ripples of pain traveled up her ass and over her pussy, tingling and making it clench at itself inside her body. Her belly fluttered as her orgasm churned and grew.

His soothing hand trailed up from the backs of her knees, to the small of her back, and back a few times. When he cupped her pussy and held it, she writhed her hips against his fingers.

Ten. Over halfway there. Help me, Robert.

He released her pussy, and soft footsteps padding out of the room was all she heard. Then there was nothing. She stayed still, straining to listen. The orgasm that had kindled within her simmered, fueled by her bound position and her tits stretching toward the floor.

In the minutes that followed, her ass flushed hot. *Blood rushing into the damaged tissue.*

Warmth spread from her ass across her pussy. Her lips tingled. The channel inside ached to be filled. Cool air confirmed that her lips were wet and blooming open. Her body needed sex. *Oh god, my pussy is on fire. And I can't get relief.*

Why is he leaving me like this?

She moved to make the nipple weights jiggle and pull. The transformation of pain to pleasure improved the more she did it. Electric pain in her breasts stoked the building rapture in her belly when its tendrils tickled its surface. It built, but she needed more stimulation to release it. She writhed, rolled her hips, and shifted her thighs, seeking in vain some pressure on her needy pussy.

Where is Robert?

Her need inflamed her body. With her head hanging down, she watched the sheen of sweat coat her chest. Her nipples were indeed purple. The weights hanging from them swung in little circles when she moved.

Good, but not enough.

Soft footsteps neared her. A nude Robert knelt and again lifted her head by the hair. Like before, he lifted slowly, helping her tired neck muscles do most of the work and not pulling so far as to strain either her neck or her scalp. Nevertheless, the message was clear. He was in charge.

Her belly fluttered at the perfect combination.

"Exquisite, how the waiting turns the pain to pleasure, and then turns the pleasure to, well, not pain, but need? Your body lingers in a purgatory between reaching orgasm and escaping the insatiable arousal. It's quite a delicious torment."

Where did he learn this? I thought he'd spank me until I couldn't sit. This is worse. And so much better. "Yes, stewing in my own juices is torture."

Robert ran a fingertip over the end of her nipple, then around it. Soft tingles cascaded from it over her breast. Then he flicked the weight, sending hot lightning through her body. This time the pain reached all the way to her pussy, where it landed on her simmering orgasm like gasoline. She writhed her hips as she groaned.

He nodded. "You are ready to progress."

Finally. Nudge him. "I notice you are dressed for it."

He stood. His cock hung soft in front of her face. "But not yet ready. Prepare me."

He lifted his cock to her mouth. She sucked him in. After so long without it, his familiar taste was like dessert. *I've missed this.*

Unable to move her head or take him deep, Alyssa sucked and slurped around him, using suction and sound rather than movement to arouse him. She tickled the underside of his head with her tongue, and he began to harden. *He knows I love feeling him grow inside me.*

When he hardened, Robert withdrew. "Good job, Alyssa."

He stepped from her view, but with her head hanging down, she saw his feet take up a position behind her side. She was ready when the smacks echoed in the room, three blows on each cheek, each one harder than the previous. Even prepared, her brain registered a fireball of pain exploding up her back and down her legs. And through her hungry pussy. It twitched inside, desperate for something to hold. She closed her eyes and held her breath, praying her body would settle before the next sensation.

Then she felt what she had wanted for weeks. The wide head of Robert's cock dragged through her wet lips, spreading them and getting wet. He would slide inside soon, and she may explode. After the time simmering in the rack, her body needed it. After the fear of Robert wanting to hurt her, her mind needed it. After weeks apart, her heart needed it. As he pushed, her pussy flexed open, granting him entry before squeezing tight in a familiar embrace. Her heart swelled, forcing a low moan from deep in her chest.

"That's what I need. Keep going."

He pulled back, then drove hard into her. His hips hit her ass, bouncing the nipple weights and tapping her cervix. Golden ropes of pleasure lashed inside her, warming everywhere they touched until they met and knotted around the orgasm building low in her belly, fueling its growing inferno.

Robert established a rhythm and fucked her hard. Her lips dragged with him as he moved, and her channel stretched as he filled her and gripped him as he withdrew, not wanting the momentary feeling of emptiness when only his head remained within her. Her release teased the limits of her body.

Then he stopped. Buried inside but still, Robert spoke.

"Who owns this pussy, Alyssa?"

Where did that come from? He's never asked me that before. He doesn't even think like that. He wouldn't know what Hayden asked me. This is a weird coincidence, but I'll play it off.

"What, Babe?"

Two slaps landed on each cheek, the pain and noise breaking her train of thought.

"Answer me."

"You own my pussy, Babe. You always have."

He fucked her hard, pausing twice to add two more slaps on each cheek. Her orgasm grew, straining against its spot inside her, the constant flares of pain from her nipples and spanks from her burning ass tamping its ability to overflow as it grew massive. *Like last time. This will be enormous. He will destroy me.*

Then he stopped.

"Am I better than your lover?"

He can't know, but the words are identical. He wasn't there, so this has to be a coincidence.

Two more loud cracks filled the air as spanks loosened her tongue.

"Yes, Babe. Of course."

Two more slaps lit stripes of fire on her cheeks.

"You're better than my lover."

He resumed fucking her, faster this time. *He wanted the same answer. How could he know?*

Her orgasm churned inside, the physical sensations growing it even as her worries closed off its escape. Her belly fluttered and her brain fogged as her body wrested control and chased rapture. The familiar tingle vibrated up and down her walls, escaping to linger over her clit. Three strokes and she would shatter.

He stopped, and four cracks filled the room. She knew the question to come and would not hesitate with the truth.

"Do you love me?"

"I love you."

He withdrew from her. Her lips spasmed open and closed, seeking something to complete her release. Her entire body quivered.

"No, Robert. Please, finish me. I'm so close."

With a few clicks, she was rotated upright. Robert stepped in front of her. He removed the nipple clamps. Pain exploded from her nipples as the blood returned and the numbness gave way to pain. It reached within her, adding to her orgasm until it strained against her very skin.

"I know something your lover didn't. You like this. Come for me, Baby."

Before Alyssa could think about what "this" might be, he raised his hand high and thundered it down on her left tit. Already screaming from the pain of the clamp, her breast sent giant shock waves of pain and pleasure through her body, just as it had months ago in Houston. Her orgasm exploded as he tilted her back and entered her in one stroke.

The roaring pain in her tits and the stretching fullness in her pussy sustained the whole-body spasms that yanked against the restraints. Deliciously agonizing waves rolled through her.

He swelled inside her, stretching her to her limit.

I need to feel him come. Stay conscious. He's close.

He exploded exactly where she needed him to. The splash on her cervix lit one final set of orgasmic fireworks in her brain. She passed out while she spasmed.

Alyssa woke but didn't open her eyes. A finger was tracing over them in a figure eight pattern, each pass slightly tighter than the last until it feathered a line across her eyelashes, then widened out at the same rate until it circled over her eyebrows and cheekbones.

I love when he does that. So relaxing.

"Hey, Babe."

"Welcome back." He stopped moving his finger over her eyes.

"Don't stop. You know I like that. Just a little longer."

He resumed brushing over and around her eyes. The leather couch still felt cool on her side and legs, so she knew she hadn't been there long. Robert's leg under her head fit just the way she wanted, and she bent her arm to caress his knee. Exhausted from the session with Robert, she was tempted to nod off under the warm throw, but her heart leaped at the knowledge she was home. She planned to enjoy every moment of this last chance.

I loved that. He can punish me that way any time he wants, especially if I get this treatment afterward. How did he know?

She flinched as fear broke her reverie.

How could he know? He knew what I said to Hayden, but how? I'd better sit up. Shit. My ass is going to kill me. So many blows. But I'll bear it if I can come home.

She pulled his hand for a kiss and sat up. Snuggling against him, she spun her legs over his and hugged his neck. She pulled his face to hers, kissing him soft and long, reveling in every ounce of love shared between their lips.

"Was I sufficiently punished?"

He nodded. "I think so."

"Have I met all the conditions to come home?"

"You have."

Alyssa hugged his neck tight, pressing her body to his. "I'll never leave again."

I need to know how bad I hurt him. "Babe, how did you decide on this punishment? You have never tolerated any hitting before."

"And I still don't like it. But you do."

"Whatever gave you that idea?"

"Hayden told me."

Ice daggers stabbed her chest from the inside. *Even he wouldn't do that. Yeah, the bastard might.*

"Oh, Robert, I'm so sorry. How did that slime get close enough to say anything?"

Robert shook his head. "The coward's way. He emailed."

"He emailed to tell you I enjoyed being spanked?"

"No, he emailed a video of you being spanked, and enjoying it more than anything I've ever seen you enjoy before tonight."

The fucker took a video. Shit. She hung her head and looked at her lap. She had never done anything crueler in her entire life, and Robert had received firsthand proof of it. "That's how you knew what I said."

"Directly from your mouth."

Make this better. "Babe, that was only sex talk. It didn't mean anything, really. I would have said anything to finish that orgasm."

He sighed. "We both know that isn't true. You meant those things. The feelings you admitted to him are why I threw you out in the first place."

He's right. I wish he were wrong, but at the time… "You knew then?"

"No. I assume you visited his house when I threw you out, because his email arrived the next morning. He sent the video to gloat."

"Robert, I'm so sorry. I was a shitty wife, but I truly never meant for you to get hurt. Please know those things I said aren't true any longer. They never should have been."

He caressed her cheek. "We can get past it."

"Is that why you spanked me so much, because you were angry?"

He pulled her close and kissed her again. "I refused to let that man give my wife more pleasure than I could. I spanked you so much because you liked it. Your orgasm proved that."

"It's the biggest one I've ever had. Thank you for it. How long was I out?"

"Nine minutes and thirty-six seconds."

She chuckled. *Maybe we will get past it.* "Of course you timed it."

"After ten minutes I would worry. I would never hurt you."

She lowered the throw to show her left breast, a red hand-print already starting to show. "This and my ass might disagree."

He held up his hand in a stop motion. "That slap only imitated what happened in Houston back in May. You loved it, and it fit with your punishment."

"I did love it, but the soreness hasn't set in on my ass yet."

"And it may not, at least not like it did in July."

"Why not? You spanked me so much more."

"Yes, more than thirty blows to Hayden's eighteen. The difference is, I intended to thrill you. He intended to hurt you."

Alyssa's stomach dropped. *He even used something special to hurt. I'm not surprised, but Robert seems certain.* "How do you know?"

"The paddle. Hayden used a large, leather-covered metal plate. It's designed to cause significant pain and leave large bruises."

"Don't they all do that?"

"Not really. I used what is called a slapper. The looped leather makes a loud sound, telling your brain that it hits harder than it does. I wanted you to perceive a hard spanking without a lot of pain and less damage. He wanted to hurt you, probably to mark you. You will be sore and have a few bruises tomorrow, but nothing like what his beating did to you."

Worry tossed Alyssa's stomach. They had never been interested in bondage or pain before. How would he know all this?

"Babe, I appreciate your luxurious torture, but how do you know all this? We've never even explored it before. Is there something I should know?"

His brow furrowed like it did when he was confused before his eyes widened and he smiled. He understood her concern.

"You thought I had some dark secret. No, Baby. When I considered letting you come back, I went to the sex store downtown and asked if they could recommend any BDSM professionals. I met a professional dominatrix. She analyzed the video and taught me about the equipment. She taught me to make you perceive more distress than was inflicted. She let me borrow the apparatus."

That's what I forgot. He gives me what I want without hurting me. He makes the effort to understand and find the best way. And I ignored his guidance every step of the way.

"You did all that because you thought I would like it, despite being separated?"

"Of course. You clearly didn't trust me to discuss your desire to explore kinky and adventurous sex. You needed to know I'm willing to help you fulfill those desires. You didn't believe my words, so I forced you to accept me into your fantasy. That way you could see for yourself."

Tears blurred her vision. She hugged him tight, afraid the joyful sob welling in her chest would steal her words. He wanted her to be home. He had heard her unfaithful words and seen her slutty actions, yet he brought her home with a gift of pleasure.

I don't deserve him, but since I have him, I will never lose him again. She pulled back to stare and smile at him.

Robert kissed her cheeks. "Why are you crying, Baby?"

"I never thought we would be together again, and here we are. I've never been happier. I love you."

"I thought we were done too. Glad we're not."

Alyssa kissed him, lingering and running her fingers through his hair as he caressed her hip.

She raised her head and sniffed. "What's that smell? Is something burning?"

Robert sniffed, then smiled and pulled their robes from the back of the couch. "We'd better get to the kitchen."

Alyssa looked across her kitchen island, where Summer stood behind dishes of herbed chicken, roasted vegetables, and salad. A bottle of wine sat in a bucket beside two glasses. She ran to hug her friend.

Summer smiled and hugged her back. "Thank god you two are finished. We worked too hard cooking to let the food get cold and yucky."

"We? Is there somebody else here?"

Keegan emerged from the laundry room. "Of course there is. This was a group effort."

Alyssa hugged the tall redhead. "It's almost eleven. What are you two doing here?"

Keegan laughed. "We are part of the staff this weekend. Technically, we are helping with Clay while you two repair your marriage, but you were so loud, then so quiet, we were…we were listening…until just a minute ago. Sorry, Robert."

Alyssa turned to Summer's red face.

"What? We can't be expected to overhear your wild reunion without listening to the sweet talk afterward. Be glad we didn't burn the food. Well, except for the rolls." Summer shrugged. "You shouldn't eat that many carbs, anyway."

Alyssa looked at Robert. "You were pretty sure of yourself. What if I had been resolute in driving you away?"

"I knew what you were doing. If you want to keep a secret, you shouldn't tell Keegan. She loves us both too much to let you ruin things intentionally."

Alyssa shot a look at Keegan, then smiled. "She had a razor on my crotch. She made me talk. Thank you, Keegan, for not letting me give up, even when I gave up." Her vision blurred as tears welled in her eyes. "You two. What can I say? Thank you for sticking with us."

The two women embraced Alyssa as she wept.

Alyssa pulled back. "And this looks delicious, even without the rolls." She went to the cabinet and pulled out plates and glasses for their friends. "You are joining us, I insist."

Dinnertime conversation confirmed that Keegan had kept Robert aware of Alyssa's well-being and her recent decision to let Robert go. Summer revealed that she had watched over Robert like Keegan had watched over Alyssa, but she had remained silent to allow Alyssa time to address her own actions and emotions surrounding the breakup.

"And I really am sorry for sleeping with Robert. It wasn't

intentional, and I never meant to hurt you." Summer winked at Alyssa. "But if your marriage ever needs me to help out that way again, I can force myself."

"I'm not sorry I sucked Robert in your basement," Keegan added, "and if either of you need to fuck me for the sake of your marriage, I'll volunteer."

Alyssa looked at Robert. "I appreciate your enthusiasm, ladies, and I don't blame you one bit. I think that phase of our marriage is over. Robert and I are returning to a monogamous marriage. I'm going to try to satisfy him, even after he has sampled your amazing and addictive charms."

Robert nodded. "She's right. It's just the two of us from now on. We look forward to being friends, without the benefits, so to speak."

Keegan looked at Summer and shrugged. "We had to try."

"We did." Summer looked at Alyssa. "We still need to get together more often, and invite Keegan. She's a breath of fresh air."

"And a tough taskmaster." Alyssa took Keegan's hand. "Thank you for everything you did to get me through. I don't know if I would have survived without you. Do you have an updated schedule for me, now that I'm back home?"

"For the next two days, make love, fuck and shower, in that order. Follow it with sleep and eat." She smiled. "After that, you don't need me to tell you what to do."

All four turned when the front door opened.

"The night shift is here," Jessica called as she and Drew walked into the great room. "What are they doing out here?"

"They had to eat sometime," Summer said with a smile.

Keegan nodded. "Besides, food is better eaten on a table than in bed, despite what the romance writers tell you."

Alyssa stood and hugged Jessica. "Thank you for taking care

of my family. You are a great friend to help us through all this. You didn't have to, you know."

"Yes, I did. You and your family are unique, and I care about you. I couldn't stand by while you struggled. I was so thrilled when Robert set this up."

Alyssa shook her head at her husband, then turned to hug Drew and kiss his cheek. "And you, watching over me, giving me advice, even sitting with me when I was alone. Thank you."

"I was glad to do it. Like Jessica said, you are unique. Not everyone's friendship could start the way ours did. Thank you for being you."

Alyssa pointed at Jessica and Drew. "So why are you here?"

Jessica shrugged. "Like I said when we came in, we are the night shift. We are helping with Clay overnight, but he'll sleep and we will handle the morning when it comes."

Alyssa looked at the tall blonde with an open mouth. "Is this necessary?"

"It's our condition of your reconciliation. We have worked too hard to let you two spend a minute apart. So finish your dinner and get in your bedroom before I carry you there."

Alyssa smiled. Warmth filled her chest, her stomach concurrently full and settled for the first time in weeks. She grinned at Robert. "If it is a condition of our reconciliation, it would be polite to stay close together all weekend."

"That was my intent." Robert led her by the hand out of the kitchen.

Alyssa stopped at the bedroom door. "If I go in here, I breach our separation agreement, and I come home. I come home for good, to live with you as your wife and as mother to our children. I won't leave again. Are you sure you want me to take this next step?"

"Actually, I don't." Robert picked her up, careful not to bump her against the doorframe. "We take this step together."

She cackled as he kicked the door closed.

44

SATURDAY, SEPTEMBER 11, HOME

"Dad?"

Alyssa kissed Robert. "I'll get him. You sleep."

She slipped on her robe and stepped down the hall to Clay's room. Jessica arrived just as she did.

"Jessica, I've got this. Go back to bed."

"He still needs a nurse's help sometimes, Alyssa. I'll take care of it."

"Don't make me show you my mama bear side. My son needs me, and I'm going in. You can watch if you want, but a hundred of you won't keep me from his side."

Jessica chuckled and patted Alyssa's shoulder. "There's the Alyssa I missed. Welcome home. I'll see you in the morning, and we will talk about letting us cater to you and Robert over the weekend."

Alyssa walked in. "Clay, honey, what do you need?"

"Mom?"

"Yes. It's me. You were sleeping when I arrived."

"What are you doing here?"

"You called for Dad. I'm letting him sleep. What do you need?"

"No, Mom. What are you doing here? Why aren't you at your apartment?"

"I live here." Alyssa sat beside him on the bed and cupped his cheek. "Your dad and I worked things out. Neither one of us enjoyed living apart very much. He and I aren't going to divorce, and I'm moving home. Is that all right with you?"

"What about your boyfriend?"

"No more boyfriends. Your dad is more than enough for me. No chance of running into strange people in the morning. Well, except for Ms. Hedgecock and her friend Drew, who are in the guest room and will be making breakfast in the morning."

"Eggs Benedict. Excellent."

"Has she cooked before?"

"At least once a week. She's a great nurse. Speaking of which, I called because I need to pee. Can you help me get to the bathroom? It's still not easy."

"Maybe I should let Ms. Hedgecock do that, since you don't seem too happy to see me."

He hugged her tight. "If you are really home, and things will be all right, I'm thrilled. Please tell me it will be all right."

"It's going to be better than all right. We are going to be great." She hugged him and helped him up.

45

TUESDAY, SEPTEMBER 13, ALYSSA'S OFFICE ONE YEAR LATER

One Year Later

Alyssa looked up as Doug walked into her office. "Good morning, Doug. What has you moving so fast this early? I just got here myself."

"You haven't heard? Frank and Patricia were in a wreck over the weekend. Patricia is in a coma. Frank is in the hospital."

"Oh my god. I hadn't heard. Is he going to be okay?"

"I think so, but he's upset, as you can imagine."

"What can we do?"

"That's why I'm here. He called me this morning. He's asking for you to come see him as soon as you arrive. Something about a change of plans."

Alyssa picked up her purse and started out the door. "Text me the room number."

Alyssa's adventures continue at

www.SageMallory.com/books.

Go there now.

ACKNOWLEDGMENTS

Thanks to North Carolina, a beautiful state and the backdrop for Alyssa's world. Nearby mountains and beaches provide such possibilities.

I must always thank Lyss, who moves the goalposts just enough with every book to help me improve without losing my sanity. If there are errors or shortcomings, they are mine, not hers.

ABOUT THE AUTHOR

Sage Mallory lives near the water, working by day and creating adventures for sexy, determined, evolving women by night. Sage enjoys cooking, hiking the mountains, deep discussions, and escaping the hectic pace of life inside a great story.